Lilac
Time

Books by Fern Michaels

Fight or Flight
The Wild Side
On the Line
Fear Thy Neighbor
No Way Out
Fearless
Deep Harbor
Fate & Fortune
Sweet Vengeance
Fancy Dancer
No Safe Secret
About Face
Perfect Match
A Family Affair
Forget Me Not
The Blossom Sisters
Balancing Act
Tuesday's Child
Betrayal
Southern Comfort
To Taste the Wine
Sins of the Flesh
Sins of Omission
Return to Sender
Mr. and Miss Anonymous
Up Close and Personal
Fool Me Once
Picture Perfect
The Future Scrolls
Kentucky Sunrise
Kentucky Heat
Kentucky Rich

Plain Jane
Charming Lily
What You Wish For
The Guest List
Listen to Your Heart
Celebration
Yesterday
Finders Keepers
Annie's Rainbow
Sara's Song
Vegas Sunrise
Vegas Heat
Vegas Rich
Whitefire
Wish List
Dear Emily

The Lost and Found Novels

Secrets
Hidden
Liar!
Proof

The Sisterhood Novels

Backwater Justice
Rock Bottom
Tick Tock
19 Yellow Moon Road
Bitter Pill
Truth and Justice
Cut and Run
Safe and Sound
Need to Know
Crash and Burn

FERN MICHAELS

Lilac
Time

LORI FOSTER • CAROLYN BROWN

KENSINGTON
PUBLISHING CORP.

kensingtonbooks.com

KENSINGTON BOOKS are published by

Kensington Publishing Corp.
900 Third Avenue
New York, NY 10022

Kensington Publishing Corp.
900 Third Avenue
New York, NY 10022

All Kensington titles, imprints, and distributed lines are available at special quantity discounts for bulk purchases for sales promotion, premiums, fundraising, and educational or institutional use.

Special book excerpts or customized printings can also be created to fit specific needs. For details, write or phone the office of the Kensington Sales Manager: Kensington Publishing Corp., 900 Third Avenue, New York, NY 10022. Attn. Sales Department. Phone: 1-800-221-2647.

KENSINGTON and the K with book logo Reg US Pat. & TM Off.

ISBN: 978-1-4967-5447-9
First Trade Paperback Printing: May 2025

ISBN: 978-1-4967-5448-6 (e-book)

10 9 8 7 6 5 4 3 2 1

Printed in the United States of America

The authorized representative in the EU for product safety and compliance
is eucomply OU, Parnu mnt 139b-14, Apt 123
Tallinn, Berlin 11317, hello@eucompliancepartner.com

Contents

SWEET AS HONEY

FERN MICHAELS

Chapter One

Thirty-four-year-old Natalie Simmons thought of herself as a tomboy-nerd, or a nerdy-tomboy. Growing up an hour from Ocala National Forest, and surrounded by state forests and wildlife management areas, Natalie took every advantage of the Florida weather and being outdoors. She loved to climb trees and would spend hours peeking through the leaves at the vibrant blue sky dotted by white puffy clouds. As a kid, her favorite outfit was a pair of overalls and a T-shirt, or a crew-neck sweater when the days were a bit crisp.

When she was in middle school, her father asked her if she ever thought she would wear a dress again, to which she responded, "I wear dresses every day to school. This is my private time." Her father couldn't argue with that logic. As she entered her teens, she felt awkward, as most adolescents do, and her antidote was to swiftly change into her overalls and head for the woods. Her older brother Nicholas shared the same passion for the outdoors, but he left for Montana to become a park ranger when Natalie was a high school freshman, leaving Natalie to find kindred spirits.

As she struggled through the pains of her teens, she found a group of like-minded nature aficionados at school. They were a group of six who ate lunch together every day and spent their weekends hiking in the forest or canoeing along the lake. Natalie and her friend Diana were the only girls in the group, and you would think that would make them very popular in their little cohort, but it seemed that the boys were much more interested in the sand pine scrub ecosystem of the 387,000 acres of the southernmost forest in the continental United States than high school dances and dating. Natalie occasionally wondered if she had any appealing female attributes, but then again, what teenager is secure in their skin?

Natalie also took an interest in computers; on the Internet, she could discover the many details of the world around her and beyond when she was forced to be indoors. When applying for college, she decided to get on the STEM highway of Science, Technology, Engineering, and Mathematics. At the time, her path was unclear. She was betwixt and between what avenue she should pursue as a career, and decided computer science would always get her a job. Somewhere. Doing something. She applied to the University of Florida in Gainesville, a little over an hour away from home and her favorite hangout, the national forest.

As she became more aware of the endless possibilities in the computer field, she honed her talents in the creative side of technology and embarked on a journey of computer graphics. Upon graduating, she was offered a job at a tech company in Jacksonville, about three hours from home, and two hours from her beloved retreat. She decided to take the job opportunity and could stop at any of her favorite woods when traveling back and forth to visit her parents.

They say time passes in the blink of an eye, and before she knew it, she was ten years into the job. Life was good. She wasn't in a serious relationship; like most of her peers, she was more interested in building her career than hunting for a mate and settling down. Plus, she always had a cat or two, and her life and routine suited her.

Natalie considered herself to be "average-looking." Average light-brown wavy hair, average medium-brown eyes, average light- to medium-tone skin. She was also an average height of five feet, four inches, and her average body weighed in at 132 pounds.

One thing that wasn't average about her was her proficiency at building websites. She had an intuition that made them come to life with the right graphics, fonts, art, and backgrounds. She believed that her rich experiences in the outdoors gave her a keen perspective in making an on-screen image feel three dimensional. Natalie also had an instinct for music. Whether it was grunge or punk, pop or rock, country or classical, she understood it—whatever "it" was they were playing—and became adept at building sites for musicians. Before she took on an assignment, she spent time listening to the musician's work, and if they were appearing, she saw them perform. Natalie gained a reputation among local musicians, which spread throughout the industry. "She gets it," was how they described her. Yes, it was the "it" factor, not necessarily how the word is used to describe the latest, greatest of whatever trend, but in what the musicians were expressing.

For several years, she reported to an office every day, wearing average attire. Business average. Skirt or tailored slacks, button-down shirt, blazer, and sensible yet fashionable shoes. Oxfords or tasseled loafers. To Natalie, that was just short of being overdressed. If she could have her way, it would be baggy shirts and baggy pants and slip-on sneakers. Her dream wardrobe became a reality when her job as a web designer became remote, which made a lot of sense. Who needed to be around people all day when you're staring at a computer? She was quite happy when the company decided to have most of the staff work remotely and meet via Zoom.

It wasn't as if Natalie was reclusive, but she found the office vibe was often distracting. And her cat, Mr. Meowzer, offered plenty of company—although he wasn't always the best office mate. There was one occasion when she received an email from a client that was just a string of question marks. When she scrolled down, she found an email that she hadn't intended on sending, at least not until she edited it. It was a bit terse, and she wanted to rethink the content. She was mortified. Then she remembered Mr. Meowzer had been sitting on her desk. Natalie quickly checked her photo files and found one of Mr. Meowzer on top of her keyboard. She immediately emailed it to the client, with the subject line: "Always the joker!" The client sent back a smiley face and said, "I like his sense of humor." Natalie wiped her brow. "That was a close one, buster," she scolded, giving the cat a side-eye.

Working from home in her apartment in Jacksonville didn't garner her any points in style. Her daily attire had become too casual. She hardly wore makeup, and her hair was either in a short ponytail or pulled back with a hair clip. She was the first to admit she wasn't material for a fashion magazine. She didn't think her appearance was important to do her job—although she would dress appropriately if she was meeting a client on Zoom. Still, unless you have a hair and makeup person on site, no one really looks great on Zoom, so why go crazy?

Natalie's best friend, Joyce, was almost her complete opposite. She always wore the latest styles. When they were together, they could have posed for the "Dos and Don'ts" photos often found in fashion magazines. It wasn't as if Natalie looked unkempt. She simply looked plain, and made the least amount of effort, if any, when it came to clothes.

One afternoon, she and Joyce were walking down the street when Natalie took notice of their reflection in a store window. Natalie grabbed Joyce's arm. "Wow . . . I look like a bag lady compared to you."

"You could easily make some improvements," Joyce said flatly. Natalie thought her friend's response was a bit harsh, but she dismissed the dig. Natalie sensed Joyce enjoyed being perceived as the "prettier" of the two, but in reality, Natalie had a beautiful face. Far from "average." But people see the first quick impression and don't focus on the details, physically or personally. That comes much later, when it is often too late.

Over the course of the past ten years, Natalie's dating record was far from spectacular, but she got into a routine with a coworker named Alec Holtzman. For the past year, every Wednesday, they went to Bennie's Tavern for a trivia night, and every Saturday they would join their friends at Gino's Pizzeria.

One Tuesday, Alec asked her to meet him that night for margaritas at Caliente Tacos. It wasn't their usual place, or their usual night, but Natalie was always game for tacos. And maybe it was time for them to take their relationship to the next level and spend more time together. Natalie decided maybe it was also time for her to put a little more effort into her appearance. Joyce's comment had kinda gotten under her skin. Natalie wasn't going to do anything drastic, but a pair of slim jeans and a white button-down shirt under a crew-neck sweater was tolerable and appropriate. She left her hair loose, dabbed a little blush on her cheeks, gave her eyebrows a little shape, and a swiped bit of gloss on her lips. She took one last look in the mirror and asked Mr. Meowzer what he thought. He gave her an extremely loud meow, which she took as approval.

Natalie was feeling perky. She did a double take as she passed a store window, because she hardly recognized herself. She had to admit she had gone too far down the rabbit hole of blah, and promised herself she would take more interest in her appearance. They say if you like the way you look, it shows in your mannerism. She happily walked the five blocks to Caliente, where Alec was waiting at an outdoor table, wearing an odd expression. Not sure what to make of it, Natalie was surprised when she leaned in to give him a kiss and he jerked his head back as if he were about to be bitten by a snake. That, too, was odd. Very odd. She kept smiling and pulled out a chair. "Everything alright?"

"We have to talk," Alec said, in that tone no one ever wants to hear.

A chill went up Natalie's spine. She knew what was coming next. Not that they were having any relationship issues, but those four words were ominous. She held her breath for as long as possible and then let it all out. "Okay. Talk," she managed to say with some dignity.

"Nat, I know we've been seeing each other for what, eight, ten months?"

The fact he didn't know was another sign the conversation was going one way, and not in a good way. Still, Natalie remained calm as she fought the tears. "It's been a year, Alec." She pushed her chair back and gripped the edge of the table with both hands to steady herself, and to keep from punching him in the face. She quickly rose and rushed out of the bar, nearly knocking into a server carrying a tray of beers.

As she walked home, she wondered how long Alec had

been unhappy. Everything seemed quite normal between them. Routine. What had changed?

She knew she hadn't given him the opportunity to explain, but what was the use? When someone wanted to break up with you, it was best to rip off the Band-Aid and spare yourself further humiliation; why stick around while your about-to-be ex tells you what's wrong with you and the relationship?

On the other hand, she didn't give him the opportunity to use the tired *It's not you, it's me* routine. It *was* him. He hadn't even taken notice of her appearance. He's such a jerk. He could have had the decency to soften the blow with a compliment. Yes, he's a huge jerk.

By the time she got back to her apartment, the embarrassment had been replaced by infuriation. That's when she realized that she wasn't in love with him. The more she thought about it, the more she realized she never really thought about love when it came to Alec. A year together, and the thought had never even crossed her mind.

Mr. Meowzer was sitting inside the door, waiting for her. Now *that* was love. Pure, unconditional love. She scooped him up in her arms and nuzzled her face against his. The big ragdoll cat eyed her suspiciously. Natalie looked into his furry face and assured him, "Yes, I am alright. Simply fine, actually." She realized she didn't even cry. The closest she came to tears was when Alec uttered those chilling four words. But she hadn't shed them. Good for her. He didn't deserve them.

She hauled Mr. Meowzer to the sofa, where she placed the kitty next to her. She turned to him and asked, "Who keeps the friends in a breakup?" He stared up at her blankly. She continued to ruminate over the subject. The guys usually stick together, and the girlfriends or wives have a fifty-fifty chance of maintaining a friendship, because as soon as the guy gets a new girlfriend, she is the one who becomes part of the group. Natalie made a promise to herself that she was not going to let another man dictate her social life or her friends. But it was going to be challenging, at least for a while. She decided to hunker down and take on more work until she felt ready to be a part of the public again.

Chapter Two

Three months after her self-imposed isolation, she decided to go to Bennie's for trivia. Just because she was single didn't mean she wasn't allowed to play.

For her first foray into the social scene, she went to great lengths to switch up her relaxed attire and put in some effort to enhance her appearance. It was akin to what she used to wear to work, with a little more attention to hair and makeup. If it didn't work on Alec, it might get someone else's attention—although that wasn't her motive or purpose. She simply wanted to emphasize her assets in case the creep was there.

And he was. And so was Joyce. Sitting on his lap.

Natalie suppressed the urge to slap the person she thought was one of her best friends. *Why do women do that to each other?* No wonder Joyce had been radio-silent the past month. Whenever Natalie invited her over, Joyce had an excuse. Did Joyce think Alec was now fair game? Didn't Natalie deserve a conversation on the subject? Not that she would have been thrilled, but a little consideration would have been nice. Natalie would have gladly given her blessing, and a warning. *Alec is all about Alec. Good luck.*

Natalie was finally over the drama and humiliation of being dumped and was looking forward to making plans with her friends and restoring her social life. Now this? Like a flash of lightning, her emotions went from shock, to hurt, to anger, to a thirst for revenge. She wasn't going to let two back-stabbers stop her from playing that night. She was more motivated than ever to beat the pants off of them. If she couldn't physically slap them around, she could certainly throttle them with her intellect. It occurred to her that might have been the reason Alec spent time with her. She always came out ahead of the pack, making them the reigning champions of trivia night. *Not anymore. Too bad, so sad, get ready to get your butts kicked.* And kick them, she did. Natalie wasn't sure what was giving her more pleasure: wiping the floor with their miserable scores, or how uncomfortable Joyce was after she leaped off Alec's lap when Natalie walked in. Natalie was not a vindictive person, but she was feeling good about herself and her trivia prowess.

At the end of the evening, Natalie walked past where Alec and Joyce were sitting. "Great game," she said, and kissed her fifty-dollar winnings before she slid the bill into her jacket pocket. She was elated. They were deflated. A little satisfaction goes a long way.

The day after the competition at Bennie's, Joyce left several voicemail messages and texts apologizing to Natalie. Too little, too late. Joyce should have called her before she started dating Alec. Unless . . . could there have been something going on between Joyce and Alec before the "we have to talk" talk that didn't happen? Is that why Alec broke up with her? Natalie decided it no longer mattered. She was done with both of them.

*   *   *

The following morning, Natalie's mother phoned. It was good news/bad news. The bad news was that her father took a fall and had to have hip replacement surgery. The good news was that it was something fixable. But her mother was going to need some help back home.

Considering all that had happened, Natalie was ready for a change of scenery.

Her father was scheduled for surgery that afternoon and would remain in the hospital for three days doing physical and occupational therapy. There was a lot to do to get the house ready for his return, so Natalie packed her laptop, some clothes, and her cat Mr. Meowzer and made the two-and-a-half-hour drive to Sumter County, northwest of Orlando. The plan was to stay with her parents for at least four weeks, until her father finished physical therapy. Although she wished it was under better circumstances, Natalie was glad to be home with the people she loved most.

Her first days home were busy. Natalie and her mother had to make the necessary preparations around the house for when her father got back from the hospital. Pathways had to be clear enough for him to maneuver with a walker. They had to remove scatter rugs that he could trip over. They had to make sure most things in the kitchen were within arm's reach. No climbing on stools allowed!

Once her dad came home, her mother went back to her job as a loan officer at a local bank, and Natalie was in charge of keeping an eye on her father to make sure he didn't overexert himself. She did her best not to baby him. His doctor said he should move around, but Natalie was ever watchful, trying not to hover.

Her mother had weekends off and insisted that Natalie get out and interact with people her own age. But where?

And with whom? Natalie hadn't lived in Sumter in almost fifteen years. Her mother suggested she could help out at the farmers market, where at the end of the day, any unsold perishables would be taken to the local food pantry. They were always in need of volunteers. Natalie thought that sounded easy enough, and she would be helping a good cause. Her mother gave her the phone number of their pastor who organized the group, and he was delighted to have someone to help. Natalie promised she would stay as long as it took to get everything cleaned up, stacked up, and organized, and she offered to work on Saturday at the pantry.

When the first Saturday approached, Natalie was in a lighthearted mood. She was excited to start socializing with people again. Even though she had been out of town for over a decade, she figured she would run into some old school chums.

She got to the market early and was about to maneuver her vehicle into a parking space when someone zipped ahead of her, causing her to slam on the brakes. She instinctively leaned on the horn but got absolutely no response from the driver. He left the motor of his truck running, hopped out of the cab, pulled down the tailgate, and yanked a case of jars from the bed. Natalie watched with interest, waiting for the man to apologize. Nothing. She was tempted to lean on the horn again but thought it might be rude. After all, this was the country, and people were more cordial. Except for this dude.

Natalie considered moving to a different parking space but decided to wait patiently for the man to return and atone for his ill-mannered behavior. Meanwhile, she noticed the exceptionally large, hairy head of a dog sticking out of the passenger-side window of the truck. She was tempted to get out of her vehicle and have a chat with the dog about his owner's rude behavior, but then thought better of it.

She checked her watch. A whole ten minutes went by before he came back. She rolled down her window, expecting an apology, but nothing. Zero. He simply got back into his vehicle and pushed the gear in reverse and came within inches of hitting her car. That was enough. She leaned on the horn, stuck her head out the window, and yelled, "Where did you get your license? A Cracker Jack box?"

He grinned, winked, and gave her a two-finger salute. At that point, Natalie was fuming and muttering, "What is wrong with people?" She noticed there was something painted in yellow on the side of the truck, but she couldn't make out what it was from her vantage point. She took a few deep breaths and gathered her composure. Chances were she would never see the guy again. Why waste her time confronting him?

Natalie spent the next four hours walking among the tables and carts, chatting with the vendors, some who went as far back as her childhood. She felt welcome. At ease. The four hours passed quickly. At the end of the day, she and the other volunteers gathered the remaining goods and packed them in their cars. She followed the convoy to the pantry.

As they pulled into the parking lot, she noticed a familiar-looking truck, the same hairy dog, and let out a groan. *Seriously? There has to be more than one green pickup truck with a hairy dog in the county.* That's when she spotted "Mr. Rude" helping unpack the goods. This time she took a long look at him. He was at least six feet tall, lean but muscular, with a mop of sun-bleached hair and some scruffy facial hair. His eyes were hidden by his Oakley Hydra sunglasses with sapphire lenses, but had he not been so rude, Natalie thought he could be attractive. Maybe. She waited for him to go inside the building, and then she hurriedly removed the boxes from her car and left them with the person parked next to her. It was becoming clear that chances were that she *would* see that guy again, but she'd rather have it be later than sooner.

She turned to the gentleman who took her boxes. "Who is that guy?"

"Oh, Garrett? The local beekeeper. Got some of the best honey around." The man heaved the boxes onto a cart.

"Huh," she muttered. Obviously, none of the honey's sweetness had rubbed off on him.

"That's his dog, Mr. Bumbles. Like the bee." The man chuckled.

She thought that was his only redeeming quality—he had a dog. It struck her that he called his dog "Mister," the same as she addressed her cat. *Just an odd coincidence,* she told herself. She thanked the man, got back into her car, and drove to her parents' house.

As she pulled up, she saw her father on the front porch, using a walker. "Hey Dad! How is it going? Are you sure you're alright out here by yourself?"

"I'm fine, honey."

Honey! Ugh. That word. She climbed to where he was getting his steps in for the day. "You sure you're okay with that? Do you need some help?" she asked.

"I'm fine, sweetie," he assured her.

"Hey, what's with those?" Natalie asked, pointing to the tennis balls on the legs of the walker.

He laughed. "They help this contraption glide easier on the wood floor."

Natalie chuckled. "I thought you were taking up another hobby."

"Well, maybe, but not this week."

"Everything else good?" she asked.

"Yep! Doc says I'm doing great. I should be graduating to a cane in about two weeks."

"Excellent." Natalie gave him a kiss on the cheek. "You're looking good. Got some color back."

"Yep. They say that the anesthesia can stay in your system for months. How about that?"

"So, you're drinking plenty of water, right?"

"You betcha. Your mother is like a prison guard. She stood in front of me until I drank the entire glass. Did that to me at least seven times today." He chuckled.

"Don't think you're going to get away with anything during the week when I'm in charge," she said, grinning.

"I have no expectations of anything less," he laughed, patting her hand.

"What about discomfort? Pain?" Natalie was concerned about pain medications. They can really mess you up, temporarily and permanently.

"Just taking Extra Strength Tylenol. Can't say I'm ready to put on my dancing shoes, but it's tolerable, and I'd rather have a little discomfort for a few days than have my body bombarded with more drugs." He shifted his stance. "Come. Let's see what your mother is cooking up in the kitchen."

Robert Simmons also worked in a bank. That's how Natalie's parents met, forty years before, when he was a teller. Now he was the branch manager, and well-liked by everyone in town. Robert liked to joke that he worked hard to win over the residents of Sumter County. Years ago, it was a rural agricultural community, but when Disney World descended upon Florida, it brought people from different backgrounds into the burgeoning area. There was a lot of resentment and suspicion toward the new residents in the beginning. Robert loved to tell the story of how, by always being extra polite and a hard worker, he earned the high praise of the locals, who would say he was "a fine, articulate country boy—not arrogant like most of them college educated folks." Over time, people became more tolerant—and the new transplants got more acclimated to Sumter County ways. At first, those from the more urban areas got frustrated at the much slower pace of "country folk," but more often than not, they soon found an appreciation for the relaxed lifestyle.

Having lived in Jacksonville for ten years, Natalie forgot how laid-back Sumter County was. When she visited for a weekend, she didn't have a lot of time to spend around the small town, but now that she was in for a longer period, she had to downshift at least a notch, more likely two. Natalie wasn't sure how well she was going to adjust to this new (or was it old?) environment, but after a few days of walking in the woods, she assumed she would feel more at home. She was already savoring aspects of country life. She hadn't realized how much she missed the air. So clean. Fresh. Not that Jacksonville was an industrialized city, but it was still a city. She would just need to relax more, take things a bit slower, and enjoy small-town charm. She thought about the rude beekeeper from earlier that day. Charm? Ha! He must have absorbed the stinger, rather than the sweetness.

As she entered the kitchen, Natalie got a whiff of her mother's famous grapefruit custard pie, fresh out of the oven. Grapefruit custard had become one of her specialties. Grapefruit and oranges were in abundance in Sumter County, and Natalie's mother Sally had decided it was time to do her own "farm-to-table" experiment. "Anyone can make an apple pie. I want to do something different," she'd said. And she did. Every year, her pies won every competition in the county. "The Keys have their limes, and

I've got my grapefruit," was how she explained her experiment with the local fruit.

"Sweetie, can you grab a jar of paprika from the pantry?" Sally asked, as she quartered a chicken. "I want to get this bird ready for dinner."

Natalie stepped inside the walk-in storage area and spotted a jar of honey on a shelf. "Mom? Where did you get this honey?"

"At the farmers market; why?"

She masked her visceral reaction. "No reason. Simply curious." Natalie picked up the golden bottle and checked the label: BEE-CAUSE. In smaller letters, it said: *One third of the world's food supply is pollinated by bees. Bee-careful when you see one. Don't swat it. Thank it and walk away.*

"How many honey farmers are at the market?" Natalie called from inside the pantry.

"Just the one. Garrett something."

Natalie rolled her eyes. *Of course.*

"I think the name and the label are rather cute, don't you?" her mother asked, referring to a winking bumblebee.

"Yeah. Adorable." Now Mr. Rude's wink made sense. She brought the paprika to her mother.

"I'm surprised you didn't meet him at the market," her mother said while seasoning the chicken.

"You could say we almost ran into each other," Natalie said, smirking. She knew that was not going to be the end of Mr. Bee-devil.

Her mother looked perplexed but didn't press the subject. She had to finish dinner.

"Can I help you with anything?" Natalie asked her mother.

"You can light the grill for your father."

"You sure about that?"

"He can stand up. He can cook." She winked at her daughter. Sally knew her husband did not want to be treated like he was disabled, so giving him a chore was good for his spirit. Professionally, Robert was a desk jockey, but when away from his office, he enjoyed the outdoors. When Natalie and Nicholas were young, he took them on hikes through the woods. As they got older and spent more time with friends and school activities, he started to play golf. He claimed, "it was better for business," which wasn't entirely a lie. The old adage that many a deal was made on a golf course had merit, considering almost one third of all big-business deals were made on the green, or at the "nineteenth hole," a nickname for the pub or the clubhouse.

Robert Simmons was not a sit-around kind of guy. His wife and daughter knew it was important to keep him busy, one of the main reasons Sally asked Natalie to come down and help. In all truth, he was perfectly capable of maneuvering without adult supervision, but he also needed mental stimulation. He would go bonkers if he were left alone with the TV remote. He wasn't much for television, unless it was a golf tournament or a good Agatha Christie movie. And do not get him started on social media. "There is nothing social about it," he'd say. To him, it was ludicrous that with all the devices and tools, no one knew how to have a conversation. Natalie would make fun of him, saying, "Every generation has its cross to bear. Tik-Tok is ours."

During one of their recent discussions on the topic, they debated the pros and cons of social media. They agreed it was becoming too much of a crutch, and people had to start to think for themselves and not accept everything they read online. That was part of the overall problem. Her father always said, "Just because it's on the Internet, it doesn't mean it's true. People need to do their research and not from that ticking thingy."

"It's called TikTok, Dad."

"More like a ticking time bomb," he said, and snickered.

Natalie laughed. True, her professional life was ensconced in technology, and she would often find herself defending it—it was, after all, an extremely useful tool for finding information, provided it was from a reliable source. But there had to be a balance, like no phones at the dinner table. Ever. "Unless you are a doctor on call, or waiting to hear if someone has come out of surgery, there is no reason for it," her father would say.

Natalie had to agree with that. She would see people at restaurants glued to their phones. "Why not just do takeout and sit in your living room?" Yes, society needed balance.

For a reason she could not explain, Natalie wondered what Mr. Bee-Cause thought about it. Was he tech savvy? Did he even care? Was he interested in his hives and his hives alone? More importantly, why was *she* contemplating this? Why did she even care? She had a stinger under her skin, and she had to pull it out. But before that happened, she planned to check his Internet presence after dinner . . . just out of curiosity.

She went out to the back porch and lit the grill while her parents chatted in the kitchen. There was a grove of trees beyond a small field where she and her brother and friends used to play soccer, softball, or anything that required you to run around. She wondered how much the woods had changed and decided to explore the next day.

Twenty minutes later, she shouted toward the house. "Grill is ready!" Then she realized her father would need help. Somebody had to carry the chicken.

Natalie's mother was steaming the string beans while her father was seasoning some corn to put on the grill. "Not too much salt, Robert. We don't want your blood pressure to get all flooey."

"I do not believe that is a medical term," he teased, and moved out of the way so Natalie could grab the platter. "Mind if I join you?" he asked.

"Who do you think is going to cook this feast?" Natalie joked.

Robert maneuvered his walker and followed Natalie to the door. She held the screen open with one hand while he shuffled to the porch. "I can't wait to get rid of this thing." He banged it on the wooden floor.

"Trust me. All of us can't wait, either." She grinned. She set the platter down on one of the stainless-steel shelves attached to the grill. "I'm going to check on Mr. Meowzer. Can I trust you to behave for a few minutes?"

"I can't promise you anything. I might try and make a run for it. That physical therapist is one tough cookie." He chuckled.

Natalie took the stairs to the second floor two at a time. She realized she hadn't seen her fur baby since she got home. The big pile of fluff was lounging in the middle of her bed. He looked like an overstuffed floor cushion.

"Oh baby-boo. Sorry I'm late. I am a terrible mother."

He stretched and yawned as if to say, "You are disturbing my nap."

Natalie cuddled with her kitty for a few minutes and told him all about the ill-mannered bee guy. "And to think he has a dog. Well, I hope he treats him with a little more respect than he did to me."

Mr. Meowzer looked up at her, and Natalie burst out laughing. "You're right. Sometimes I prefer animals over people. Actually, most of the time."

She got up and checked his bowl for food. All good.

"Maybe we'll let you explore the rest of the house tomorrow when I can keep an eye on you and make sure there are no escape routes available for your inquisitive soul." She gave him a kiss on the head. "I'm going to have dinner with grandma and grandpa. See you in a bit."

When Natalie returned to the kitchen, she savored the aroma of the grilled food, while her mother was garnishing her string beans almondine. "Honey, can you check on the potatoes?"

Natalie cringed again at the word *honey. How can one man completely ruin a word?* And again, she wondered why he vexed her so much. Was it his sinewy muscles that were exposed from his shirt with the ripped-off sleeves? Or his mischievous grin? Was it the sassy wink? The salute? He unnerved her. That was one thing of which she was certain.

Natalie grabbed an oven mitt and retrieved the spuds from the lower oven. "I'll go see how Dad's doing."

"Perfect timing," he remarked as she stepped outside. He used tongs to remove the chicken and corn from the grill and placed them on the platter.

"You haven't lost your touch." Natalie smiled. "I'll bring these in and get the door for you."

The three gathered at the table. It was a glorious-looking spread. Robert insisted he could manage to get in his chair without any help.

"Remember, I am in recovery, so it's important that I do as much as I can without compromising my surgery. A chair, I can manage. Just don't ask me to go horseback riding." He chortled. "But in all seriousness, they wouldn't let me out of the hospital unless I was able to climb a flight of stairs and put on a pair of socks with my handy-dandy sock helper." He was referring to a plastic contraption that looked like it was made from an empty bottle of bleach and two pieces of rope. "This group of doctors are top-notch. They had me watch a ten-minute video, and I had my own personal physician's assistant go over everything from A to Z."

"I'm happy you opted for daily visits to physical therapy. You will heal much faster than if you had someone come to the house three times a week," Sally noted.

Robert leaned in toward Natalie and winked. "I call it 'ortho-boot-camp.' I have to admit, I am enjoying the shower seat."

"That is going to be the first thing to retire to the garage," Sally quipped. "I have to move it out of the way if I want to take a bath."

"Try the shower seat. It's a nice experience. I feel like I'm at a spa."

Sally huffed. Having the house retrofitted to accommodate Robert's recovery was only a small inconvenience, but it was not a look Sally wanted to keep any longer than necessary. A second railing was installed on the staircase so he could have support on both sides. The bathroom required a temporary raised commode. They exchanged the glass shower doors for a curtain, a safety bar, and a new handheld shower head. The half-bath on the main floor also needed a raised commode.

"I'm glad you didn't listen to some of your friends, who insisted you put a hospital bed in the dining room," Sally said.

"Even my surgeon agreed on that point. So much of recovery is psychological. You do the work, and you get on with your life," Robert replied.

"Let's say grace," Sally suggested as they held hands. "Thank you for this wonderful meal, our family, and all the blessings in our life. Amen."

"How was your first day at the farmers market?" Natalie's father asked.

Natalie shuddered at the thought of discussing her encounter with Mr. Bee-Cause, however fleeting it was. "I met some wonderful people. The atmosphere was lively, and it was busy."

"It's the first weekend of the season," her mother remarked. "Was the cheese man there?" Sally was referring to an older gentleman who migrated from Italy via New York. "He has brought us the most amazing mozzarella." She pronounced it *mutts-a-rell* as opposed to *mozz-a-rella*.

"Oh, aren't we the continental one?" Natalie teased.

"Respect, dear." Sally grinned. "And the proper way to say tomato sauce is *mar-eh-nah-ra* and not *mari-nari*."

"She's fluent," Robert teased.

"I can see that." Natalie dug into her juicy chicken.

"And it's *fo-ca-chia,* not *fo-co-chia*," Sally laughed.

"I see you've learned to master an Italian menu," Natalie said between bites. "But to answer your question, he was not at a table today, but I heard someone say he would be there tomorrow. Someone said he had to go to New York to get a few pounds of provolone. Did I say that correctly?" Natalie joshed.

"Molto bene!" Sally replied.

Robert looked over at his wife and knitted his brows. "Don't tell me you are having an affair with Mr. Giambelli?"

"Darling, he's almost eighty years old."

"That didn't stop Rupert Murdoch," Robert retorted with a devilish grin. "He was eighty-five when he married Jerry Hall. And she was fifty-nine."

Everyone burst out laughing. Natalie felt a rush of dopamine. Laughter was the best medicine, especially when you are sharing it with your family—and good friends, if she still had any.

Lively banter filled the room as they enjoyed their meal.

Natalie felt a pang of guilt. One of the reasons she moved to Jacksonville was because it wasn't that far away from home. It could be as short as a day trip if necessary. But when was the last time she came to visit? Why didn't she go home more often? She felt she may have come to a crossroad. Lots of questions and thoughts were forming in her head: *Who can you count on? Who do you trust? Where do you belong? Maybe going with the flow wasn't the ultimate ideal. At least look around and see where the water is taking you. You could be headed for dangerous rapids.* She thought about her friends in Jacksonville. Were they even her friends? How long had they known that her "best friend" was hooking up with her ex-boyfriend? They, too, were splashing about with little direction. Had her generation become lazy? Uninspired? Indifferent? The fact that she was thinking about it was good. One day away from her routine, and already she was taking steps to figure out her life.

Several minutes passed. "Natalie? You okay?" Her mother noticed her daughter had become pensive.

Natalie snickered. "Yes. I am quite okay." That's when she decided to tell her parents about Alec and Joyce. She got up and began to clear the table. Once the plates were stacked near the sink, she put on a pot of coffee. "I hope we're getting some of that pie tonight." Natalie raised her eyebrows in anticipation and nodded toward the pie cooling on the counter.

"I was going to save it for tomorrow, but there is no reason why we can't have a slice tonight." Sally got up from her chair and brought clean plates and the pie to the table. She handed each of them a piece.

Natalie began, "So . . ." She took a long pause. "There is something I want to tell you."

Sally's eyes went wide. "Honey, is everything alright?"

Natalie had a silent gag at the word *honey* again. "Yes, everything is fine. Really. Alec and I broke up a couple of months ago."

"And you didn't tell us?" Her father's voice sounded troubled.

"No, because I was working a few things out. I think the biggest revelation was that I didn't shed a tear."

"So, you broke up with him?" Sally queried.

"No, he broke up with me," Natalie said calmly.

"But why?" Her father's voice was in a slight state of disbelief.

"We never got to that point," Natalie continued. "We were meeting for dinner, and when I got there he said, 'Nat, we have to talk.' That's all I had to hear. There is no good outcome. Somebody was about to get hurt, and there was a target on my back."

"I don't understand," her mother prodded.

"Mom, when someone says those four dreaded words, you know where it's going. If it had been something good, he would have had the conversation with me at home. In private. But he picked a restaurant. A public place."

Her father was nodding. She continued, "The 'we have to talk' is a preamble to either 'it's not you, it's me, or 'I think you're swell, but . . .'"

"What did you do?" Sally asked.

"I hope you punched him in the face," her normally mild-mannered father snarked.

Natalie laughed out loud. "That's exactly what I wanted to do, but I grabbed hold of the table, got up, and left."

"Then what happened?"

"Nothing. He never called or sent a text. Ever."

"Oh dear. That is so rude," Sally said.

"But wait, there's more. After three months of self-evaluation and self-imposed isolation, I prettied myself up. Dad, you would have been proud. No dress, but business casual, hair, and makeup."

He was smiling at his daughter.

"I decided to go to Bennie's for trivia night. There are no rules that say ex-girlfriends are not allowed, especially ex-girlfriends who always win. Anyway, when I walked into the pub, there was my so-called friend Joyce, sitting on Alec's lap!"

"Oh my. That is terrible! I thought she was your friend," Sally said.

"So did I, but that would be a big *no*. But here's the best part. I won the fifty-dollar first prize in trivia."

"Well, good for you!" her father exclaimed.

"Actually, the best part was when I sauntered past them with the bill in my hands and said, 'Great game.' Then I kissed President Ulysses S. Grant's picture. It was epic."

Sally laughed. "Well, good for you!"

"That's my girl," Robert said, chuckling.

"What happened after that?" Sally asked.

"Joyce left a few voicemails, but I haven't returned any of her calls. For what? To ask her if they had been cheating behind my back? How long had it been going on? It didn't matter. I could never trust her again."

"And you are okay with all of this?" her father asked.

"Yes. Yes, I am. Don't take this the wrong way, Pop, but you couldn't have broken your hip at a better time." She got up from her chair, stood behind her father, and gave him a wraparound hug.

"Glad to be of assistance," he laughed, patting her hands.

"What are your plans for tomorrow, besides the food pantry?" her mother asked.

"I really don't have any. Maybe take a walk through the woods. See how much has changed."

Her father gave a little frown. "Don't wander too far. There is a housing development about a mile from here." "Don't tell me they tore down the woods?" Natalie was aghast. "Not all of them, thanks to the local farmers and city council. For every tree they cut down, they had to plant two, and not just some scruff pine or shrubs. They had to be the equivalent of what they were removing." "That's sort of what they do in the lumbering industry," Natalie noted. "Yes. That's where we got the idea. Your brother put us in touch with an organization for reforestation, and they did a survey for us. Free of charge, I might add," her father said proudly. "Well good for you and everyone else. It drives me crazy when I see bulldozers plowing down everything in sight. It's becoming a problem near me." "It's a problem everywhere, honey," her father said. "I know a lot of people make fun of the 'tree huggers,' but trees provide the oxygen we need to breathe. And don't get me started on what they are doing to the Amazon." He took a deep breath. "We are excessively big consumers of the earth's natural resources, and a lot of people turn a blind eye, but I don't think it is unreasonable to expect land developers to replace what they ruin."

Natalie couldn't argue with that—not that she would.

"Speaking of preservation, you know that honey in the pantry?" her mother asked, giving Natalie a nudge toward indigestion. "The beekeeper gives a tour and does a talk about bees and pollination. You should sign up for it."

"Yeah, maybe," Natalie said casually, while thinking, *only if you hold my feet to a fire.*

It was close to eight o'clock by the time they finished their chat and cleared the kitchen.

"I'm whipped. Do you mind if I take a shower and hit the sack? I think Mr. Meowzer will be getting cranky if I don't pay attention to him."

"Of course, dear," her mother replied. "You know, you don't have to keep him locked in your room."

"Thanks, but I don't want him to get under Dad's feet."

"Good point," her father said.

"I'll see how antsy he is. If he's chilling out, then I'll leave him to his own devices. He has toys, and I left the radio on for him. He's partial to classical music." She grinned, kissed her father on the top of his head, and gave her mother a hug. "You need any help getting upstairs?"

"My doctor would be appalled if I said I did." He smiled. "Get a good night's sleep, sweetheart."

"'Night," Natalie said as she climbed the stairs. Just as she thought, her fur baby was curled up right in the middle of the bed, unbothered by her absence.

"Hello, baby-boo. Did you miss me?"

He yawned and rolled over. It was time for his belly rub.

"Would you like some dinner?" She opened a pouch of his favorite kitty tuna, and like a flash, he hopped off the bed.

"I'm incredibly happy you are adjusting well. In fact, I think I'm also adjusting well. It's nice to be here."

Natalie got undressed, put on a robe, and headed to the adjacent bathroom, where Mr. Meowzer's litter box was situated under the sink. Her parents had their own bath, and the one Natalie was using had two doors: one from her room, and another from the hall. After her shower she did a rough blow-out, slipped into a fresh pair of pajamas, and got into bed. She flipped on the TV to see if she had missed anything important besides *Jeopardy!* Many of her friends encouraged her to try out for the famous game show, but being a local trivia champion was good enough for her.

Mr. Meowzer finished his dinner, went into the bathroom to do his business, and returned to his spot on the bed.

"Hey, move over, dude," Natalie said as she pulled him closer to her. "What do you think of Hotel Simmons? Is it to your liking?"

He purred his answer. *So far, so good.* As soon as her head hit the pillow, Natalie was out like a light.

Chapter Three

The sun peeked through the curtains around six the next morning. She blinked several times, remembering she was back in her former bedroom. Mr. Meowzer was already sitting on the windowsill, watching the birds swoop down on the feeder below.

"Good morning, baby-boo. Did you have a good night's sleep?"

The cat turned his head toward her as if to say, *Yes, and where is my breakfast?*

Natalie patted the bed. "Come here, you little furball."

He was no dummy, and immediately obliged. She gave him a few noogies, slipped out of bed, and filled his bowl with crunchy dry food. "Here you go." Mr. Meowzer rubbed against both of her legs before he began to eat his morning meal.

Natalie listened for any movement in the rest of the house. All quiet. She decided to go downstairs and fix a pot of coffee. "I'll be back in a bit," she said as she secured the door behind her.

The sun was shining brightly into the kitchen. It warmed

Natalie physically and emotionally. A fleeting thought about moving back home permanently ran through her head. She could work from anywhere. She no longer had a half-baked boyfriend. Her friends were sparse and made it clear they were *his* friends in the breakup. But then she considered she may be having a knee-jerk reaction. It's easy to do when what you *thought* was your world got tilted on its side. Perhaps this was a good time to go with the flow. At least for the next couple of weeks. There was no rush to make any decisions. Her big challenge would be to avoid the bumblebee guy.

After the coffee finished brewing, she filled a mug and took it outside. The bird feeder was far enough from the outdoor table and chairs so as not to interrupt the bird's morning and evening feeding times. The yard was meticulously landscaped with a variety of vegetation, rocks, and flowers. To the side of the house was her mother's vegetable garden, lined with an assortment of fruit trees. There were strawberry plants, plums, blackberries, and figs. She wondered what her mother's next special pie would be for the fair. Sally Simmons could not be expected to bake the same blue-ribbon pie two years in a row. That would never do. Each year it had to be something different.

About an hour later, both her parents made their way down the stairs and into the kitchen. "Nothing like the aroma of freshly brewed coffee," her father called out to Natalie. "Thanks, sweetie."

"My pleasure," she responded, as she got up and went inside. "I was checking out your garden, Mom. What kind of pie are you going to create this season?"

"Funny you should ask. I was thinking about making a plum cake instead of pie. My grandmother Matilda used to make a delicious cake with fresh plums, a hint of cinnamon, and a yummy streusel topping, but I don't have the recipe." Sally sighed. "I'm hoping I can recreate it from memory, but I think I just have to experiment until I get it right."

"You can certainly experiment on me," Robert said cheerfully.

"Count me in!" Natalie echoed, pulling out a chair and taking a seat.

"The plums aren't ripe enough yet, at least not mine."

"I'll check out the market next Saturday and see if anyone has some," Natalie volunteered. She took a sip of her coffee and offered, "Shall I make breakfast?"

"That would be swell," her father replied.

"Oh, honey, you don't have to go to any trouble," her mother said.

"No trouble. French toast? Pancakes? Bacon and eggs?"

"Ooh. All of the above?" Her father chuckled.

"You have to pick one," Sally scolded. "Just because Natalie is here doesn't mean you can get all flooey with your diet."

"There's that word again," Robert said, cackling.

Natalie went into the pantry to see what was available. Then she remembered she was in her mother's house—everything was available. She spotted a loaf of challah bread. Perfect for French toast. And there was that jar of honey with the bumblebee winking at her. She shook her head and turned the jar around so the bee could wink at the wall. She quickly grabbed the bread and returned to the kitchen. "I vote for French toast." She held up the bag of bread, then set it on the counter. Her mother pulled out a carton of eggs, milk, and cinnamon.

"Nat, can you grab the honey?" her father asked.

Ugh! Honey. "Sure. No problem." She went back into the pantry, lifted the jar, and stuck out her tongue. "Don't you wink at me, Mr. Bumble."

"What did you say?" her mother called from the kitchen. "Nothing, Mom. Just muttering to myself." She held the jar of honey as if it were hazardous material. "Okay, now everyone out of the way." She shooed her mother and father. "I am the captain of this ship right now. Go sit outside. I'll take care of everything."

"Natalie, you don't have to . . ."

"Mom, please. I want to do this, so take Mr. Bionic Hip to the porch. It's a beautiful day."

"Aye aye, captain." Sally grinned. She turned to her husband and said, "Come on, dear. You heard her." Sally resisted the temptation to help her husband out of his chair. The more he moved around, the quicker he would heal, provided he didn't overexert himself, which was not about to happen over the twenty feet he had to finesse. Sally opened the door as Robert shuffled his walker over the threshold.

Natalie turned on the radio and moved to the beat of "Sweet Dreams (Are Made of This)," by the Eurythmics. The next song was by Marvin Gaye, from 1981. It dawned on her that both songs were recorded before she was born, yet she knew all the lyrics. Contemporary music just couldn't compete. For someone who collaborated with musicians, she could not think of one song recorded in the last year that stuck with her. None of them were memorable. The radio station continued to play '80s music, songs you could sing along with, or dance to, or both. She wondered how many of the contemporary hits would have longevity. Time would tell, but that wasn't her concern. That, too, gave her pause. Was she selling out by taking on work she really didn't believe in? She twisted her mouth in thought. *Nah. Just trying to make a living.* She decided to do some homework when she got back to Jacksonville. Check on the contemporary artists she actually liked.

As she flipped the first batch of French toast, it occurred to her she was having more than one revelation. She smiled as she moved on to the next slices of the egg-battered bread. When everything was done, she plated the aromatic bread on a platter, sprinkled a little powdered sugar, and garnished it with sliced strawberries. She stepped back and admired her culinary talent. Another thing for her epiphany list: *Cook more.*

Natalie carried the breakfast fixings on a tray, purposely leaving Mr. Bee on the counter. "That looks delicious," her father beamed. "I had no idea you were an ace in the kitchen."

"I'm full of surprises," Natalie said and smiled, although she wasn't sure what kind.

They were halfway through their meal when someone finally noticed the missing nectar.

"Honey, can you get the honey?" her mother asked.

Natalie couldn't help but laugh, and her parents joined in with her.

Natalie retrieved the jar from the kitchen counter and handed it to her mother.

"You know, I never told you about my brief encounter with the bee guy."

"I thought you said you almost ran into each other?" her mother asked curiously.

"That's the point. The jerk pulled in front of me while I was trying to park, completely blocking the space, left his truck running for almost ten minutes."

"You waited?" her mother asked casually.

"Well, yes. I was expecting an apology, but nooo. He was so rude."

"So, what happened when he got back?" her father asked as he wiped powdered sugar off his chin.

"That's just it! Nothing!"

"Did you say anything to him?" her mother asked.

"Yeah. I said, 'Where'd you get your license? A Cracker Jack box?'"

Her father let out a guffaw. "That's my girl."

"Oh, but he just grinned, winked, and gave me a little salute. Ugh!"

"Sounds rather harmless," her father noted, still grinning.

"I suppose." Natalie shrugged. "His only saving grace is that he has a beautiful dog, Mr. Bumbles."

"Don't sell him short. He's doing something important with his apiary."

"Whatever." Natalie plunged her fork into a chunk of the sugary carbs in front of her. She had to admit, she made an impressive French toast.

When everyone had their fill, Natalie began to clear the table. "Honey, you don't have to do that," her mother said, rising.

"Mom, can you please let me feel useful?" she pleaded, tilting her head. "Please?"

"Of course, dear. But you're our guest."

Natalie frowned. "I don't want to be treated like a guest. I want to be treated like, like I live here. I mean, I *used* to live here."

"Oh, dear, this will always be your home, and you are welcome to stay as long as you want," her father said, as he placed his hand on her platter-filled arm.

"Thanks, Dad. I really appreciate it." Natalie piled the dishes on the counter and called back outside, "I'm going to check on Mr. Meowzer and get ready to go to the food pantry."

"I think you can let your cat out when you get back. Your father and I are planning on going for a drive this afternoon."

"I don't want to go stir crazy," her father added.

"You can go out, but we're going to keep you on a tight leash this week." Natalie chuckled and winked at her mother. "Oh, by the way, I was thinking about cooking dinner next Saturday when I get back from the farmers market."

"What did you have in mind?" her mother asked.

"I thought I'd cook something Italian. Maybe make a primavera pasta. There are a lot of great-looking veggies at the market."

"When did you become Julie Child?" her father teased.

"It's Julia, Dad. And she was known for her French cooking, not Italian. I want to make pasta. I found a simple recipe by Giada De Laurentiis."

"You are going to spoil us," her mother said as she brought the remaining plates inside.

"Is that a problem?" Natalie raised her eyebrows in mocked skepticism.

Her mother chuckled. "Not for me, honey."

Now if Natalie could only get her parents to stop calling her that. "Then it's settled. Mr. Giambelli is supposed to be back this week. I'll grab some of his Parmigiano Reggiano, and a loaf of bread. He may have fresh pasta, too."

"You are going to make us fat if you keep this up," her father teased, as he dragged his walker through the door.

"It's healthy, Dad. Fresh food. You've heard of it, correct?" she said over her shoulder as she began to climb the stairs.

"Yes, your mother keeps reminding me every time I mention Chick-fil-A."

Natalie went into her room and found Mr. Meowzer sitting on the windowsill, enjoying the comings and goings of the birds.

"Good thing you can't get out there. I'm sure you'd make quite a ruckus."

Natalie could have sworn he winked at her. "Oh, don't you start doing that, too."

She gave him a few rubs behind his ears. "Are you enjoying your vacation so far?"

He nudged his head against her arm.

"I know you're used to me being around twenty-four-seven, but you seem to be doing okay." She picked him up and set him on her lap. "I am going out to work at the food pantry, but when I come back, we are going to take a tour of the house. Would you like that?" He nudged her arm again. She wondered if he was content in his little hideaway. It was a comfortable space. Big windows. His feathered friends to watch. Food. Water. Bathroom. He had his own hotel suite.

Natalie went into the bathroom to brush her teeth and make herself presentable. But for whom? "You never know," she said to her reflection in the mirror.

The weather was going to be sunny and hot, so she decided on a sleeveless tank, cargo pants, and a straw porkpie hat. She slathered herself with sunblock, tucked her hair behind her ears, and let it fall to her collarbone. She added some blush and pale lipstick as a final addition. Today she was only half a tomboy. She gave her fur baby a hug. "I'll be back in a bit," she promised, and then headed down the stairs.

"Well don't you look bright and perky," her father noted.

"And yet, no dress," she said, and grinned.

"Enjoy the day, sweetheart," her mother said, as she finished making sandwiches for her and Robert's outing.

"Going any place special?" Natalie asked, as she plucked her keys from the console in the entry hall.

"We have to mind the terrain, so we're going to a park where they have a concrete path and picnic tables."

"Be careful out there . . ." Natalie gave each of them a peck on the cheek.

"Don't let any bees get in your bonnet today," her father teased.

Natalie rolled her eyes and headed toward the food pantry a few miles away.

The work was gratifying, and she met a ton of new people from the town. The bee man was notably absent, and Natalie was glad for it. The more she could avoid running into him, the better.

Chapter Four

The week flew by. Natalie was in charge of bringing her father to physical therapy and picking him up. In between, she would run some errands, and once back at the house, she would work on clients' websites while keeping an eye on Robert. Before she knew it, Saturday and another day at the farmers market had arrived.

When she reached the parking lot, she was expecting another altercation with the bee guy, but he was nowhere in sight. She was struck by a hint of disappointment. *Now where did that come from?* She wondered. She walked around the market, stopping to say hello to several people she knew, then she spotted Mr. Giambelli and waved. She wanted to be sure she bought some of his delicious offerings before he sold out. Good Italian products were in short supply in their corner of Florida. And good luck trying to find good pizza, but if anyone knew, it would be Mr. Giambelli. She tucked that idea into the back of her head. With the influx of New Yorkers and Jerseyites, there was a high demand for the delicacies, and Mr. Giambelli's reputation was widely known throughout the county.

"*Buongiorno!*" he greeted Natalie. "*Come stai?*"

"*Molto bene!*" Aside from food products, that was the extent of Natalie's Italian. "I heard a rumor you went all the way to New York to bring us some of that wonderful cheese."

"Ah, *si*. I bring-a few kinds." He rattled off his list. "And some prosciutto!" he added.

"Fantastic. I'm making dinner for my parents tonight. Pasta primavera."

"Ah, and a nice antipasto!" He handed her a loaf of semolina bread. "You eat with the antipasto, yes? Not with-a the pasta."

"Whatever you say, Mr. Giambelli. Any other tips you can give me?"

"Depends. What kinda vegetables?"

"Zucchini? Tomatoes? Broccoli?"

"Use plum tomatoes. Sliced. Smash a few garlic cloves, sauté in olive oil but don-a let it get brown. Just a nice golden color. Then you take it out. Add some white wine, a little chicken stock, some shaved parmesan, a little shave of provolone to give it some-a zing. Make-a sure the pasta is al dente, and no overcook the vegetables."

"I think I need you to come over and supervise," Natalie laughed.

"No. But I give-a you my phone number in case you have any questions." He smiled.

Natalie thought about the banter between her parents the week before. At eighty-something, Mr. Giambelli was quite charming. No wonder her father was teasing her mother during breakfast. She asked him if she could pay for everything and leave it with him until the end of the day, which he was happy to do.

"Tell your Mama I say hello."

Natalie thought that would give her father another opportunity to tease her mother about Mr. Giambelli. Did her father really think her mother was capable of having an affair? She shrugged to herself. *I suppose people are capable of anything*, she thought, and she reminded herself of the stunt her "good friend" Joyce pulled on her.

Natalie walked from stall to stall, picking the vegetables she planned to use in her pasta. She noticed a young woman sitting at the honey booth. *Was that his girlfriend?* she wondered. Then Natalie remembered she hadn't checked out the website or if he had any social media presence. She made a mental note to do that as soon as she got back to the house. Then she wondered why she was slightly obsessed with the guy. She strolled past the booth, where the young woman sat behind a table with a red-and-white-checkered tablecloth. Natalie mustered up the courage to approach the booth and nosy around.

"Hello," the young woman greeted her. "Do you like honey? We have samples if you'd like to try some."

Natalie was caught off guard. "Uh, yes. Sure."

"Any particular kind? We have clover and orange blossom."

"May I try both?" Natalie asked politely.

"Of course."

The woman pulled two small wooden spoons from a jar, wrapped them with a small napkin, and dipped each one into the individual honey. She handed the sweet delights to Natalie.

"Most people don't realize there are many kinds of honey, depending on the flora that surrounds the apiary, and the time of year."

Natalie licked one spoon and then the other. "Yummy."

"I'm glad you like it! Garrett would be pleased. That's my brother. He's the beekeeper, and I run the market and our store. He's not here today, otherwise I'd introduce you. He had to go to Orlando today to pick up some supplies."

Natalie was relieved and disappointed. She wanted another look at the guy. *But why?* "Your brother and you run the business?" she asked, licking the last drop.

"Yes, our parents had a farm but sold some of the land when they retired. Garrett and I always loved the farm, so we kept ten acres and made it our own. Well, it was really Garrett's idea to turn it into an apiary. I was always squeamish when it came to bees, so I wasn't exactly enthused, as you can imagine."

Natalie chuckled. "I can totally understand that."

"But Garrett convinced me that we were doing something good for the planet and could also make a modest living at it."

"Very noble." Natalie nodded.

"You should come to one of our demonstrations. Garrett does one a month, usually on a Monday. The public is invited for free." She paused before adding, "Oh, we have beekeeper suits for everyone to wear, so you don't have to worry about getting stung." She smiled up at Natalie.

"That's good to hear." Natalie picked up one of the flyers with the dates and times of the demos. "Do I have to register in advance?"

"We encourage it, because we only have a dozen suits, and obviously no one is allowed to attend without one."

"Obviously," Natalie said with a grin.

"You can sign up on our website. It's not very fancy, but the contact information is at the bottom." She pointed to the address. "My name is Georgia, by the way."

"Natalie."

"Nice to meet you, Natalie. Do you live around here?"

"I grew up here but live in Jacksonville now. I'm visiting my parents for a few weeks."

"Well then, you must come by before you go back home." Georgia gave her a dazzling smile.

"I'll check with my family. My dad has to go to physical

therapy, and I'm helping out. He broke his hip playing golf. He slipped on something, and down he went."

"I hope he's okay." Georgia sounded sincere.

"Yeah. I think he needs six more weeks, and then he'll be good as new. Well, almost," Natalie said. "Not sure how this is going to affect his golf game. I guess we'll find out." Natalie picked up a jar of each of the honey. "What do I owe you?"

"Six for one jar, but you get two for ten."

"Sounds like a good deal to me." She handed the woman a bill. "Thanks."

"Thank you, Natalie. Hope to see you at the apiary."

Natalie tapped the flyer in her hand. How could she refuse such an interesting invitation?

She spent the next few hours giving people a hand when their booths got busy. Her contribution was weighing the produce while the vendors exchanged the money.

One of the flower vendors looked familiar. "Diana? Diana Cunningham?" Natalie asked.

"Natalie Simmons? Oh my gosh! I haven't seen you in ages!" The woman came around to the front of her stall and gave Natalie a big hug. "You haven't changed a bit!"

Natalie took a long look at her childhood friend. "Neither have you!"

"Ha! You're sweet, but you can't miss this change." Diana chuckled, patting her very pregnant tummy. "Actually, this is my third. I already have Jordan, who is five, and Lindsay, who is three. Their new baby sister is due in three months. Three girls—can you believe it??"

"So, you and Ryan got married after school?" Natalie was referring to Diana's college sweetheart.

"Ryan? No. He turned out to be a big dud. Still lives with his parents." Diana chortled. "I dodged a bullet there. I married a genuinely nice guy who has a real job."

Natalie had to laugh. "And doesn't live with his parents."

"Exactly. His name is Jeremy Russell. He's an environmental engineer."

"Impressive."

"We met at a rally to save the Everglades."

"You were always a bit of a rebel," Natalie noted.

"The funny thing about it is, he was on the other side of the fence. I kept yelling at him all day and he finally said, 'How about I take you to dinner and you can explain your position without screaming in my face?' He was so cute. Still is. How could I say no?"

"Sounds like it was a good move. Tell me about your flowers," Natalie prodded.

"I own a little shop in town. Greenhouse Flowers. Not very original, but it's to the point. We have a greenhouse and grow most of our flowers, but we also make specialty arrangements. Check out our 'Look Book.' "

Natalie noticed three large photo albums on the table. She flipped through the book in front of her. "Very impressive. You were always the artsy type. Aside from your tree hugging." Natalie laughed.

"I'm happy I've been able to combine them." Diana showed her the next book that was filled with photos of their greenhouse. There were photos from every season, including dwarf Christmas trees, wreaths, and garland.

"Outstanding!" Natalie gushed.

"That degree in botany was worth all the dirt up my nose." Diana laughed. "Still get my fill every day!"

"I would love to see your place," Natalie said.

"You still do the trivia thing?" Diana asked.

"I do." Natalie cocked her head. "Why do you ask?"

"Because we have a place that hosts trivia on Tuesdays. I would love it if you could be my partner next week. I heard someone was bringing in a former *Jeopardy!* contestant. Not a champion, but . . ."

"Count me in!" Natalie was thrilled at the idea of doing something she enjoyed with an old pal.

"Great! You can come by the house, and I'll give you a tour of the greenhouse before we go. Trivia starts at seven thirty, but I usually get there around six to have a bite to eat. Can you be at my place, say, around five?"

"Perfect. I have to pick up my dad from physical therapy at four. Should be plenty of time."

"Fantastic!" Diana squealed. "And you can meet my rug rats. My mom is watching them today. Jeremy is at a seminar in Ocala."

"Will I get to meet him, too?" Natalie was excited to meet the man who swept her pal off her feet.

"Yes, but he will be babysitting. Tuesdays are my night out. He gets Wednesdays and plays on a softball team."

"Sounds like a sweet life," Natalie said with admiration.

"It has its moments." Diana chuckled.

Natalie laughed, "Doesn't everything?"

"Yep. So, tell me, what brings you to Sumter County?"

"My dad needed a hip replacement, and I'm helping chauffeur him back and forth to physical therapy."

"How is he doing?"

"Great. He has an excellent attitude, and so does my mom. It's been nice spending the past week with them."

"What about work? What are you up to?"

"Designing websites, mostly for bands and recording artists."

"Sounds exciting!"

"Eh. It's a living." Natalie shrugged. "It's ironic, but I don't particularly like some of the music, but I understand what kind of message the bands want to get across."

"You always had good instincts," Diana said.

"When it comes to that sort of thing, yes, but still trying to figure out what I want to be when I grow up. My instincts are not giving me any signals," she said, chuckling.

"I doubt that. I remember when you would second-guess yourself, and then want to kick yourself in the pants afterwards."

"Many times." Natalie grimaced. "Being here has made me slow down and give pause. Reflection, I think."

"Philosophical, eh?"

"I suppose. A change of scenery was most welcomed."

"Oh?" Diana tilted her head.

"Long story." Natalie sighed. "Well, not really. I had been seeing someone for about a year. Three months ago, we were meeting for dinner, and he gave me the 'we have to talk' routine."

"Uh, boy," Diana said with sympathy.

"I didn't even bother to have 'the talk,' " she said, using air quotes. "That's the kiss of death. So, I left. He didn't even know how long we had been seeing each other, which was another big red flag that the relationship was going nowhere. I could say the worst part was finding one of my best friends sitting on his lap at a pub, after I came out of hibernation."

"Whoa. That's really nasty."

"Yes, but I won the trivia prize that night and almost literally rubbed it in their faces." Natalie described her taunt.

"Well played," Diana said respectfully. "Did either of them get in touch with you afterwards?"

"Joyce left a few 'I'm so sorry' voicemails, but I ignored them. I could never trust her again," Natalie added thoughtfully. "Trust. I am going to have to get over my skepticism; otherwise, I could be closing myself off to opportunities."

"You really sound like you've been in a reflective mood."

"Yes, but in a good way." Natalie gave Diana a hug. "I better get going. Need to help pack up. I'm working with the food pantry."

"Wonderful. They could use the help."

"See you Tuesday." Natalie waved as she walked away. She was excited to meet up with an old friend and have something to look forward to. She bounced her way to the first stall and began to collect the leftover corn. After she made her rounds, she returned to Mr. Giambelli's to fetch her dinner fixings. "Remember to give my best to your mama!" he reiterated.

"And my papa, too!" Natalie gave him a devilish grin. "No complications over pasta!"

He chuckled. "Ciao, bella!"

Natalie put her groceries in the front seat and packed the back with the boxes of leftover produce, jams, and a few jars of honey. She picked up one of the jars and stared down at the bee on the front. "We'll just see about that apiary."

Chapter Five

After she delivered the boxes to the pantry, Natalie stopped at a liquor store to buy a bottle of wine. Her father wasn't on meds, and the doctor said one glass wouldn't hurt. In fact, he told her father that a glass of wine was far less lethal than the drugs people take for pain. "But just one," he cautioned. "No getting tipsy on my watch."

When she got back to the house, her parents were still out on another countryside jaunt. She set the groceries down and went to check on Mr. Meowzer, who was snoozing in the remaining sunlight.

"Well, hello there," Natalie cooed. "Are you in the mood to explore the kitchen with me?"

He stretched, rolled over, and went back to his nap.

"I guess not. At least you are chillaxing here. I'm going to fix dinner for Grandma and Grandpa." She scratched the top of his head and gave him a nuzzle.

Natalie separated her bounty and put the antipasto items on a platter, covered it with wrap, and set the dish in the refrigerator. She went into the pantry, grabbed two pots, and an apron. She didn't know why, but she had an unusual giddy sensation. It had been an interesting day, and she had social plans. Good reason to feel uplifted. She smashed the garlic like Mr. Giambelli suggested and sauteed it in the extra virgin olive oil. He stressed not to have the heat too high. "You don-a wanna burn the olive oil or the garlic. Make it nice ana easy." Natalie watched the cloves turn a light golden color and then removed them from the pan. She added some vegetable stock, and the fresh herbs from the garden.

As soon as the aromatics from her concoction filled the air, she shut the burner. She didn't want to start the veggies before the pasta was ready, and she didn't want to start the pasta before her parents got home. She put the pot of water on the stove, and turned up the heat so it could come to a boil. By then, everyone should be back and ready to eat.

Her timing was perfect. The car pulled into the driveway, and she could hear her parents coming up the porch steps. "You're doing great, Robert," her mother cheered him on.

"That's because something smells delicious." He chuckled. The two entered the kitchen. "This is very impressive," he went on. "Where did you learn how to cook like this?"

"I got a few tips from Mr. Giambelli. By the way, he said to say hello." She winked at her mother.

Her father let out a playful growl. "And did he say hello to me as well?"

"Not that I recall," Natalie teased.

"Huh," her father said with mock dismay.

"I told him that if he didn't say hello to you, there would be a lot of flying pasta in the kitchen." Natalie laughed.

"You didn't . . . ?" her mother asked warily.

"Not exactly." Natalie chuckled as she relit the burner,

where the herbs were infusing the olive oil and stock mixture. "Do you have any white wine? I bought a bottle of red for medicinal reasons."

"There's some white cooking wine in the pantry."

Natalie cringed at the idea of coming across the winking bee again, but then remembered she'd turned it around. She grabbed the bottle of wine and scooted back into the kitchen quickly, as if the dreaded bee would turn around like in a horror movie.

Natalie handed her father the bottle of red wine and the corkscrew. "I think you can manage this."

"I'll give it my best effort."

She began to add the vegetables to the pan, then tossed a cup of grated cheese on top so it could melt into the mixture; then she popped the pasta into the boiling water. While everything was cooking, she brought the antipasto platter to the table.

"Holy smoke!" Her father beamed. "This is quite a treat."

"Dear, this looks delicious! What can I do to help?" her mother offered.

"Sit. Relax. *Mangia*!" Natalie pulled the chair out for her mother, and then her father, who was waiting patiently to dig into the fresh mozzarella and prosciutto.

Ten minutes later, the pasta was ready to go into the vegetable mix. Natalie drained it, then mixed everything together. After she placed it in a large serving bowl, she grated more fresh parmesan on top, and garnished with a few sprigs of basil.

Moans and groans of delight filled the dining area. "Are you sure you have to go back to Jacksonville?" her father asked as he dunked his bread into the saucy vegetables.

Natalie didn't know how to answer the question, since she wasn't sure if he was joking. Instead, she said, "You're not supposed to eat bread with pasta."

"Then why is it on the table?" he asked, wiping a few crumbs from his face.

"That was for the antipasto."

"Antipasto, pasta, pesto. It's all going in the same place. My mouth!" He grinned and dunked more bread in his plate.

Halfway through the meal, Natalie mentioned she ran into Diana, and they were going to have a girls' night on Tuesday.

"That's wonderful, dear," her mother said between bites.

"And it's a trivia night." Natalie raised her eyebrows.

"You may get run out of town," her father joked.

"Ha! A former *Jeopardy!* contestant is going to be there."

"A contestant, or a champion?" her father asked, still dunking away.

"A contestant. I wonder if I'll recognize him. I think I've watched every episode in the past ten years."

"As long as you have fun, that's all that matters."

"I totally agree," Natalie said between bites. "Did you know about Diana's flower business?"

"Yes, I often buy arrangements for the church from her. She does lovely work."

"Oh? You never mentioned it," Natalie questioned.

"I usually order over the phone, and have it delivered, so I really haven't seen her in person for a long time."

"She looks the same. Married with two kids and another on the way. I am going to her place first to get a tour of the greenhouse. Then we'll head over to Clementine's, grab something to eat, and to beat the pants off Mr. Former Jeopardy Contestant."

"I've heard so much about her greenhouse. I am embarrassed to say I haven't been there."

"Her husband is an engineer and designed it for her." Natalie went on to explain how the two met.

"That's rather comical," her father noted.

"I think it's romantic," her mother chimed in.

"She seems very happy, and she looks great," Natalie mused.

"I'm so happy you have someone to go out with while you're here," her mother added.

"Me, too." Natalie nodded and smiled.

After dinner, Natalie told her parents to relax while she cleared the table and cleaned up the kitchen. Just as she was finishing up, her mother appeared in the doorway.

"You know you can stay here as long as you like—even after your father's physical therapy is over."

Natalie gave her an "it's possible" kind of nod. "You sure you can put up with me? I'm feeling a little guilty about Mr. Meowzer, although he seems content watching the birds and napping in the sun."

"Are you going to see if he's interested in investigating the rest of the house?"

"I'm just worried Dad might trip over him."

"He'll be fine. I'm sure your kitty will scoot far enough away from that contraption he uses, although the doctor said he might graduate to a cane in a couple of weeks."

"Maybe I'll give it a try tomorrow while you guys are out."

The next morning, Mr. Meowzer was the first to wake up as the sun peeked through the curtains. He nudged Natalie in the head.

"Hey, bubbie, isn't it a little early?" Natalie murmured as she checked the bedside clock. It was six o'clock.

He nudged her again.

"Okay! Okay!" She rolled out of bed and put a cup of kibble in his bowl. "What do you say we go on an adventure this morning? I'll bring you downstairs when Mom and Dad go to church."

He glanced up at her and gave her the cat version of a

shrug, meaning he went back to eating his food. Since she was wide awake, Natalie decided to go downstairs and make coffee. It was another bright, beautiful day. The morning paper was sitting outside the front door. She smiled at the "old-school" tradition of reading a printed newspaper. When she was growing up, her parents would split the paper, with her mother reading the lifestyle section and her dad reading sports and international news. She poured herself a cup of coffee and took both her mug and paper to the patio and began to skim the pages. Even though there was much turmoil in the world, she felt a sense of peace and serenity where she sat. *Was it the comfort of family? Being back in her childhood home? Seeing an old friend? Spending her afternoons doing something worthwhile?* As she pondered, she decided it was all of it.

As the sun began to rise, she was deep in thought. Life is filled with distractions, many of which can derail you from what's profoundly important. We set goals for ourselves and become razor-focused. Diana, for example. They had been friends since childhood. They even attended the same college. But over the years, they drifted apart. Not because of anything in particular. It happens without any intent. She pondered the pros and cons of "going with the flow" once again. Natalie decided there was a time and a place for that philosophy. For now, she was going with the warm flow of feeling content.

An hour later, her parents joined her in the kitchen for coffee.

"I don't suppose you're going to spoil us with breakfast this morning?" her father teased.

"Oh, Robert. Stop being a pest. You know we're going to meet the Mullans for brunch after church."

"Dang! Foiled again." He laughed. "Good thing they have a ramp at the club, although I really hate people watching me hobble around like an old fogey."

"Dad, people younger than you have surgery all the time." She stopped abruptly. "Wait right there."

Natalie headed out the back, past the herb garden and fruit trees, and wiggled her way into the garage. Just as she remembered, her old bicycle was leaning against the far wall. She squeezed past pieces of furniture, boxes, and an old lawn mower. "Geesh. This place is packed with all sorts of no-longer-needed stuff." When she finally reached the bike, she unhooked the classic trumpet-style horn from the handlebars. She gave the rubber bulb a little squeeze and giggled at the *whomp* sound it made. She dusted it off with her pajama top, squirmed her way back to the door, and moved quickly to the house. When she returned, both her parents had curious expressions on their faces. Natalie bent over the walker, attached the horn, and gave it another squeeze. *Whomp! Whomp!*

Her father burst out laughing. "I like it!"

"Since you can't ignore the fact that you are temporarily impaired, you might as well announce it," Natalie proclaimed.

Her mother was also on the verge of hysterics. "That's very funny." She turned to her husband. "But are you sure you want to go to church with that?" she asked.

"I promise not to interrupt the pastor's sermon."

"I shall pinch you until you are blue, if you do," Sally made an empty threat.

It was almost eight when Sally announced she was going back upstairs to get ready. "Service starts at nine."

While her parents were in church, Natalie would be at the food pantry. It's not that she didn't believe in God, she just preferred to worship in her own meditative way. She lit candles when people were ill, or to celebrate a birthday or anniversary, and said her morning prayers every day. She believed God loved her no matter where she prayed.

She once said to her mother, "As long as I have faith, He'll watch over me." Her mother couldn't argue with that, and neither did their pastor, Reverend Brooks. He knew Natalie was a good person and appreciated her volunteer work with the food pantry. He also believed that actions were often more important than words. It was your deeds that really mattered. While some friends and neighbors were in church, she was serving food, and making bundles for families to take home. It was all good.

Her father had already taken his shower and was dressed. Even though getting up and down a flight of stairs was manageable, it also required some oomph. He didn't want to tire himself out at such an early hour.

Robert gave his new toy another honk. "This is going to be fun."

"Try not to embarrass Mother, please," Natalie said, giving him a side-eye.

"I'll do my best"—he raised his eyebrows—"but can't promise you anything."

"I'm going to get Mr. Meowzer. Don't go anywhere," she instructed her father, who seemed content where he was.

"Don't forget to bring down my roller skates," he joked.

Natalie went back to her room, where Mr. Meowzer was sitting on the windowsill, his head bobbing up and down as he followed the flight of the birds.

"Hello, Bubbie. Want to do some exploring?" She picked him up, slung him over her shoulder, and carried him into the kitchen, making sure all the doors were closed. "Say hi to Grandpa." She bent toward her father so he could give the kitty a pat on the head.

"I forgot what a big boy he is."

Mr. Meowzer didn't seem to mind the attention and

change of scenery. Natalie eased him onto the floor, where he quickly began to rub against her father's legs. "Be careful there, buddy. We don't want Pops to trip over you."

The cat began to do what cats do. He sniffed around and meowed loudly. "What do you want?" Natalie asked.

He turned his face up to her and gave her a look that seemed to say: *What do you think? Food, lady. Get busy.* Natalie laughed out loud, as if she actually could read his thoughts. But, then again, she did. "Food? Did you say food?"

He responded with another loud meow.

"Impressive. Your cat speaks English," her father said dryly.

"True. There are no communication issues between us, which is more than I can say for my ex-boyfriend." Natalie realized that was the only reference she had made about Alec since she first told her parents about their breakup.

"Tell me something, sweetie. Did that guy break your heart?" her father asked compassionately.

Natalie paused for a moment before answering, "No. He made me angry. Angry, because it was obvious that our relationship didn't mean much to him, and he wasted a year of my life pretending he was interested."

"I know you can't get that time back, but now you will be more cognizant of the early warning signs."

"Yeah, apathy for one," she cackled. "I knew, in my heart, we weren't in love. It was more of a matter of convenience, and to be honest, laziness. We had gotten into a routine, and neither of us had the energy or the guts to move on."

"Sweetheart, you are young, vibrant, and smart. If you want a relationship, you will find one."

"I know you're right. I just have to pay more attention the next time, and not be afraid to make a change."

Sally returned to the kitchen. "Mr. Meowzer. So nice to see you out." She leaned over to give him a long stroke. She turned to Natalie. "What kind of change are you talking about?"

"Life. Men, or in my case, boys. I was telling Dad that I wasn't heartbroken over Alec, but I was angry at both him and myself. I should have moved on, or at least out of the relationship when I knew it was going nowhere. You know what I mean? That little nagging voice inside that screams, 'Run! Run as fast as you can!' I made a promise to myself that I would pay more attention to my intuition."

"That's a good plan, honey," her mother replied.

That word again!

Her parents left a few minutes later while Natalie kept an eye on her fur baby. He was tentative but not skittish. A good sign. Natalie had always thought her cat was well adjusted, considering he came from a house where a hoarder was arrested because she had almost thirty animals in the house under terrible conditions. That was two years ago, when Mr. Meowzer was a little over a year old. Natalie concluded that the cat was relieved he had been rescued from a hellacious menagerie, and therefore showed his gratitude by being mellow and affectionate. She watched him slowly walk from the kitchen to the living room, stopping to sniff a few things. When he reached the bottom of the stairs, he looked back at Natalie, then jumped up the steps and headed to the bedroom as if this were something he did every morning: *Go downstairs, sniff, eat, go back to the window.* Natalie followed him as he got back on his perch. Natalie could understand his position. It was like watching an IMAX *National Geographic* special on local birds. The cat was thoroughly entertained.

Natalie changed into her work clothes, which consisted of her cargo pants and a T-shirt. She checked herself in the mirror and made a face. A little makeup wouldn't hurt.

And she should do something with her hair. *There is no shame in connecting with your feminine side,* she said to her reflection. She may be doing grunt work, but she didn't have to look like one. She found a headband that matched her T-shirt. She took another look in the mirror. "Respectable, yet functional." She gave her cat another hug. "See you later. Behave." Natalie closed the bedroom door. Even though the kitty seemed to be relaxed roaming the house, Natalie didn't want to take any chances.

The shelves at the food pantry were organized as if it was a small market. Natalie's job was to walk people through and help them with their items. There were limits on some of the goods due to shortages. It was important to monitor the milk, eggs, and meat. Natalie was touched by the humility and gratitude people showed. She was humbled by the experience, as well.

By four o'clock, the weekly truck from a local supermarket arrived. That meant restocking the shelves. Every Sunday, the largest grocery store chain delivered several pallets of canned and dry goods. The pallets had to be broken down and the items shelved. It usually took a little over an hour, depending on how many volunteers were left. That particular day, there were enough to get the job done quickly.

Before she headed home, she phoned her folks to see if they were interested in pizza, although Natalie couldn't think of a place that had good pizza. She realized she hadn't ordered pizza here in over fifteen years. Maybe she should call Mr. Giambelli. If anyone knew where to find good pizza, he would.

He was delighted to hear from her and was more than happy to suggest his nephew's place, Sal's Pizzeria. "He's-a from-a New Jersey. It hasta to be good!" Mr. Giambelli joked. More good food! Natalie was in culinary heaven, even if it was something as simple as pizza.

Her parents were all in favor of no cooking or pots and pans, so Natalie placed her order with none other than Sal himself, who suggested a plain Margherita pizza with fresh tomatoes, mozzarella, and basil. "No sauce!" She also ordered a Caesar salad to make sure there was something green on the table besides the basil. She punched the address into her GPS and made the five-mile trip to Sal's.

It was a typical bistro-sized restaurant with red and white tablecloths and straw-clad Chianti bottles holding melted candles at various stages. It was warm and inviting, and the aroma was divine. She introduced herself and was handed a large, insulated bag chock full of eatery delights. "I slipped some garlic knots inside," he said, and winked at her. *Was winking a thing in Sumter County?* she wondered. She didn't find it offensive, just interesting. And it was more of a friendly gesture than a flirty one. Besides, Sal's wife was working the register. "You can give my uncle the bag on Saturday. We have over a dozen. We want every pie to be piping hot when it gets to the table." He helped her with the door. "Ciao! Hope to see you again!"

As she drove home, Natalie realized she had a huge grin on her face. She was quickly easing her way into the friendly and casual lifestyle of Sumter County. Had it changed since she was a kid? Or, did she forget? Had she become jaded living in a city? By the time she meandered through those thoughts, she was pulling into the driveway. She carefully brought her bounty into the kitchen, with a waft of deliciousness surrounding her. Plates, napkins, and forks were lined up on the counter.

Natalie fixed a plate for her father and carried it to the patio.

"That looks and smells delicious."

"It's from New Jersey," Natalie joked.

"I've heard that's where you get the best pizza," her mother chimed in.

"It only cost three hundred and fifty dollars," Natalie said with a straight face.

"Huh?" Her father squinted.

"Airfare. It's gone up quite a bit," Natalie teased.

When they finished stuffing their faces with their latest food find, Natalie cleared the table and put the dishes in the dishwasher. "Anybody need anything else?" she asked. Natalie realized she still hadn't checked on the bee guy's Internet presence. That was something she was itching to do. "I have a few things I need to check on."

"We're fine, honey. You do what you have to do."

Honey! Ugh! Then she reminded herself to be nice, until he gave her another reason not to. "See you in the morning. Sweet dreams," she called, and blew her parents a kiss.

"You too, sweetie."

Natalie slowly opened the door of her bedroom and discovered Mr. Meowzer dozing on the bed. He lifted his head, blinked, and went back to sleep. "Aren't you the enthusiastic one?" She snickered. Natalie pulled the chair from under her desk and powered up her laptop. There was one message from work. Another band needed a website update. The Sledgehammers. *Swell.* She sighed and marked the message as unread. She'd get to it during the regular work week. It was still Sunday, and she wasn't going to work on the weekend.

She opened the search engine and googled *Bee-Cause Honey.* A very rudimentary site popped up. One page with a contact form to sign up for the beekeeping demonstration. There were a few sentences about Garrett, a short mission statement about the importance of pollination, but little else. There was no place to order the product. She jotted that down. First was to enable it to generate income. Wait. What was she doing? She wasn't hired to update their website. *I guess I could do it as a favor. For Georgia, of course.* But what if they didn't want to expand that far? She jotted that down, as well. She'd ask her first before she offered her advice. She moved on to the more important matter at hand—Bee-man, himself. Just as she was about to search "Garrett Webster," her phone rang. It was Diana.

"Hey girlfriend! What's going on?" Natalie said with a smile, and closed her laptop.

"Just wanted to chat a bit."

"Everything okay?"

"Oh yeah, everything is fine. I had a few free minutes and thought we could have some girl talk. I know we're going to see each other on Tuesday, but we may not have time for ourselves. It gets pretty rowdy, especially if there are guys shooting pool in the other room."

Natalie faked concern. "Oh, my. Where are you taking me?"

Diana laughed. "It's a nice place, but you know how a few beers and some competition can raise the decibel level."

Natalie chuckled. "I do, indeed."

"Any more dirt on that cad of a boyfriend?"

"Nope. And I really am okay with it." Natalie paused, then continued, "Is it that hard for some people to believe? The fact that I didn't cry or get depressed? Embarrassed, yes. POed? Yes. But sad? No. Like I said, it wasn't love."

"Okay. Not that I didn't believe you, but sometimes people put up a false bravado." Diana was being kind.

"Have you met me?" Natalie said dryly.

"The Natalie I remember always put on a good, strong face. Just checking," Diana said warmly.

"It may be years since we palled around, but I still consider you one of my besties. I'm sorry we drifted apart."

"It happens without any ill will," Diana stated.

Natalie let out a chuckle. "I was thinking the very same thing."

"I'm glad we reconnected," Diana added.

"Me, too." Natalie wanted to talk to her friend about an extended stay in Sumter County. Would it be a good idea? She decided she should spend more time thinking about it before she started talking about it. That was going on her check list. Think. Talk.

The two women chatted about nothing, and laughed at several somethings, when they realized they had been on the phone for almost two hours. "Jeepers!" Diana exclaimed. "We've been blabbing forever. I better go check on my kids and my husband." Diana laughed.

"Okey dokey. I shall see you Tuesday. Looking forward to it." Natalie ended the call, got into her pajamas, gave Mr. Meowzer a kiss, then pulled the covers over her head.

Chapter Six

Monday morning greeted her in the same sunny fashion as the past several days. Her big boy kitty was engaged in his birdie entertainment.

"Hello, cutie pie," she called out to Mr. Meowzer, who turned to look at her and then immediately went back to bird-watching.

Natalie climbed out of bed, picked up her cat, gave him a hug, and set out some breakfast for him. She noticed the flyer for the beekeeping demonstration next to her laptop. At first, she tried to ignore it, but it was as if it had a life of its own. That darn winking bee was following her around the room. She made a mental note to continue her online search for the beekeeper, but that would have to come later. She pulled on a robe and padded down to the kitchen, where her mother was enjoying a cup of coffee.

They chatted a bit about what was on the day's agenda. Sally was going to work from nine to three, and Natalie was taking her father to his physical therapy. She hadn't formulated a plan for what she was going to do between projects. But then, totally against her inclinations, Natalie succumbed to her parents nudging her to go to the beekeeping demonstration. She'd managed to avoid the guy since their first encounter, but she decided it was better to face her demons, whether real or imagined. At least she would be in a beekeeper safety suit. Hopefully, he wouldn't recognize her. Besides, Natalie liked Georgia's vibe. Mellow, but without being dull. Sweet, but without being sickening.

Natalie went to the website and signed up.

After Natalie dropped off her father, she drove to the apiary. There were over a dozen bee-curious attendees, all clad in white and mesh. She thought they looked like a bunch of astronauts ready to take off. In reality, she was ready to take off in the opposite direction. She couldn't fathom why the man irked her to the extent he did. True, he was rude. But it was only one encounter. Don't people deserve a second chance to redeem themselves? Sometimes. Joyce and Alec did not. Garrett? She'd find out soon enough. That is, if she didn't bolt.

Georgia spotted her immediately and waved her over.

"Oh, I'm so glad you came. Here, take one of these suits and catch up with the tour. It just started, so you didn't miss much."

Natalie followed the group, purposely positioning herself so Garrett couldn't see her face clearly. What was she afraid of? Would he mock her? And if so, for what? Who knows if he'd even remember her. She couldn't call their first encounter an altercation. He wasn't mean. He even smiled and winked. And what was that all about? A bit cheeky, as far as she was concerned. She resigned herself to formulate a better assessment at the end of the day. She hoped she had learned something about jumping to conclusions and being judgmental. It was only fair.

The group followed Garrett to the apiary area, several yards from the building where they sold their honey. Garrett explained the distance was for obvious reasons. Traffic noise could disrupt the bees' process, and people who know nothing about beekeeping should stay away. He added that the best location for an apiary is facing south in a sunny area.

There were over a dozen man-made hives that looked like large boxes, approximately thirty inches high by twenty inches deep. Some were made of cedar and some of nonporous plastic. Garrett explained he was studying whether the bees preferred one over the other. Each hive was on a platform to make it easier to work with.

He described the parts of the hive, starting with the telescoping top cover to protect against rain. The inner cover was used for feeding. From there was a honey box, the queen excluder, then a brood box that held beehive frames with wax in order to make it easier for the bees to build honeycombs. The brood boxes held ten frames, spaced eight millimeters apart.

Natalie was struck by the intricacies of a man-made hive, and the passion Garrett showed for the bees and honey-making process. When he opened the lid of one of the hives, he used a smoking device that looked like a watering can, and explained how it calms the bees, and they retreat into the box.

"Keeping the hives in a state of good hygiene is as important as patience. It's a slow incremental process, and I inspect them at least once a week." Someone noted the large number of ants, to which Garrett explained they "clean house." He went on to say that one hive can produce up to two hundred pounds of honey a year. He also explained how important bees are to our agriculture and food production. Sounds of awe emanated from the screened-in spectators.

Natalie wasn't sure what was making her brain buzz. Was it the amount of information she was trying to process, or was it the bees themselves? She realized it would take more than one session to completely understand and appreciate the method and technique. It wasn't something you could glean from a YouTube video. She had to admit, she was impressed. Several people asked questions. She chuckled to herself, thinking she should ask him if he's always rude in parking lots.

After the demonstration, the group went back to the building, where they were checked for any rogue bees before removing their protective clothing. Natalie hoped Garrett wouldn't follow them inside. Instead, his sister Georgia ushered everyone into the storefront, where they were given a small wooden crate with several kinds of honey. "Natalie, right?" Georgia addressed her.

"Yep. That's me." Natalie blushed.

"I really am so happy you were able to come to one of our demonstrations. Most people have no idea how complex the process is."

"For sure. I think I only remember one or two things." She laughed. "It was quite interesting. I shall have much more respect for bees when I see them."

"Good! That's the whole point." Georgia smiled.

Out of the corner of her eye, Natalie spotted Mr. Bumbles bounding toward them. He had something in his mouth, and it was alive! Natalie gasped. "Oh, my goodness! What is that?" She thought it might be a rat. As the dog got closer, she realized it was a kitten.

"Mr. Bumbles! Bring her here!" Georgia commanded. The dog obediently and gently offered the kitten to Georgia's open hands.

"She's adorable!" Natalie gurgled at the furry, black kitty. "But show me a kitten who isn't."

"We sorta rescued a pregnant feral cat. She had four babies. We kept the mommy, and she's adjusting quite well to a more domesticated life. We were able to get all the kittens adopted except for this little darling. I suspect it's because some people think black cats are bad luck." Georgia grimaced.

"Aw, that's nonsense. I have a big, hairy, solid black ragdoll. The sweetest thing."

"Does he need a playmate?" Georgia pitched the idea at Natalie and handed her the fur baby.

Natalie froze. "Uh, well, I'm not sure how he'd take to a kitten, especially since he's in a strange environment right now. He's doing fine, but I don't know if introducing him to something else might make him bonkers." Natalie couldn't resist rubbing her cheek against the cat. "She *is* cute." The kitten began to purr, which melted Natalie's heart. "I wish I could." She handed the furball back to Georgia.

"Think about it." Georgia smiled.

Natalie sighed, "Oh, I will. Thanks again for the invitation"—she held up the little crate—"and the honey." She noticed Garrett walking toward the store and made a beeline for her car. No pun intended.

Once she got behind the wheel, she realized what a dolt she had been and decided it was time to give the bee dude a break. The next time she saw him, she would mention she had attended the demonstration and how impressed she was. Okay, perhaps she wouldn't go *that* far, but she would say hello.

When she left the apiary, she drove to the clinic, where her father was finishing his physical therapy. She met him at the entrance and helped him into the car.

"What's this?" He held up the small crate that was sitting on the console.

"Honey," Natalie said blankly as she pulled out of the parking lot.

"Ah, so you decided to go?" Her father inspected the jars.

"Yes, Daddy dearest. I took your and mom's advice. It was pretty interesting, actually."

"I bet it was." He grinned. "I've heard only good things about that fella."

"Yeah. Yeah," Natalie responded, and changed the subject. "How many more sessions do you have?"

"Two weeks."

"And then?"

"And then it's twice a week for six weeks."

"You mean I am going to have to be your chauffeur for another month and a half?" Natalie was teasing.

"Only if you want to. I can always take an Uber or Lyft."

"Or do you not want me to stay longer?"

"We would love for you to stay longer. Stay as long as you want. You have your best buddy kitty, your mother, and me. What else do you need? Besides your laptop."

"I've been thinking about it. The farmers market is open until Labor Day, and the food pantry needs help every Sunday. I'd hate to let them down, especially during their busy months. I have nothing going on in Jacksonville right now. I just don't want to get in the way of you and Mom."

"Never! And if you keep cooking, we'll never let you go back," he said, laughing.

That sealed it for Natalie. Her summer was now booked. The only thing left was to pay the rent for a place she wasn't living in. She had returned twice to check her mail and get more clothes. It struck her that when she was there, she realized she didn't miss it. Any of it.

"Listen, your mother and I were talking about converting the garage into a studio apartment. We thought about renting it out. Get a little more income to put in my retirement account."

"Retire? You?" Natalie couldn't recall hearing her father talk about retirement.

"Not right away. But the building is just sitting there housing a bunch of stuff we don't use. To tell you the truth, I don't even know what's in there besides gardening tools, and I built a separate shed near your mother's garden so she wouldn't have to drag everything back and forth."

"Well, we know my old bicycle is still in there."

Robert reached around to the back seat and gave his horn a toot. "The other idea was to turn it into an artist studio and rent it out that way. It just makes no sense to have a building that could generate some income, rather than a storage unit."

Natalie's wheels were turning. If they emptied the garage, it could be a very cool space with a loft bedroom. "I think it's a great idea, Dad." She failed to mention she thought it was a great idea for herself. She didn't want to make any hasty decisions. She had only been back for a little over two weeks. Two genuinely nice, comfortable weeks. Still, no reason to rush into anything.

"I do have a lot of free time, Dad. I'd be happy to go through some of the stuff. You can sit on that old milk can and boss me around."

"I just might take you up on that offer." Robert's wheels were also turning. It would be nice to have his daughter close by.

Sally and Robert never pressured either of their children to "settle down" or stay nearby. They raised them to be adults, adults with their own path.

The subject of a traditional "married with children" lifestyle was never a topic of discussion. Procreating was a good thing, but it wasn't for everyone. There were a lot of children with parents that were ill-equipped. Robert once remarked that you had to take a driving test in order to get a license, so shouldn't you have to take one to have a baby? There were no qualifications for parenthood. No training required.

Natalie and her brother were relieved their parents accepted them for who they were and respected their personal decisions. If it were up to Natalie, she would have more cats and a dog. Another checkmark in the "plus" column of the garage conversion. She had enough work and money to pay the rent for her unoccupied apartment for a few months, so it wasn't a pressing situation. She decided this was one of those "go with the flow" situations.

Chapter Seven

Once Natalie and her father returned from his session and he was situated with one of his books, Natalie went to her room. She logged onto her computer, back to where she left off. She wanted to resume investigating the bee guy.

She searched under Garrett Webster. That's when she hit pay dirt. There were a number of articles about his bee farm, lectures, and seminars he gave, and a video demonstration, similar to what she saw that afternoon.

She couldn't imagine why none of it was included on the website. Her first instinct was to recreate the site for them. What was the worst that could happen? They could tell her, "Thanks, but mind your own business," or they could be overjoyed. She wasn't going to second-guess herself this time, but she would also tread lightly. Natalie decided to engage in another conversation with Georgia the following Saturday. Natalie planned to bring her laptop and show Georgia her ideas. And she would offer it for free. Perhaps that was it: they didn't think they could afford a redesign? Or they suffered from technophobia—Natalie's word for people who feared technology. Another favorite term was the ever-popular "techno-challenged," a category many people fell into. But it wasn't really a fault or deficiency. Natalie knew how quickly technology changes, and unless you are involved in that fast-as-lightning industry, there is nothing to be ashamed of if you can't keep up. She would often tell clients, "That's why there are people like me. To get you through it. It's not unlike a vehicle. If you are a mechanic, then changing the oil isn't a problem. But if you're me, it's a problem. I don't know a crankshaft from a cylinder head."

She skimmed a few of the articles that featured Garrett and his explanation of the importance of bees and pollination. He talked about how precipitation, temperature, pesticides, and deforestation were having a huge impact on the pollinators. She read that the number of pollinators decreased sixty percent in the last fifteen years, something Garrett stressed during the demonstration. She thought about his demeanor. It was to the point but not preachy. He wasn't trying to lay a guilt trip on anyone. His goal was to enlighten people, not badger them. She laughed out loud, thinking about the expression *You can catch more bees with honey.* Garrett Webster learned a lot from his vocation.

Natalie felt a surge of excitement and enthusiastically drew up notes for the proposed website. She was deep in thought when her mother called from the hallway, "Natalie, dinner will be ready shortly."

Natalie blinked. She was so engrossed in her new project that she hadn't noticed the sun had gone down. "Mr. Meowzer, you haven't asked for your dinner."

At the word *dinner*, the kitty licked his lips.

"You really do understand English." She laughed. She gave him a pat on the head and answered her mother. "Be down in a minute." She opened a pouch for her furball, filled his bowl, and quickly moved to the main floor.

"Mom. I am so sorry. You should have asked me to help."

"Don't be silly, dear. I know you were working."

"I was doing some research. They have a new band they want me to take on." Natalie was telling only half of the story. It was true she had a new project for her job, but she left out her personal project. At least for now. She was familiar with The Sledgehammers and knew she could create their site in a short time. She turned to her mother. "I'll set the table."

Robert rolled his walker into the dining area. "Maybe two more weeks with this gadget, but I must confess, I'm a little nervous."

"About what, Dad?"

"It gives me the confidence I need to do what I have to do."

"And you will be able to do what you have to do without it soon. How many weeks with the cane?" Natalie asked.

"It depends. They would like me to be independent by Independence Day," he said, and snickered.

"That's a good goal. You'll simply have to be more mindful of your movements," Sally reminded him.

"I guess that means no bowling," he said, making a frowning face.

"When did you start bowling?" Natalie furrowed her brow.

"I haven't." He chuckled. "I couldn't bowl before, and I'm not going to bowl after."

Natalie laughed along with him. "What about golf?"

"If I do my homework, I should be able to play in twelve weeks."

"Driving? Not that I am looking to give up my part-time job."

"Hopefully, the week after next. As soon as I can ditch

this." He patted the walker. "But I have to take a little test with the doctor. He's going to have me drive in the parking lot before he gives me the 'all-clear.' "

Natalie became a little apprehensive. "So, you won't need me?"

"Of course we need you!" her mother quickly said, putting her arm around her daughter.

"You can still drive me around." Her father smiled. "But I'll sit in the back seat like a proper passenger with a chauffeur." He dragged out the *r* with a slight French accent.

Once everyone was seated at the table, said grace, and passed the platters of roasted chicken, potatoes, and vegetables, Natalie brought up the subject of the garage.

"Dad was telling me that you've been thinking about converting the garage into a rental of some type."

Sally looked up from her plate. "Yes, we've talked about it, but when I think about it, I get overwhelmed at the amount of work that's involved."

"What if I do most of it? I'll drag everything out, and we can have a yard sale or donate what you don't want."

"That's a very good idea," Robert said.

"Then once the place is cleared out, we can do an assessment. We can inspect the building and see if there are any big issues. If not, then I can draw up some sketches. I have a computer program for it."

"You're making this sound easy," her mother said.

"It doesn't have to be difficult if we plan it right," Robert chimed in. He was all for it and was glad he planted the seed in Natalie's head.

"Should we turn it into an apartment?" her mother asked.

Natalie took a deep breath. Was she ready to commit? Not yet. Maybe in another day or two. She wanted to run the idea past Diana. Natalie wondered if she would miss Jacksonville. Could she have a fulfilling life in Sumter County? If so, what would it be? Could she find it in Sumter County? In one way, it was a big move. But in another way, it wasn't. She began to think more about what she was moving *to*, instead of moving *from*.

"Do you have a budget you're considering?" Natalie questioned.

"I figure if we put in a full bathroom, an open kitchen with an island, a staircase to a loft space, it will probably run somewhere around twenty thousand," her father said, indicating he had spent more time on this than he had let on. "The building is twenty-four by thirty, so it's seven-hundred-twenty square feet. If we use the upper floor as a loft, then that could possibly add another two, hundred square feet."

Natalie's eyes were sparkling. "That would make a very cool studio. But I think there should be a shower upstairs and a half bath downstairs."

"You just added another five thousand to the project." Her father chuckled.

"What if I chip in?" Natalie offered.

Both her parents did a double take.

"Really?" said her father.

"Seriously?" said her mother.

"Why not? It's an investment," Natalie offered.

"You mean you don't want to spend that money jet-setting?" her father kidded.

"You mean traveling to the Greek Islands? The French Riviera? Boring," Natalie mocked in return.

"I think if Natalie wants to invest in this project, we should let her." Sally was convinced it was an excellent idea.

"Alright! We have a deal. I shall begin to go through it

this week. Anything that is too big for me to move, I will put on a list, and we can have those items removed professionally."

"Big items?" her father asked.

Natalie recalled what she observed recently. "There's an old generator, a commercial-grade ice chest, and ride-on lawn mower."

"You still have that lawn mower?" her mother asked her husband with surprise.

"Yes. I was going to get it fixed, but now that we have Lester tending the lawn, well, I never got around to it."

Sally rolled her eyes and muttered, "Why do men have such a hard time getting rid of things they never use?"

"I'm sorry. Did you say something?" Robert poked at her.

"Yes. You need to get rid of that stuff. You don't even know what's in there," Sally huffed.

"Neither do you," he taunted with a smile.

"Alright, you two. Knock it off or no dessert," Natalie ribbed.

Robert held up his hands. "I give up. Natalie, this is all on you. You do whatever you think is necessary. Just consult with me before you toss anything."

Sally gave him a raised eyebrow and stink-eye stare.

"What I meant to say was you do whatever your mother wants," he said, and guffawed.

Chapter Eight

Morning routines were becoming the status quo. Mr. Meowzer and Natalie would wake around six thirty. She would give him his breakfast, then head to the kitchen to make coffee. She watched some of the morning news programs in the kitchen until her parents came down. The three would have coffee on the patio, discuss anything and everything, including plans for the rest of the day. Sally was usually off to work before nine, and Natalie and Robert would be on their way to physical therapy either late morning or early afternoon, depending on whether or not he had hydrotherapy—a fancy word for exercising in the pool.

While Robert was going through his paces, Natalie waited in the lounge area, working on her laptop, which was when she worked on her employer's projects. She saved her side project, aka Mr. Bumbles' family business, for her evenings. But she wouldn't be working on the website this evening. Tonight, she was going to Clementine's with Diana. Natalie had to admit she was feeling atwitter. Excited.

The day moved along quickly. Robert and Natalie went

back to the house after physical therapy, and Natalie decided to change into a more appropriate outfit. It was her first night out since she won at Bennie's. One would think she was getting ready for her prom. Natalie laughed at herself. Was she that in need of a night out? Apparently, she was!

She rummaged through her clothes and found a navy-blue polka-dot maxi skirt. It was *almost* a dress. A navy sleeveless T-shirt, a string of white mala beads, and silver ballet flats completed the simple, yet stylish outfit. *Now what to do about the hair?* She searched the "everything drawer" that contained everything from scissors, to tape, to paperclips, to a few unidentified washers, screws, and several spools of ribbon. A piece of navy-blue grosgrain caught her eye. It was the right length to turn it into a headband. She bent over and brushed her hair, slid the ribbon behind her ears, then flipped her head and let her hair fall to her shoulders.

Now what to do about makeup? That was going to require a little finagling. She had tinted moisturizer, cream blush, light brown eyeshadow, and brown pencil. The pencil would have to do double duty for her eyebrows and eyeliner. A tired-looking tube of mascara was at the bottom of her bag. It still had a bit of gel left, just enough to do the job. If she liked the end results, she'd consider investing a few dollars in new makeup.

After she finished getting dolled up, she turned to her kitty. "What do you think?"

He stared at her.

"Is that a 'you look fabulous' expression, or 'put a bag over your head' expression?"

He blinked again and rolled over.

"Am I to assume that is an affirmative that I am passable?"

He rubbed his head against her hand.

"I shall take that as a 'yes.' Thank you." She gave him a kiss on the head. "Wish me luck!"

Natalie went downstairs to the patio, where her parents were enjoying the pastel colors of the early evening sky. Her father jolted upright. "Natalie! You look lovely!"

Natalie did a little curtsy. "See, I *can* wear a dress, but only when *I* want to."

"I agree with your father. You look lovely," her mother added.

Natalie gave them each a peck on the cheek. "Wish me luck!" She wasn't sure what kind of luck it would be, but she was feeling optimistic. Big changes were coming. Welcomed changes. Even if she had no idea what was ahead, the idea that looking at life with a new point of view was happily accepted.

"Good luck. Have fun!" Her mother waved.

"Don't go breaking any hearts tonight," her father said brightly.

Natalie snickered, "As if."

Settling herself into her car, she entered Diana's address into her GPS. According to the device, it should take twelve minutes to get there. Natalie was surprised and delighted that her friend was only a short distance away. When she arrived at the address, she noticed two driveways. One led to the greenhouse and flower shop; the other led to the main house. As expected, the grounds were beautifully landscaped, with a wide variety of lush tropical plants pouring magnificent colors into the scenery. Natalie pulled in front of the house and kept staring at the floral eye candy. Diana opened the door and joined Natalie outside.

"This is spectacular!" Natalie gushed.

"It's a work in progress," Diana said, smiling.

"I am so impressed. This is paradise." Natalie gawked at the bright fuchsia bougainvillea that draped along the side of the front patio.

"I have to give Jeremy most of the credit. He designed it. Come on back. You can see the rest of our production. And believe me, it can be a major production when a bride's specialty flowers are running behind. Talk about stress."

Natalie chuckled. "Most people don't associate flowers with stress."

"If you want to talk about stress, let me tell you, *Bridezillas* is not just a horrifying reality show. It lives and breathes here, too." She cocked her head in the direction of the greenhouse. "Follow me."

Diana opened the insulated doors. The area was teeming with colors and textures. To one side was a vast assortment of succulents; on the other, dozens of ferns draped their leaves in hanging baskets. Diana pointed out most of the obvious plants. The enclosed room led to another greenhouse, where rows of fresh flowers were in bloom. "This is beyond words," Natalie said in awe. "How many people work here?"

"There's six of us, including me and Jeremy. He is such a good sport about all of this. He works all week and then tends the greenhouses on the weekends." Diana opened the rear door that led to an area of large tropical plants. "I almost feel guilty. Almost." Diana chuckled. "I keep reminding him that all of this was his idea."

Diana cocked her head, listening. "Here they come!" Giggles from her two little girls got louder as they approached. "Mommy! Mommy!" One of the tykes wrapped her arms around Diana's legs.

"This is Jordan." Then the other child wrapped her arms around her mother's legs. "And this is Lindsay."

Diana placed her hands on the girls' shoulders. "Say hello to Natalie. She's one of my good friends."

Both girls politely said hello and then hid behind their mother's dress. A tall, handsome man had been lagging behind. "And this is the mastermind, Jeremy."

Natalie held out her hand. "Very nice to meet you, Jeremy. This place is stunning."

"Thanks. It's all Diana. I just do the grunt work." He smiled as he shook her hand.

"That's not what I've been told." Natalie smiled at the beautiful family. She crouched down and spoke to the two shy girls. "Do you help with the flowers?"

Jordan was the first to peek out. "Yes, but we aren't allowed to use the knife."

"That's an excellent rule." Natalie nodded. "And what about you, Lindsay? Do you help, too?"

Lindsay pulled the dress away from her face. "Yes, when Daddy is here."

The group began to walk back inside and through the sheltered plants. "I think I could live in here," Natalie cooed.

"It gets really, really hot sometimes," Jordan announced.

"I am sure it does," Natalie replied.

When they approached the front of the building, Jeremy said, "Come on, girls. Mommy is going out to play with her friend. Say good night to Natalie and give your mommy a big kiss."

In unison, the girls said, "Good night, Natalie."

"And?" their mother prodded.

"Nice to meet you," the children responded.

Diana gave the girls a kiss and then gave one to Jeremy. "Don't have too much fun!" Jeremy waved.

"You should probably notify the authorities," Diana quipped back.

"Shall I drive?" Diana pointed to her SUV.

"Sure. I've been *Driving Miss Daisy* every day," Natalie joked. "He's threatening to sit in the back. I just might let him," Natalie chuckled. "Your parents must be over the moon that you're staying here for a while." Diana hopped into the driver's seat.

"Yes, and so am I. Did I tell you I am going to be here for the rest of the summer?" Natalie said as she buckled her seat belt.

"That's great!" Diana turned to her with a big smile. "You can be my trivia partner every week."

Natalie laughed. "Let's see how I do tonight."

"I have no doubt you will be mopping the floor with everyone else. *Jeopardy!* contestant? Ha!"

It took less than ten minutes to arrive at Clementine's. The parking lot had well over two dozen cars.

"Gosh. I haven't been here in forever." Natalie stretched her neck to scan the parking lot. "I don't remember it being this popular. It was always kind of a down-market joint."

"New owners took over, cleaned it up, and made it a much more suitable place to bring the kids."

Diana pulled into a spot and turned off the engine. She continued to explain the transformation as they walked to the main entrance. "They have all sorts of activities, including a 'Grown Ups Only' time slot so you can have a quiet dinner." She swung open the brass and glass doors. "It's become a very popular spot."

"I can see that." Natalie scrutinized the room. "And all the men are wearing shirts with sleeves." She cackled.

"And no bare feet," Diana added.

The hostess greeted them. "Hi, Diana. Same table?"

"Yes, and this is my friend Natalie. She grew up here and is spending the summer with her family."

"Welcome!" The young woman smiled at Natalie. "Hope you enjoy yourself."

Soft rock music floated above. "They've really classed it up." Natalie noted the polished tables, which matched the light oak floors. The walls were also paneled in a light oak with large, framed drawings of indigenous trees. A long slate bar ran along one side. A low wall with the same slate and hanging ferns separated the dining area. Natalie noted the baskets. "Your handiwork?"

"Yep! I told them they needed to bring some life into the place."

"Good move." Natalie took in the new design and concept. "Big difference from the old, skunky, dark, and dank place."

"Everyone in town was overjoyed with the remodel. We needed a place like this."

People waved in their direction. Diana waved back, and Natalie smiled. It seemed like such a nice crowd. She could definitely see herself feeling comfortable here.

They were seated at a table in the rear corner, where the rest of the players would gather in a little over an hour.

Natalie perused the menu. "What do you recommend?"

"The short ribs. No question."

"Well okay, then." Natalie closed the menu and placed it on the table.

Natalie began to tell Diana about her parents' plans to convert the garage. At first, she hesitated to reveal her idea about moving back. But why? Would saying it out loud make it real? She took a deep breath. "I'm thinking of moving back. Permanently. Well, as permanent as anything can be."

Diana grabbed Natalie's hand. "Really? That would be so incredible. A year-round trivia partner, and a good friend nearby? I'll be in heaven."

Natalie was grinning from ear to ear. It felt good to say it, and extra good to see Diana's reaction. "There's nothing for me in Jacksonville. My chapter there is over. Time to write a new one."

"Wow." Diana took a deep breath. "This is huge, right?"

"Right!" Natalie's face was beaming. "I guess I should start getting used to this place."

Someone caught Diana's eye, and she smiled and waved. Natalie casually turned her head to see who it was. The Bee Guy!

"You know him, I suppose?" Natalie's face went slack.

"Garrett? Sure. He's a bee farmer. Nice dude."

"I went to a demonstration at the apiary yesterday," Natalie said, with a slight bit of trepidation. Why? She wasn't sure.

"Oh, cool. Fascinating, isn't it?" Diana gushed.

"Very much so. There are a lot of moving parts, including the bees." Natalie was back to relaxation mode. "So, what's his story?" Natalie had to ask. It had become abundantly clear she was going to be interacting with him at some point down the road.

"Divorced. Married a beauty queen, but when she realized he wasn't leaving his hives to help promote her career, she bolted."

"How long were they married?"

"I think it was about five minutes."

Both women burst out laughing.

"But seriously," Diana said, regaining her composure. "I think it was a year, maybe a little more. She was Ms. Orange Blossom and thought she had hit the big time."

Natalie couldn't help but ask, "Is he dating anyone now?"

"Not that I know of. I think he closed the door on that idea. At least for now."

"I totally get it," Natalie sighed.

A server came over to the table. Natalie was ready to place her order, but before she could say anything, the waiter said, "Mr. Webster would like to buy you ladies a drink."

Natalie almost choked. "Um . . . I'll . . . um . . . I'll have a cranberry and soda. Thank you."

"Club soda with lots of limes for me," Diana added.

"Tell him thank you very much," Natalie said begrudgingly, and then went on to tell Diana about her first interaction with Bee-man.

"He may have been busting your chops," Diana offered an explanation.

"He doesn't even know me," Natalie sputtered.

"I think you are letting your well-earned hostility toward men cloud your judgment."

Natalie pursed her lips. "You may be right. I was unreasonably rattled. I think the smile and wink pushed me into irrational indignation," she said, smirking.

Diana chuckled. "You're excused."

If Bee-man had any intention of coming over to talk to them, something must have changed his mind, because the women ordered and ate their meal without a visit from him.

The short ribs did not disappoint, and they finished their dinner several minutes before the rest of the challengers arrived. Natalie wondered if Bee-dude was a trivia buff, but he remained seated at the bar, watching a baseball game.

The trivia manager handed out pre-printed cards with five boxes on each, and placed tabletop bells in front of the contestants. "Write your name at the top. You will be given five questions. When you have completed the questions, ring the bell. The first card with the correct answers will win the round."

Natalie was excited. This was a different technique than Bennie's, where people would ring the bell and answer out loud. The round went quickly, with Natalie and Diana the first to slam the bell. That was how the rest of the evening proceeded. After winning a half dozen rounds, people were stage-whispering "ringer." And where was Mr. *Jeopardy!* contestant? If he was there, he wasn't letting his presence be known. At least, not yet. It wasn't until the final round, when his friends booed him, that there was confirmation that he was even there. "Are you sure you were on that show?" one of his mates whined.

It was good clean banter, and the women bought a round of drinks with their winnings.

"See you next week!" Diana announced. More moans and groans followed them out the door. Natalie had forgotten about her imagined nemesis at the bar until she heard a voice—"Good night, ladies"—and he gave them the two-finger salute.

"Don't you find him annoying?" Natalie asked, and locked arms with Diana.

"Garrett? No! He's a doll."

Natalie was still not convinced, but then she thought about what Diana said about her attitude toward men in general. "You're right. I need to get over my 'all guys are creeps' mentality."

"That's my Natalie!" Diana gave her friend a hug. "I had so much fun tonight. I don't think I've ever won more than three rounds. But twenty-five? I am now a trivia star, thanks to you!"

"You did half the work." Natalie slung her arm around her friend. "And agreed. That was a lot of fun."

By the time Natalie got home, her parents were already in their room. She bounded up the stairs and found Mr. Meowzer sitting comfortably on the bed.

"Miss me?" He stretched. Natalie opened a pouch of food that he gladly accepted. "Mommy aced the contest tonight." Mr. Meowzer was too involved with his dinner to respond.

Natalie changed into her pajamas and powered up her laptop. She was more intent than ever to work up a website for the beekeeper.

Chapter Nine

By the time Saturday rolled around, Natalie had a rough model for the Bee-Cause website. The home page was a video close-up of a honeybee. As the bee exited, the headline POLLINATORS: BENEFICIAL FOR OUR ENVIRONMENT popped up. Under that was a welcome message with a brief description of why pollination is integral to our existence. Natalie pulled a few quotes from Garrett's symposium and posted them on the page. There was also a box the user could click to watch a demonstration. The website was simple for an average user and directed the viewer to the ordering page. That was where she stopped. Could they, *would* they, want to do e-commerce? She left that spot blank. Natalie walked herself through the website as if she were a first-time visitor and was pleased with the results. If Georgia and Garrett weren't, then it was no big deal. If nothing else, she was honing her creative chops.

Saturday morning was another bright, beautiful day. Natalie tucked her laptop into a tote, gave Mr. Meowzer a kiss on the head, and went into the kitchen. She made coffee and a slice of toast and wrote a note to her parents explaining she was leaving early for the market. She didn't say why, but it was because she wanted to spend a few minutes with Georgia before the market opened to the public. When she arrived, there was a lot of hustle and bustle, with people setting up their booths and putting their wares on display. The market was divided into several categories. There was the fresh produce area, baked goods, seafood, and prepared food such as chicken pot pies, cheeses, and a variety of home-canned goods, such as Natalie recalled what she'd observed recently. A separate section was devoted to handcrafted items such as jewelry, leather goods, paintings, and pottery.

Natalie found her way to Georgia's booth. "Hey there! Need a hand?" Natalie offered.

"Hi, Natalie. Yes, thanks. That would be great. Garrett usually helps, but he's running a little late today."

"I have something I wanted to talk to you about," Natalie said casually, while she placed the jars of honey on a table.

"Sure. What about?" Georgia handed Natalie another case of honey.

"I was really impressed with the demo and your shop."

"Thanks. We do our best."

"So . . . I went to your website."

"Oh, gee. It's really not up to speed. We just haven't had time to do anything with it. Busy season, ya know?"

"I understand. Did I tell you I am a web designer?"

"Uh-boy. I bet you were underwhelmed," Georgia replied.

"I hope you don't mind, but I took it upon myself and came up with an idea." She pulled her laptop from her bag. "May I?"

Georgia gestured to the table. "Of course."

Natalie powered up her device and opened the link she created for their site. "Now, it's just a concept."

Georgia looked over Natalie's shoulder as Natalie explained the simple pages. The only words from Georgia were, "Wow. Oh my. That's amazing."

"I didn't know if you wanted to include e-commerce, so I left it blank."

"This is really impressive, but to be honest, we can't afford it right now."

"Oh, I am not going to charge you for my work, and I'll be happy to maintain it for you. All you would have to do is let me know what flavors are available and fulfill the orders that come through."

Georgia was dumbstruck. "This is incredible. We've been talking about getting up to speed so we can generate more income. This could be a game changer for us." Georgia stared at the website.

Natalie could sense Georgia's uncertainty. "Consider it my contribution to pollination. What you and your brother are doing is admirable. I am happy to help."

"I really don't know what to say." Georgia was genuinely speechless.

"I am sure your brother will have some thoughts. Can I email this link to you so you can show him?"

"Of course. That would be swell!" Georgia blinked several times. "I am blown away."

"That was the reaction I was hoping for. Now let's hope your brother agrees."

"I don't see why he wouldn't. Thank you so very much." Georgia gave Natalie an awkward hug.

"I'll see you at the end of the day. Is Garrett going to be here?"

"Probably. But if not, I will show it to him tonight. How can I reach you?"

Natalie pulled a business card from her pocket and handed it to Georgia. "Talk to you later."

Natalie was almost skipping past the stalls. Then she spotted them. A stall had baskets full of plums. Just what her mother wanted. Natalie bought a basket and asked the farmer to hold them until the end of the day.

The day moved quickly, but still no sign of the bee guy. By the time everything was packed, Natalie noticed he was still nowhere to be seen. She shrugged. *Later, gator.*

When she arrived at the pantry, Reverend Brooks was holding a large box. It was filled with flyers for the Fourth of July Jamboree. "Natalie, I was wondering if you could help put some of these up in town?"

Natalie set her box down on a table and looked at the flyer. "Sounds like quite the extravaganza."

"Yes, we have become the most popular July Fourth celebration. Contests, music, food trucks, and fireworks in the field behind the bandstand." Pastor Brooks was proud of his personal holiday project. "They say we may have close to three thousand people this year."

"And it's only for one day?" Natalie asked.

"Yes. We tried to make it a two- or three-day fair type of thing, but people needed to go to work, and it wasn't worthwhile. Now we pack everything into one day, including half the county residents. We might have to find another locale for next year. Our modest fairground will be filled to the brim. Good thing the local middle school offered use of the parking lot, and we have shuttle buses."

"Pastor, you have done an extraordinary job."

"With the world moving so fast, and people staring at their phones, I wanted to have at least one event where people could gather, enjoy the company of their neighbors, and celebrate our country." He leaned closer and whispered, "Without all the politics."

"I am so with you. We need good, family fun. No fighting, no whining."

"Natalie, you have always been one of my favorites, and I was happy to hear you are going to be with us for the rest of the summer."

"Maybe longer." She gave him a wink. *Ah, now she understood the friendly, co-conspirator wink.* It was one way of conveying a number of thoughts.

"You are forever welcome here." The pastor stopped short of mentioning church services. He wished more of his parishioners had the integrity and generosity that Natalie possessed.

"Thank you. And I will be sure to paper the town with these. Can you set aside a box while I unpack?"

"Absolutely." Reverend Brooks took a box that contained one hundred flyers and placed them on an outdoor picnic table. "They'll be here when you leave."

"Thanks, Rev," she called over her shoulder, and finished her chores for the day.

When she got home, she carried the basket of plums into the kitchen. "Look what I found!"

"I am so happy!" Her mother clapped her hands. "You and your father will be my guinea pigs."

"Count me in!"

That evening, Natalie got an email from Georgia. "We are beyond grateful. This is fantastic! Thank you so much! Talk on Saturday!"

Natalie was walking on a cloud. Life did have a way of turning things around . . . if you paid attention.

The following week, Natalie put signs in every window she passed. Everyone was excited about the annual festival. Once again, she was all atwitter. She was truly looking forward to an old-fashioned holiday celebration, and the start of her garage project.

Diana's husband graciously offered to help with the contractors once the garage was cleared out. Natalie underestimated how much grunt work was involved and hired Diana's people to help. With the two men, they were able to pull everything from the inside to the driveway. It looked as if a junkyard had moved in. Sally came outside and gasped. "All of that was in there?" She pointed to the now-empty building.

"Yes, it was. Now we have to figure out what to do with all of it."

"I'll go get your father." Sally hurried inside, as if the rubbish police were hot on her tail. Robert carefully traversed the sidewalk that led from the kitchen, past Sally's garden, and to the driveway.

"What is all this?" he asked, half joking.

"Most of it is yours, dear." Sally stood with her arms folded. "Can you honestly say that you want to keep all of it?"

"Keep it? I forgot I had it!" He laughed. "Isn't there a number you can call? Something like, 1-800-get-rid-of-it?"

Natalie laughed. "Yes, Pop. I'll manage the details. Just give it one quick look-over and let me know what you want to keep."

"He doesn't want to keep any of it," Sally proclaimed. "You know what they say? If you haven't used it in five years, then you don't need it."

"Who said that?" Robert teased.

"Doesn't matter. Gone. All of it." Sally suppressed a

smile and then winked at Natalie. *There it was again. A wink.*

The following day, Natalie began to make phone calls to have the remains of the garage removed. There was nothing she found salvageable for her needs, nor did either of her parents. "I'm gonna miss that lawn mower," her father kidded.

Chapter Ten

The few weeks leading up to the celebration were busier than usual: Robert had graduated to a cane; the bee site had been launched, with Georgia getting a tutorial from Natalie; and Natalie had the rough plans drawn for the garage's renovation. Before she knew it, July was upon the world, and with it, the biggest celebration in the county, within fifty miles, not counting Orlando.

It had been a month since Natalie began working at the farmers market, and she hadn't seen Garrett since the night at Clementine's. She didn't want to admit she wondered about his whereabouts, and she certainly was not inclined to ask. She assumed he was busy making honey since the site went live. It had only taken two weeks for the honey business to start getting orders from all over the country. Georgia was elated, but also busier than ever, and she hired some part-time staff to help pack and ship.

Two weeks after that, Georgia found Natalie among the booths at the market. "Natalie! You have turned our lives around!" she exclaimed, giving her a huge bear hug.

"Do tell!" Natalie was thrilled she'd been able to make a worthwhile contribution using her skills.

"I don't know what you did, but we have been getting dozens of orders every week. Garrett said he's going to have to put up a few more hives. The extra money from the mail orders will enable him to purchase everything he needs to expand without getting us into debt." Georgia was out of breath from her excitement in delivering the news. "He's been busy as his bees! He also said to tell you how much he appreciates what you've done, and he's sorry he hasn't had the time to tell you in person."

Natalie smiled. "I totally understand. And, as I said, happy to help."

Georgia finished their conversation with, "I hope we will see you at the Jamboree."

"I wouldn't miss it," Natalie said, as she walked away on air.

"Hey Nat?" Georgia called out. "That kitty still needs a home."

Natalie grimaced. She was torn. "Let's chat about this later."

The fair was a week away, and Sally tried several recipes for the bake-off contest. She was determined to enter her plum cake but needed the final approval from Robert and Natalie. The two previous attempts weren't quite right, and Sally hoped she had hit her mark this time.

After dinner that evening, Sally presented them with her latest creation. Natalie couldn't eat it fast enough between her mutterings of delight. "Mom! I think you've got a winner here!" She picked up the crumbs with the back of her fork and licked them off.

"You may have another slice," Sally said gleefully.

Robert held up his plate and made puppy eyes. "Please, may I have some more, too?"

"Speaking of more," Natalie chimed in, "I'm thinking about getting another cat. This one is a kitten and needs a home."

"Do you think Mr. Meowzer would approve?"

"That's my only concern. He's quite mellow, and I don't think he'd mind having a playmate."

"Can't you take it with the stipulation that your cat must accept another kitty?" her father suggested.

"That's a brilliant idea. I'll phone Georgia later. Meanwhile, another piece, please?"

After dinner, Natalie phoned Georgia and explained her terms. Georgia understood the circumstances and was happy to oblige. "I'll ask Garrett to bring her over tonight, if that's okay."

Natalie suddenly got the jitters. *Garrett? Here? Tonight?* What could she say?

"He'll bring litter, a pan, and food."

Now she had to say yes. "That would be fine. What time should I expect him?"

"Hang on, I'll go ask him." Georgia took a moment to find her brother while Natalie's legs turned to Jell-O. "He can be there in an hour. Is that alright?"

Natalie gulped. "Yes. Fine. Great. Thanks." She gave Georgia the address and ended the call.

She immediately checked her image in the mirror. It needed a little tweak. She brushed her hair, retied a ribbon around it, dabbed on some blush, and swiped some gloss on her lips. She reminded herself once again that it was okay to be in touch with your feminine side, as long as you didn't give up and abandon who you are: smart, creative, caring, and able to stand on your own two feet.

She sat at the edge of the bed and began to explain to her big, fluffy boy that he was about to get a sister. He stared, blinked, and yawned.

"I think you are going to be very happy having a pal, someone to keep you company and someone to play with."

He blinked again and stretched. Natalie took it as a sign that he was willing to try it.

Within the hour, the doorbell rang. Natalie's heart was beating fast. She took several deep breaths. Why was she so nervous? A new member of the family for one thing, and the bee dude for another.

Natalie answered the door. Garrett seemed larger than life, with his firm muscles pushing against the fabric of his shirt, his bright eyes, and a very charming smile. "Hello, Natalie," he said in a clear baritone voice.

"Hi, Garrett." She swung the door open. "Please come in." She peered inside the carrier, where a little black ball of fur meowed. She approached with a soft voice. "Hello, sweetie. Everything is going to be okay." Then she turned her attention back to Garrett. "Thanks for bringing her and everything else over." She noticed a large box on the front step that contained everything Georgia had listed.

She took the carrier from Garrett as he brought the box inside. "Where do you want this?"

"You can leave it at the bottom of the stairs."

Several minutes later, Sally and Robert appeared in the hall. "Garrett, these are my parents, Sally and Robert Simmons."

Garrett politely shook their hands. "Nice to meet you."

"We buy your honey all the time," Sally said with a smile.

"Thanks. We appreciate it." Garrett paused before continuing, "Did you see the incredible job Natalie did with our website?"

Sally looked surprised. "I haven't seen it. Have you, dear?" she asked, turning to her husband.

"No. Natalie hadn't mentioned it," he said with a smirk.

"Just trying to help out. No biggie." Natalie tried to blow it off.

"Don't believe her. It really is a biggie. It's generated over two thousand dollars in the past month."

"That's our girl," her father said proudly. "And modest, too." He gave her a wink, the new sign language.

"I better get going. Nice to meet you. Hope to see you at the festival. I hear the fireworks display this year is going to be over the top."

"Looking forward to it," Robert answered, knowing he was going to have to limit his movements, but he wasn't going to miss the pyrotechnics.

Natalie moved toward the front door to let Garrett out. "Thanks again."

"No, thank you, Natalie Simmons." Garrett gave her the two-finger salute as he turned and walked outside.

Her father was the first to proclaim, "Nice young man."

Natalie was about to say something snarky but stopped herself. Garrett hadn't been anything but kind and gracious, even if he did slightly embarrass her with his compliments. He just made her feel . . . unbalanced. But she wasn't sure why.

Natalie shook the thoughts out of her head and turned her attention to the new member of the family. "Hi. Do you want to meet your new brother?" She looked at her parents and said, "Wish us luck."

Natalie climbed the stairs and took a deep breath as she opened the door.

"Look who I have here, Mr. Meowzer. It's your new toy. This is for you."

Natalie remembered that when you introduce a new pet, you should make it sound like it's a present for your current one. She placed the carrier on the bed, and Mr.

Meowzer went straight to sniffing it out. The kitten backed into the corner of the carrier, and Natalie continued to speak to both of them in hushed tones. She opened the door of the hard-cased pet taxi and decided to leave them to their own to explore the situation and feel each other out.

Mr. Meowzer sat on the outside of the carrier, sniffing and staring. No hissing so far.

"I'll be right back," Natalie said to them, and then went downstairs to tell her parents that she was going to supervise the introduction and get some work done. When she returned to her room, the kitten had moved closer to the opening of the carrier.

"That's my girl. And my boy."

Mr. Meowzer hadn't budged, but at least he didn't run away, or worse, make a move to threaten the kitten.

Natalie opened her laptop and began to finish her latest project for her job. She contemplated the difference in her enthusiasm between the sites she developed for Bee-Cause Honey and The Sledgehammers. It was obvious. The challenge of the honeybee website was definitely more satisfying.

A lightbulb went on in her head. Why not turn some of her focus toward nonprofits or community groups? She could maintain her day job. That was easy. Boring, but easy. Stretching herself to more worthwhile projects would be gratifying and add balance to her life.

Spending time at the market and the food pantry changed her point of view. Or it actually gave her one. A much larger one, at the very least. She reflected about the irony to have found a bigger perspective and purpose in a smaller place.

Natalie had been engrossed in her thoughts when a purring caught her attention. She quickly turned toward the sound. There was Mr. Meowzer, gently holding the kitten down with one paw while he licked the top of her head and all over her face. It was a *meow* of delight.

"Welcome to your new home, little one."

Natalie realized the cat didn't have a name, or if she did, neither Georgia nor Garrett shared it. Natalie often referred to Mr. Meowzer as "Bubbie" and chose "Boo" for the new fur baby. Easy to say, "Bubbie and Boo." *That's Miz Boo for anyone who asks.*

Natalie decided to check on her folks and give them an update. They were in the living room, watching reruns of *Columbo*. Her father turned toward her and remarked, "Fifty years later, and it's still entertaining."

"Better than a lot of stuff these days." Sally chuckled. "Do we sound like old fogies?"

"No. You sound like intelligent people who want to be entertained by talented writers and actors, whether it's comedy or drama."

"A very articulate response," her father replied.

"And flattering," Sally added. "So how are my grandchildren getting along?"

"So far, so good. When I came down, Mr. M was grooming Miz Boo."

"You named her already?" her mother asked.

"It just came to me. I usually call my guy Bubbie. Boo seemed to fit."

"Bubbie and Boo. Sounds like a duo to me," her father remarked. "By the way, that Garrett fellow. Seems like a nice young man."

"Yeah, you said." Natalie waved him off. "Good night."

Chapter Eleven

The excitement in the county was palpable. You could feel it in the air. Two days before the event, strings of lights zigzagged their way around an area the size of several football fields. People assembled the bandstand riser and placed one hundred folding chairs in two split rows, on top of a portable dance floor. The first row was reserved for dignitaries, like the mayor and sheriff and committee members. Natalie had volunteered to help and was an official committee member, so she made sure she secured two seats for her parents, and three for Jeremy, Diana, and herself. She scrawled their names on the placeholders. The rest was first come, first seated, and everyone else was welcome to sit on the grass. A few people brought their own lawn chairs and marked their territory without fear of someone stealing them before the festival. It was the honor system. There were also a few off-duty police officers who volunteered to keep an eye on things. It wasn't a big city, but it also had over ten thousand people living in the area.

Once again, Natalie was faced with the big challenge of what to wear. She engaged the assistance of Diana a few days before. "I know I'm doing this at the last minute, but I feel like I need to get something to wear for the Fourth. My first big outing, ya know? Want to come shopping with me?"

Diana was thrilled to have some girlfriend time and loved to shop. Even though it was her busy season, an hour diversion was welcomed.

It didn't take long for the two to agree on a pale peach linen dress. It had a V-neck, short sleeves, and hit at the calf. It was casual but put together. Feminine but not frilly. A pair of low-wedge espadrilles and a straw tote rounded out the outfit. Perfect.

The Independence Day jamboree began at noon, with food trucks, contests, and music, featuring several local bands. The evening concert was scheduled to start at eight, with a big band playing many of the old standards. An area between the seats and riser was open for anyone who cared to dance.

Jeremy and Diana planned to bring the girls for a little afternoon fun. The evening was reserved for adults, and Diana had gotten a babysitter. Natalie agreed to catch up with them when they returned.

Sally entered her plum cake in the bake-off that started at four o'clock. After several attempts, she'd finally hit upon a recipe that was close to her grandmother's.

It took no one by surprise when Sally won the ribbon for "Best Family Recipe," with no crumb left in sight.

Natalie agreed to scoot home after the contest to pick up Robert and bring him to the evening festivities. Although he had come a long way in six weeks and was able to move about most of the time without his cane, Sally and Natalie convinced him that it would be better if he just came to the evening concert. Robert didn't even want to bring his cane but, out of an abundance of caution, his doctor recommended he bring it, because it was a signal to the people around him to *try* not to bump into him.

Natalie pulled the car near the area where the band's sound truck was parked. It would make it a much shorter walk for Robert. Diana, Jeremy, and Sally were standing near the seats, having an animated conversation, with gestures toward the ribbon pinned on her chest.

"Looks like your mother did it again." Robert smiled proudly. "But did she save any for me?" He feigned a whine.

Sally reached into her small straw tote and presented Robert with a slice of the winning cake.

"You deserve this," she said, as she handed him the mouthwatering delight.

Just then there was a small stir on the band riser, indicating that the entertainment music was about to begin. Sally, Robert, Diana, Jeremy, and Natalie took their seats.

An announcer walked onto the stage and did the usual, "May I have your attention please?" He went on to thank everyone who made the day possible, then introduced the band.

The sound of "Boogie Woogie," reminiscent of the Tommy Dorsey band, got the crowd bouncing. Then came "In the Mood," and it sounded as if it were the Glenn Miller Orchestra playing it. The band was really good, and a few couples took to the dance floor, dazzling the crowd with their version of a jitterbug. The next song was "Moonlight Serenade." Then a female vocalist took the stage and began to sing "Let's Do It (Let's Fall in Love)."

Natalie was startled when someone tapped her on the shoulder and whispered, "They're playing our song."

Natalie stared into the eyes of Garrett Webster. She was flustered but stood gracefully, took his hand, and followed him to the dance floor. It was as if they had done it a hundred times before. He began to sing along. *"Birds do it. Bees do it."*

Natalie placed her head against his shoulder and swayed with him. *"Even educated fleas do it."*

He pulled her closer and whispered in her ear, releasing a quiver up her spine. "Please accept my apology for my rude behavior the first time we, um, met. I should have stopped and said hello. Then, when I offered to buy you a drink at Clementine's as a peace offering I thought that would break the ice, but I wasn't sure you wanted anything to do with me. I figured I should just accept that, but when you presented us with that amazing website, you really spun my head around."

Natalie was stunned. "And here we are," she whispered.

He lifted her chin and brushed a lock of hair from her cheek. "Yes, here we are," he said softly.

She sighed and melted deeper into his arms. "Life may not always be a bowl of cherries, but it can certainly be sweet as honey."

Grandma Matilda's Plum Cake

Ingredients

Streusel
1 cup flour
⅓ cup sugar
¼ teaspoon ground cinnamon
4 tablespoons cold butter

Cake
2 sticks butter, softened
1 cup sugar
3 large eggs
1 cup Greek yogurt
2½ cups flour
1 cup ground almonds
1½ teaspoons baking powder
1 teaspoon ground cinnamon
¼ teaspoon salt
2 pounds pitted plums, quartered

Instructions
1. Preheat oven to 360.
2. Line a 9 x 13-inch cake pan with parchment paper.
3. Make the streusel: Mix 1 cup flour, ⅓ cup sugar, and ¼ teaspoon of cinnamon in a small bowl. Cut in the butter until crumbs form. Chill until ready to use.
4. For the cake, cream the two sticks of butter with 1 cup sugar and 3 large eggs. Mix until light and fluffy, about 5 minutes. Slowly mix in the Greek yogurt. Once incorporated, slowly mix in the flour, ground

almonds, baking powder, cinnamon, and salt. Mix until batter is smooth.

5. Spread the batter in the cake pan. Place the plums on top, evenly spaced. Slightly press the plums into the batter. Sprinkle the streusel evenly over the cake.

6. Bake 35-40 minutes, until a toothpick inserted in the middle comes out clean.

7. Cool in the pan on a wire rack. Eat and enjoy!

EVERYTHING SHE'D EVER WANTED

LORI FOSTER

Chapter One

A ray of blinding sunshine cut through the heavy storm clouds, adding a layer of steam to the first day of spring. Ah, sunshine. She'd missed it so much during the long dark winter.

AnnaBeth Sanders turned her face up, ready to enjoy the warmth, to bask in the renewal of promise that was springtime.

Almost immediately, a rumble of thunder shook the ground beneath her feet, and heavy clouds rolled in to obscure the sun, causing her to huff.

Obviously, it was too much to ask for the unseasonably mild weather to last. In Ohio, spring usually came in rough, bounced around a bit with winter, and then landed hard in rainy season.

It had drizzled off and on all day, but she'd briefly hoped for a pretty sunset. No such luck. She looked out at her tiny Chiweenie dog, Ruby, who for the moment seemed undecided on where to do her business. "Hustle up, Buttercup."

The dog, of course, ignored her to investigate yet another patch of soggy ground. Ruby stretched her leash as far as she possibly could, which meant AnnaBeth was going to have to haul herself up off the porch steps any minute now.

"Your paws are going to be mud-covered. For real." Not that it was a huge issue with a four-pound dog. Cleanup was usually a breeze.

Ruby glanced back at her in a dismissive doggy way, then suddenly turned to stare up the street, her posture alert.

That got AnnaBeth on her feet. "Yup, right on schedule." True, the sunshine was nice, but the main reason she and Ruby were outside had more to do with her neighbor's hot nephew. He visited around this time every Tuesday and Thursday, and often on weekends, as well.

AnnaBeth had been playing it cool around him for a year, but Ruby, who'd fallen head-over-paws in love with the guy's five-year-old daughter, never hesitated to show her devotion.

Seconds later, Devlin Connely's familiar SUV came careening toward his elderly uncle's driveway, which ran alongside *her* driveway.

AnnaBeth stared. "What in the world?" He wasn't exactly speeding, but he was definitely going faster than usual.

She and Ruby watched as he shot diagonally into the driveway, jammed the vehicle into park, then launched himself out of the driver's seat and scrambled around at a fast sprint to the opposite back-seat door.

He fumbled, cursed low, got it open, and fumbled some more, then lifted out his daughter . . . just in time for Mia to projectile vomit.

For real, it shot through the air . . . and landed mostly on AnnaBeth's driveway.

"Whoa." AnnaBeth wrinkled her nose. The dog strained against her leash, more than ready to visit her friend—and possibly investigate the mess. Gross.

Super-fine Devlin Connely didn't even seem to see her standing there, gawking at him.

All his attention was on his daughter as he jerked off his open flannel shirt and used it to wipe the little girl's mouth. He said in a low, crooning voice, "It's okay, sweetheart. Take a breath."

Ambling closer, AnnaBeth asked, "What's up, other than her stomach?"

Kneeling, gently rubbing the little girl's back, he said, "Too much ice cream, I suspect."

"*Dad,*" Mia complained, and promptly gagged again.

"Yeah, Dad," AnnaBeth echoed. "No mentioning f-o-o-d to a chick who's puking."

Brown eyes, sinfully dark and heavily lashed, glanced up at her. "You're not helping."

"Should I help?" She knew Devlin was often over-whelmed, poor guy. As a single father who was also re-sponsible for his aging uncle while holding down a full-time job and running a household, he juggled a lot.

Pretty much everything AnnaBeth had ever wanted—namely, family who depended on him, who loved him. Dev-lin might go to bed frazzled, but he never went to bed feeling completely alone in the world.

"Ruby," Mia whined, reaching out for the dog. The lit-tle girl and the littler dog were anxious to cuddle. Nothing new in that. The pooch that used to be AnnaBeth's had quickly become Mia's, at least whenever Mia was around. Apparently, a little throw-up wouldn't change anything.

"Not just yet, honey," AnnaBeth said. "Ruby seems a little too interested in what your stomach no longer wants. If she starts nibbling, we'll all be chucking buckets."

"AnnaBeth," Devlin complained . . . until Mia giggled.

Grinning at him, she scooped up Ruby and asked, "What can I do?"

He looked undecided about involving her.

"Dude, I'm just standing here. As you said, I can help."

"I didn't exactly say that." Devlin stroked back Mia's pale blond hair. "Better?"

"I don't know." Mia held her stomach.

Taking over as she often did, AnnaBeth said, "How about I get dog and kiddo into your uncle's house while you properly park? Once you're inside, I'll hose off this mess—that is, if rain doesn't wash it away first." A glance up showed bloated, angry clouds tumbling over one another.

Rubbing the back of his neck, Devlin asked, "You wouldn't mind?"

"Are you kidding? Mia and I are gal pals, ain't that right, Squirt?"

In answer, Mia stepped around the mess and leaned on her leg. "Can I hold Ruby?" she asked in a pitiful voice.

Already the dog squirmed, wanting what Mia wanted. Shame that Chiweenies tended to bond so strongly with one person.

That person was now Mia.

Oh, when Mia wasn't around, Ruby tolerated Anna-Beth just fine. But the second she spotted Mia, the dog switched allegiance in a blink. "Once I get you settled, okay? You'll need to change clothes and rinse your mouth and all that stuff we girls do so we aren't too gross."

"Am I gross?"

"Just a tiny bit." AnnaBeth put her hand to the middle of Mia's narrow shoulders and started her toward the front door, but then paused. "Hey, is the house unlocked?"

"Shit, no." Digging out his keys, Devlin jogged past the two of them, bounded up the porch steps, and unlocked the door. He yelled in, "Uncle Sony, AnnaBeth is coming in with Mia."

No answer, which wasn't surprising, since Uncle Sony often forgot his hearing aids.

Mia said, "Well, shit," which made AnnaBeth's eyes open wide as she choked down a laugh.

Devlin was not amused. "Mia," he chastised. "You know better."

In reply, the little girl wrapped her arms around her stomach and groaned, "Oh, I'm sick."

Of course, Devlin softened. Typical dad reaction.

With a snort, AnnaBeth said, "You little actress. It's not nice to tease your dad. You can see he's out of sorts."

Devlin started to dispute that, but then Uncle Sony appeared in the hall wearing only baggy boxers, a long-sleeved T-shirt, white crew socks, and slippers. He looked startled to find them all standing there, then shot a ferocious look at Devlin. "You coulda warned me we had company."

Aggrieved, Devlin started forward, but AnnaBeth put a hand on his chest. *Such a nice chest.* Okay, so she might have copped a little feel under the guise of reassuring him. A girl had to get her thrills where she could.

"I've got this," she promised. "Seriously. Go park, and take a breath while you're at it." To dissuade him from arguing, she stepped forward, with Mia's hand in her own. "Uncle Sony, if you'll excuse us," she shouted so he could hear. "Mia tossed her cookies. I'm going to use the upstairs bathroom to clean her up. We'll be back in five, so grab some britches, okay?"

Sony saluted her, pivoted around on his slippers, and headed to his first-floor bedroom.

She heard Devlin say, "I'll be right back," and then the front door closed.

Good thing their houses had identical layouts. "Can you walk, Squirt? I don't know if I can carry you and Ruby both."

"I could carry Ruby."

"No can do," she said. "You have a few chunks on you,

which means Ruby will get chunks on her. We already agreed that's icky, right?"

Mia cracked another grin. "Grandma gives me everything I want 'cuz I'm special."

"Special, indeed, but I'm still carrying Ruby—for now."

Another grin. "I like you, AnnaBeth."

Her heart did a somersault. "I like you too, Squirt." *More than you know.*

"You don't give me everything." Holding the banister, she proceeded slowly up the stairs, left foot up, right foot up. Her short legs made it more time-consuming. "Dad won't, either. He says he loves me too much to give me everything."

"Your dad is a wise, wise man."

"He says I get sick at Grandma's because she gives me *too* much."

"Oh?" AnnaBeth didn't mean to pry, but what else could she say to that? She knew Devlin and Mia well—Uncle Sony, too—but she'd never met the grandma.

"He told Grandma only two cookies, but she gave me five."

Five? One more step up. "I thought it was ice cream?"

"Yeah." Another step. "After the cookies."

Good grief. At this rate, they'd still be in the middle of the stairs when Devlin returned. "Did you eat lunch?"

"Grandma said I didn't have to."

Sounded like Grandma went overboard on indulging the little girl. "Which grandma is this?"

"Grandma Olsen. Grandma Connely lives in Flor'da, but we visit. I like it most when we go there, 'cuz then I can play on the beach."

So it was the maternal grandma loading Mia up on sweets. Since Mia's mama had passed away three years ago in a pile-up on the interstate, maybe Grandma Olsen was misplacing her grief by spoiling her only granddaughter.

That thought made AnnaBeth sad for all of them—and even more determined to lend Devlin a hand. With sudden inspiration, she said, "Okay, Slowpoke, I'll race ya to the bathroom."

And just like that, Mia took off, bounding up the steps while AnnaBeth pretended to labor beside her. Once they reached the top, though, Mia looked a little green again.

"Come on, sweetie. We'll get you cleaned up, and then you can settle on the couch and maybe watch a cartoon."

"With Ruby?"

"Sure. Ruby would love that." In the bathroom, Anna-Beth closed the door, set the dog on her feet, and whisked off Mia's jacket and shirt, dropping both into the bathtub, which Sony didn't use anymore. Not only did the elderly man struggle with the stairs, but if he sat in a tub, he might not be able to get back out.

Devlin had helped to get his uncle set up downstairs over a year ago, not long after AnnaBeth had moved in next door. Now, on the days when Devlin couldn't visit, she made a point of checking on Sony in case he needed anything. Her number was saved in his contacts, as well as held on his fridge with a magnet.

She wet a washcloth under the faucet with warm water, and when she turned to face Mia, the girl had skinned down to cute little flowered panties. Nonplussed, Anna-Beth asked, "Was it on your pants, too?"

"Yup." Mia sat down on the floor so Ruby could get closer. "It was everywhere, even on my shoes. But now Ruby can cuddle with me, huh?"

"Yes, and look how happy it makes her." The dog crawled onto Mia's lap and stared at her adoringly. Seeing them both so happy made it almost worth losing the loyalty of her pet.

Kneeling down, AnnaBeth gently wiped the girl's face

and neck, and then cleaned a little sticky stuff out of her hair. "Do you have any other clothes here?"

"Yup. In the room I use."

A knock sounded on the door, and Devlin asked, "Everything okay?"

"AnnaBeth's giving me a bath."

The door immediately cracked open, and Devlin peeked in, looking confused—until he saw them on the floor.

"No bath," AnnaBeth explained. "Just some cleanup. I'll rinse out the clothes and put them in Sony's laundry."

"I can do it." He held out a plastic cup of water. "You want to rinse, Mia?"

"Yup." Instead, she guzzled down the water and handed the cup to AnnaBeth.

"Good enough." After setting it on the sink behind her, she wiped Mia's mouth once more. "Better?"

"Yeah." Mia put a loud kiss on Ruby's head.

AnnaBeth looked up at Devlin—something she wouldn't mind doing for a day, a month . . . the rest of her life. "The squirt says she has clothes here?"

He held out a sweatshirt and sweatpants. "Already got them."

"Wow, way to be proactive." After accepting the clothes, she again shooed him away. "Make sure your uncle found his pants, too."

There was a beat of silence before he said, "I took care of it." Folding his arms, he leaned in the doorway and surveyed her as she rinsed the rag, wrung it out, and returned to Mia. "I'm not incompetent, you know."

"Ha! Definitely not." AnnaBeth snorted for good measure. "I've known you an entire year, and it's like you're a superhero, dealing with anything and everything that comes your way."

Mia looked back and forth between them.

Yeah, she felt it, too. There was an extra zing in their conversation, beyond their usual teasing. Or maybe that was wishful thinking on her part. "You should get a bag for her clothes. They're pretty messy."

Smug, he pulled a plastic grocery bag from his back pocket. "You're awfully comfortable giving me orders."

"Yeah, well, I do that sometimes." It was one of her biggest flaws, and God knew she had many. She cleaned Mia's small hands, saying, "You have such cute fingers, kiddo."

Devlin gave her a funny frown, not one of disapproval but more like puzzled awareness or something. "She does, doesn't she? Cute toes, too."

"Very cute toes." Without thinking about it, AnnaBeth lifted one tiny foot and sniffed it. Ruby tried to lick her face when she did, which was the dog's protective reaction. Ruby considered Mia her own, but since she wasn't a biter, she licked. "Oh, good, no puke smell." Wrinkling her nose, AnnaBeth said, "A little sweaty, though."

Mia snickered while cuddling Ruby against her chest.

Trying to ignore the fact that six feet, two inches of sexy male stood behind her, AnnaBeth sighed. "You know, Ruby used to be *my* dog. She was totally into me, and she's so small I could take her everywhere. We were like this." She held up two crossed fingers. "Then you and your cute fingers and toes showed up, and Ruby jumped ship."

"Did I steal her?" Mia asked, not sounding the least bit sorry.

"You stole her heart, that's for sure. She loves you. Watch this." AnnaBeth leaned in, as if to kiss Mia's head, and Ruby snuffled kisses all over her face again. "That's how she proclaims you as her own. No one else is allowed to smooch on you."

Laughing, Mia said, "Dad, you try!"

"All right." Lowering himself to his haunches, he said to AnnaBeth, "I'm not going to get my nose bitten, am I?"

"Ruby would never," she replied in mock affront. "She's a licker, not a biter."

"Hmm." He gave her a quick, heated look that completely took her off guard.

"I mean, that is . . ."

With a half-smile, he turned to kiss his daughter.

Ruby attacked his face with licks until he pulled back with a comical grimace. Mia cracked up, falling back against the side of the tub, while Ruby scampered around in excitement.

Quickly standing, Devlin lifted the bottom of his T-shirt to wipe his face—and left AnnaBeth agog. "Holy hotness, Batman."

He paused, raised a brow, and had the audacity to ask, "What?"

I saw your happy trail, up close and personal, that's what. She didn't say it, luckily, but as heat rushed through her, she did quip, "A man shouldn't go about flashing a woman like that. What if I'd swallowed my tongue?"

"You've seen me without my shirt before, when I cut my uncle's grass."

"From across the yard, not . . ." She flapped her hand between them. "Two feet away."

He looked right at her and replied, "You could get even. I wouldn't mind."

Her jaw loosened. Did he want her to flash him? Nope, not happening. AnnaBeth took advantage of Mia's distraction with the dog, and quickly pulled the girl's clean sweatshirt down over her head.

"I love Ruby." Mia punctuated the words with a cuddle, which got the dog's skinny tail swinging wildly.

"Arms through, kiddo. I'll hold Ruby only until you're done getting dressed, okay?"

With that promise, the deed was completed with alacrity. Fingers grasping air, Mia sweetly demanded the dog back. Ruby practically leaped into her arms, forcing Anna-Beth to juggle her until Mia had a good hold.

I used to have a dog, she thought again. Ruby had been her only real family . . . for a few months, anyway. As soon as girl and dog met, it was love at first sight.

"You need socks," she decided, and in an effort to distract herself, she started to push to her feet.

Devlin caught her arm, helping to haul her up. Unfortunately, their combined efforts caused her to stumble in the small space of the room. The back of her landed against the front of him and . . . yeah, she froze. In shock. In pleasure.

May as well savor the moment, she decided.

Near her ear, he whispered, "This is nice . . . except my daughter is watching."

He liked the contact, too? Then the rest of what he'd said sank in. Oh, Lord. AnnaBeth jerked away from him with an absurd laugh. "Clumsy me. Sorry. I didn't bruise your . . . chest, did I? I mean, I'm sure I didn't, you being so hard . . ." Her eyes flared. "So *solid*, I mean."

The man had the audacity to find her amusing. "I'm fine, AnnaBeth. A little warmer, maybe, but no, not bruised."

A little warmer. What did he mean by that? And seriously, Mia was still watching them both, her attention rapt. "Socks!" AnnaBeth declared. "Where will I find them for the pipsqueak?"

"You call me the funnest things," Mia said.

" 'Cuz you're the funnest gal—that's why."

"Funniest," Devlin corrected, and AnnaBeth wasn't sure if he was speaking to Mia or herself.

"*Funnest* sounds better to us cool chicks." She ruffled Mia's hair, then lingered a moment, appreciating the silkiness of the long, pale locks. One day, Mia's hair might darken like her daddy's. It seemed possible, since they shared the same beautiful brown eyes. When she turned back to Devlin, she found those warm brown eyes scrutinizing her. She cleared her throat.

"Socks?"

"In my uncle's old bedroom, down the hall on the right. Bottom drawer of the dresser, mixed in with a few of my things. Grab her something warm. The storm brought in cooler temps."

"Sounds like a plan." She wanted out of the too-small bathroom, where she seemed to be surrounded by him and his appeal, his oh-too-attentive daughter, and her faithless dog.

With a provoking smile, he stepped slightly to the side, which allowed her to inch her way out around him, but not without breathing in his "hot guy" scent and feeling the warmth of that tall, solid body, and yeah, wanting him, which, okay, she'd been doing since the day she'd first set eyes on him a year ago.

"Excuse me." She double-timed it down the hall.

He called after her quickly retreating back, "I'll take Ruby and Mia downstairs."

"Yup, you do that. I might be a minute." She ducked into the bedroom and, now out of sight, put her hands over her face. Oh, how humiliating.

Sex-starved, that's what she was. It was the only explanation for her bizarre behavior. Even as she thought it, her spine tingled in remembered excitement at making contact with him. *Her spine*—hello, new erogenous zone.

Being "up against a man" shouldn't be such a thrill, but for real, when that man was Devlin Connely, thrills abounded.

'Course, her arm was still tingly, too, from where he'd caught her to help her up, and her ear—that ear he'd whispered into—well, that ear would clearly never be the same. As she listened to Devlin's fading footsteps and the muted conversation he was having with his daughter, she fanned her face. She had to get it together. Help him, that's all he wanted her to do, so that's all she could do.

In the time she'd known him, he'd been friendly, polite, kind, even attentive, but he'd never, not once, made a real move. In her head, she'd made many. But only in her head.

So now, she'd be the helpful friend he needed, and nothing more. She sealed that vow with a bracing breath and marched to the dresser. Bottom drawer, she recalled. The dresser was an ancient burl-wood piece of furniture that was part of a handsome bedroom set. Sony had probably had it for several decades. Maybe he and his wife had bought this set together.

Family.

What would that be like? To start a home together, have each other for sixty-plus years of marriage, so many good memories—and some that were bad, but still shared—and all that love . . .

But then to be the one left behind? Thank God, Sony had Devlin and Mia. She knew how they brightened his life. They were wonderful people, close and caring.

It would be amazing to be a part of it all. But she wasn't.

She was just a neighbor with no family of her own, so the least she could do was be the best neighbor possible.

She opened the drawer and found the socks.

In the year since Devlin had met AnnaBeth, she'd been friendly, fun, thoughtful, always ready to lend a hand, but she'd never, not once, made a move.

It confounded him, because more and more every day,

he wanted her, but there'd never been a single sign that she was interested. Most of the time, she treated Uncle Sony with the same open, teasing friendliness that he received. Didn't matter how many times he'd imagined more; she was his uncle's neighbor, so he was respectful of her implied boundaries.

Yet it didn't escape his notice that the tension he so often felt in his neck and shoulders had started to ease the moment he saw AnnaBeth tending to his daughter. It wasn't only that AnnaBeth was helpful, because that wasn't unusual. It wasn't only that she made Mia happy, though she always did. And it wasn't merely her casual way of taking over, which so often amused him.

He couldn't blame it on her looks, either. Sure, she was sexy. *Really* sexy, if he was honest about it, with her teasing blue eyes and long, light brown hair. Of course, he'd noticed her body, with those curves in all the right places. And the way she moved, so fluid and graceful but without artifice. There was no extra sway in her hips, no sideways glances or other flirting gestures that he sometimes noticed from other women.

But with AnnaBeth? She moved with a purpose, and he *always* noticed. Sweet personality, check. Good looks and gorgeous body, check. Great camaraderie with his family, check.

It was more than all that, though.

There was the sincerity of the small smile she wore whenever she spoke with Sony. The gentle touches to his daughter's hair, and the generous way she shared her dog with Mia. How adept she was at handling the worst sort of cleanup—teasing, as if she actually enjoyed the duty.

And the way she watched him so intently? Hot. He had a feeling they'd burn up the sheets. Was she ready for that? Was he?

His body was, for sure.

She presented a powerful and appealing combo of attributes, both physical and emotional, and he was far from immune.

"What was it this time?" Uncle Sony shouted.

Knowing his uncle referred to Mia's upset stomach, he explained, "Cookies and ice cream."

"If you don't get a handle on your mother-in-law, our girl's gonna turn into sugar."

Very true. Cindy Olsen often tried his patience with her refusal to follow any parental guidelines at all, regardless of how her behavior affected Mia. She loved her granddaughter; there was never any question about that, but she indulged her to excess. Since losing Dana, her only daughter, she'd poured every ounce of affection and attention she had into Mia. It was why he made sure Mia visited twice weekly, even on days like today, when it wasn't convenient.

In his mind, a child couldn't have too much love, even when that love often ended in a bellyache, or like today, with her—how had AnnaBeth put it?—tossing up her cookies.

Already stretched out on the couch with a throw blanket over her, Mia sleepily watched cartoons while Ruby curled up under her chin, her little nose tucked into Mia's neck.

AnnaBeth was right. His daughter had more or less stolen the dog. Not deliberately, but girl and Chiweenie had quickly bonded, and now, whenever he was at his uncle's, which was often, AnnaBeth was nice enough to let Mia visit with Ruby.

Which, of course, meant he interacted with AnnaBeth, too. He'd come to anticipate seeing her. Around Anna-Beth, things were never boring.

She was fun, laid-back, and easy to talk to. She never flirted, so there was no awkwardness around his eagle-eyed daughter. That had been refreshing . . . at first.

For the longest time after losing Dana, Devlin had barely noticed women or thought of himself as a man. All the responsibilities tied to parenting, extended family, the household, and work, had landed on him. In the middle of his grief, he'd learned that Dana had juggled even more than he'd ever realized.

Shared responsibilities were so much easier. Doing it all alone? That took a lot more coordination, but he was determined to keep his daughter's life as full as possible.

Sony shouted, "She's a good girl."

Devlin glanced at Mia, who was used to Sony's loud voice and only yawned.

He saw that his uncle was trying to get his hearing aids in right, so he didn't bother reminding him to lower his voice. "She's about to take a nap."

"I meant the other one. The pretty girl."

Mia said, "I'm pretty," in a sleepy voice.

Of course, Uncle Sony didn't hear her. "You're beautiful," Devlin confirmed, watching as Mia smiled and closed her eyes.

With a short laugh, Sony said, "She's a looker."

"I'm aware. I do still have eyes, you know." By the time he'd met AnnaBeth, he'd been a widower for two years. Besides, AnnaBeth wasn't the type of woman anyone could ignore. If her physical presence didn't grab you, her big personality would.

Finger in his ear, his uncle made adjustments. "You need someone smart and sexy to snuggle up with at night."

"Uncle Sony," he said with a sigh, "you're still shouting." He again looked at Mia, but he could tell by her deep, even breaths that she was asleep.

"You should make a move."

Devlin rolled his eyes heavenward. "She's been clear that she doesn't want that."

"I bet she does."

"Keep yelling, and she'll hear every word."

"Already did," AnnaBeth said as she stepped into the room, "and you're right, Sony."

His uncle grinned, and finally in a lower voice, said, "You see, Devlin. A man could do a lot worse than the sweet girl next door."

"Right you are." She sat on the couch near Mia's feet and expertly slipped the socks on her feet without disturbing her sleep. "What if a man got involved with a spy, or a serial killer, or someone just after his money."

"I don't have that much money," Devlin told her, ready to play along. "I'm comfortable, but it's not like I'm loaded or anything."

"Hypothetical," she replied, seemingly unbothered by his uncle's matchmaking shenanigans. Carefully, tenderly, she tucked the blanket around Mia, stroked two fingers over Ruby's neck, and smiled.

It was astounding to Devlin, how at ease she was with his daughter. Eye-opening, enlightening, and extremely pleasing. It was as if his body reacted to her sexiness, while his heart reacted to her nurturing nature.

And now all the teasing? "Exactly how much did you hear, AnnaBeth?"

"Enough to know you two were joking."

Devlin started to correct her, but Uncle Sony spoke up. "Spring weddings are the best. I married Evelyn in the spring. It rained like hell, but we didn't care."

AnnaBeth smiled at him. "Were there flowers blooming?"

"Nah. My parents had a pig farm down south. Pigs woulda eaten any flowers. Once we moved up here, though,

Evelyn planted flowers everywhere." He eyed Devlin critically, then switched his gaze back to AnnaBeth. "Like you do."

"I love flowers, and I love spring." She glanced toward the window. "Even when it rains."

So they were just going to act as if all the wedding talk hadn't happened? Seemed so. AnnaBeth had done an admirable job of turning Sony's attention while giving him an opportunity to reminisce. That, too, was one of her skills.

"I like this cartoon," Sony said around a yawn. Using the lever on the side of his lounge chair, he tilted it back so his feet were elevated. "Mia has me hooked. Would you mind making some tea while I relax and watch it?"

Before Devlin could reply, AnnaBeth said, "Of course I wouldn't mind." She stood, and then tucked a second throw over his uncle. "You want some, too, Devlin?"

He stared at her. Damn, she was good at taking over, at attending to Mia, and even at pampering his uncle. "I can make it."

Her smile never slipped. "I don't mind. You had a rough day."

"No, I didn't." Did she really see him as weak, or frazzled, or incapable of dealing with . . . well, everything? That bugged him, so he gestured for her to lead the way. "We can get the tea together."

"Now you're talking," Uncle Sony said.

When Devlin turned to tell him to cease and desist, his uncle's eyes were closed, and he looked ready to doze off, as well. "Faker," he muttered, which only made AnnaBeth nudge him.

They left the dim, cozy living room together, went down the short hall side by side, past the first-floor bedroom on the right that his uncle now used, and the recently remodeled bathroom on the left that better suited his uncle's needs than the one upstairs. With every step, Devlin was acutely aware of her lengthy stride, of her light, fresh scent, of her *nearness*. It'd be so easy to touch her—shoulder to shoulder, or to take her hand.

He didn't. With AnnaBeth, he'd never been able to tell if the growing, nearly overwhelming attraction was one-sided, or if she had other reasons for staring straight ahead, now without a smile. Admittedly, he was far out of practice, but even so . . . he knew there was something between them. He was still a man, never mind that he'd been on ice for three years. Around this one particular woman, his instincts were alive and kicking.

As they entered the kitchen, the biggest and brightest room in the house, AnnaBeth said, "Grab a seat," and began opening cabinets with practiced ease.

Bemused, Devlin leaned on the counter. "I take it you've done this before." He knew she and his uncle were close, but he'd never before had a good reason to spend time alone with her during his visits. Never would he exclude his daughter, and his uncle was always far too observant for him to simply slip away with her.

"Sony does love his tea. And he's such a sweetheart; I enjoy visiting with him."

She was the sweetheart, but yeah, Uncle Sony was a charmer, too. "He told me you've cleaned his house a few times."

She went still for a second, then lifted one shoulder. "I've tidied up for him here and there. No biggie."

"AnnaBeth—" he started, trying to find the words to tell her that she didn't need to do so much, but she cut him off.

"You know people call me AB Positive, right? Or just AB. You don't have to work through that mouthful."

He heard a note of defensiveness, and it bothered him. Was the nickname given out of kindness, or something else? "I like your name. It's pretty."

Her quick smirk proved she didn't believe him. "Anna-Beth Posey Sanders. Who gives a kid the middle name of Posey, especially following AnnaBeth?"

"I'd never heard your middle name, but all together, it's melodic." When she didn't reply, he said, "I'm sure your mother had a reason." He watched her get out three mugs instead of cups, open a canister of tea bags, check the sugar bowl, and then refill it. All without speaking, so he tried another tack. "Is Posey the name of a relative?"

"No idea." She flashed him a forced smile. "I never knew any of my relatives."

Never knew. . . . His heart seemed to freeze up in his chest, and sympathy overshadowed every other emotion. "How is that possible?"

For only a second, her shoulders slumped. Then she brushed back her light brown hair, pivoted to him with a smile, and said, "I lost my parents when I was real young, too young to remember anything about them. I lived with a distant aunt for a while, but when she got divorced, she turned me over to the state. Foster homes here and there, you know how it is."

No, he didn't have a single clue, thank God. The urge to reach out to her, to draw her close, was hard to resist, but she had an emotional wall around her now. "I'm sorry; I didn't realize."

"Eh, why sweat the small stuff, right?" The kettle started to whistle, and she quickly removed it from the heat. "Grab a seat, Pete."

"Pete?"

"It rhymes."

That made him smile. He'd often heard her use goofy rhymes. To better put her at ease, he pulled out a chair as she requested, then replied, "Done, hon." See, he could play that game.

"Not bad, but not great. Keep practicing." She glanced at him with a questioning smile. "Sony likes two sugars in his tea. How about you?"

"One sugar, please."

"Don't tell Mia, but I load up. Tea is nasty. I don't know how any of you drink it."

One surprise after another today. "If you don't like it, then why do you drink it?"

"Sony likes it, and he likes company while he drinks it, so I practically turn mine into syrup and visit with him while we share—*ick, yuck*—hot tea."

Because she was just that nice, and maybe a little lonely, too. Over the past twelve months—basically, since the day he'd met her—he'd paid attention to her comings and goings . . . and hadn't noticed any visitors.

With almost territorial interest, he'd waited to see who—and how often—she dated, but he'd seen no one at all, either of the romantic or friendly variety.

It struck him as odd. Not that she was odd, never that, but an incredibly attractive woman in her early twenties should have had an active social life. God knew, in his twenties, he'd enjoyed dating, hanging with friends, balancing work and school with plenty of fun.

Yet anytime he visited his uncle—days, evenings, or weekends—AnnaBeth was around. And alone. Maybe lonely?

As carnal curiosity about her consumed him, he pushed out of his seat. "I'll take my uncle's tea to him. He'll fake sleeping, because he's decided to throw us together."

"He means well," she said, defending Sony as if he were her very own uncle. "Don't worry that I'll take what you said seriously. In fact, since you're here and they're both asleep, I could just head home, I guess."

He wanted her to take it seriously. And he wanted her

to stay. "If you keep me company here in the kitchen, I promise you don't have to drink your tea. Uncle Sony will never know."

She hesitated, but when he held her gaze, doing his best to convince her, she drew a breath and nodded. "Solid plan. I like it." She waved him off. "Go. Leave his tea on the table beside him, but make sure it's far enough from his elbow that he won't accidently bump it—"

"AnnaBeth," he murmured, gently chiding. "I know how to take care of my uncle, I promise." Then he added, "You don't mind staying to visit?"

Pretty blue eyes, always so direct, stared into his as she softly replied, "I'll enjoy it. Thanks for asking me."

Chapter Two

AnnaBeth had her hands wrapped around the warm mug of tea when Devlin reentered the kitchen. Muted light filtering through the windows shone on the long, wavy hair draping the sides of her face as she stared down at the table. She appeared lost in thought. Outside, drizzling rain turned into a downpour, darkening the skies and adding shadows to both the kitchen and her pensive expression. He could flip on the overhead fluorescent lights, but here, with her, dim and shadowy felt nicer. More intimate.

Not an hour ago, Devlin had been beat after a long workday and another conflict with his well-meaning mother-in-law. For the entire ride to his uncle's house, Mia had been miserable, close to throwing up. Seeing her like that never failed to level him. He could have canceled the visit with his uncle, but Sony looked forward to seeing them, and his house was closer than Devlin's anyway. On top of that, Mia had wanted to see Ruby . . . and he'd wanted to see AnnaBeth.

Now, thanks to AnnaBeth, he felt rejuvenated.

Seeing her in profile like this, he noticed the length of

her eyelashes, the straight line of her nose, the curve of her cheekbone, and the lush shape of her lips.

He'd thought about those lips far too often.

Quietly, so he wouldn't startle her, he said, "They're all three out."

Her lips curling into a smile, she looked up. "Sony is asleep for real?"

"Complete with loud snores. Ruby buried herself under the blanket on Mia's chest. Is that okay?"

"She loves to burrow. It's fine."

He reseated himself across from her. "I'm sorry about . . ." He didn't know how to put it. "Mia and Ruby. She wanted a dog, but then she met yours and stopped asking. It seemed like an easy solution for me, since a dog would be one more thing to care for."

"Wise choice. I swear, Ruby waits for me to get busy to decide she wants to go out. Or that she needs a treat. And she loses her favorite toys all the time, then whines at me to find them. I think she does that on purpose, though, when she decides I've worked too long and it's time to play." She smiled, showing him she didn't mind that game at all. "Pets take a lot of time and patience, but she's an adorable little companion."

A companion that AnnaBeth clearly loved. "I'm sorry I never considered how it might feel to you."

"For real?" She scoffed. "No worries. I love seeing the two squirts together. Besides, Ruby would have been completely heartbroken if Mia had gotten a different dog. This way, they're both happy."

But what about her? How happy could she be giving up half her time with her pet? "It's nice of you to share."

She shrugged. "I still get to sleep with Ruby at night. When Mia's not here, the dog loves me just fine."

She shared her bed with the dog. Did she share it with any humans? "Still . . ."

"Dude, seriously. I love seeing them together." Humor slipped up on him, causing the side of his mouth to lift. "You're the only woman I know who calls me *dude*."

She flashed him another grin. "I'm weird, I know." Tilting her head and making a silly face, she said, "AB Positive."

It bothered him the way she put that. "I never said you were weird, AnnaBeth. You're not. You're definitely fun, though. I enjoy your company, and both my uncle and my daughter adore you." The emotions Devlin felt for her were a little more complicated—and getting more so by the minute.

"Adore them right back. They're terrific." She glanced around the kitchen and came up with a topic change. "Sony told me this room was updated twenty-five years ago, and he hasn't changed anything since."

Devlin laughed. "By updated, he means they changed the countertop from cracked tiles to laminate, switched out the cabinet knobs, and instead of yellow-flowered curtains on that window over the sink, they got red-checked curtains. This old tile floor is the same as I remember when I was a little kid. Same maple cabinets. Same . . . feel. I always liked visiting my aunt and uncle."

AnnaBeth watched him. "What was she like, Sony's wife? He talks about her a lot."

"Yeah." Devlin thought of his uncle, currently slumped in his chair, how different he was now that he approached ninety. He'd slowed down for sure, and he often napped twice a day. Yet in many ways, he was the same man with the same robust opinions and open affection that Devlin remembered from his youth. "He still loves Evelyn. Always will." That would never change. Though Devlin had loved Dana, too, they'd only had a few years together before she'd passed away, not the lifetime Uncle Sony and Aunt Evelyn had shared.

Dana would always hold a special place in his heart, but his fondest memories—those of their daughter growing from a baby into a little girl—didn't include her.

A thought struck him, and he studied AnnaBeth.

"What?" She quickly smoothed her hair, even sat a little straighter.

His mouth curved. "Just because I look at you, you assume something is wrong?"

She said, "Um . . . no?"

That deserved a small laugh. "You're worrying, but you don't need to be. Not with me."

Brushing that aside, she asked again, "What were you thinking?"

"That Evelyn was the fun aunt. She'd say silly things and tell outrageous stories, and every so often, she'd curse, and it'd crack me up. She had an enormous heart and was always interested in people." He stared into AnnaBeth's eyes, noticing things he hadn't before. Like the way a ring of darker blue circled her irises. How her long lashes curled at the outer corners. The way her brows pinched together when she was concerned about something.

Her gaze made him want to get a whole lot closer. With AnnaBeth, he felt seen in a different way. Her attention felt sensual.

Did she realize how she looked at him?

Her lips twitched. "Am I growing horns? You're staring."

"Because you're so attractive."

Her smile went crooked.

"In a lot of ways, you're like Aunt Evelyn. Natural and easy. Everyone who meets you likes you. You make people feel comfortable and special, just as she did. It's a gift."

Color bloomed in her cheeks, turning her skin splotchy. Not a great look, but even her embarrassment seemed endearing. "Why are you blushing?"

"Because I don't make people comfortable. Just the opposite, probably. Like you said, I'm bossy, and sometimes I joke when I shouldn't." Anxious to make a point, she said, "Like when Mia was sick. I should have been sympathetic, not teasing."

"Wrong." It seemed the most natural thing in the world for him to reach across the table and take her hand. A small hand, soft and warm, seemingly delicate, but he knew better. AnnaBeth had to have incredible strength to go through life alone and still be so generous.

The second they touched, she went completely still, unblinking, her gaze fixed on his.

Devlin kept his hold loose, his palm up so she could pull away if he'd made her uncomfortable. She didn't budge, though, so he brushed his thumb over her knuckles. "Sympathy isn't always what you say. It's more about what you do and how you make people feel. You helped Mia to feel better, you distracted her, and you offered me some much-needed help. Even when I resisted, you just did what you could."

"Pushy," she muttered. "That's me."

"Take charge," he corrected. "It's a good quality to have." Needing her to believe him, he explained, "When Mia is sick, it leaves me undone. I probably would have babied her, and then she'd have been crying, and that would have made us both feel worse. Instead, you were plainspoken and practical, and you got her to grin." That was likely the moment the fog had lifted for him, the very second that he'd decided it was time to take a chance.

To move forward. And he knew where to start.

"She'd just been moaning in the car," Devlin said. "Then she emptied her stomach. And you got a grin out of her." He gently squeezed her fingers. "I appreciate you, AnnaBeth. *We* appreciate you."

She stared at their linked hands, then into his eyes again. It was a small thing, but her fingers gently curved to his. "I was glad to pitch in."

"I know. Because you're the same type of person my aunt was. A doer, not just a talker."

"I like how you see me. It's nice."

Nice. He should be happy with that, but instead, he wanted more. Today was different from all the days leading up to this moment. It was as if they'd just crossed some boundary, and in doing so, the grief he'd felt for so long faded a little more, still there but not as prevalent. Not such a big part of him. "So, AnnaBeth, are you seeing anyone?"

Her brows lifted. "What do you mean?"

"Are you dating anyone special?" He probably should have asked before taking her hand, but again, this all felt new and special. He didn't want to mess it up. "I mean, are you involved with anyone?"

"No." She glanced at their linked hands. "I'm guessing you aren't, either?"

"I haven't dated since my wife died." Saying it out loud was harder than he'd thought it would be. Not just the finality of acknowledging Dana's death, as if stating he was ready to move on, but also the worry that he might have just erred. Only a man sorely out of practice would mention his deceased wife while enjoying the company of another woman.

Hoping to retrench, to give himself a moment to think, he released her hand to drink his quickly cooling tea.

As if she'd felt his hesitation, his brief withdrawal, she no longer looked at him. Though neither of them had changed positions, she now felt farther away. He was making it awkward, and he knew it, but at the moment, he didn't know how to salvage the situation.

A flash of lightning illuminated the kitchen, followed by the rumble of thunder.

"Your wife," she suddenly said, drawing his attention back to her. Silent seconds ticked by before she asked softly, "Would you tell me about her?"

The question took him off guard. Few had ever asked him to do that. Certainly not the women who'd shown interest in him. They'd flirt a little, and he'd politely respond without any encouragement at all, so they'd kindly retreat. He'd had zero interest, and no time to invest in a relationship, no matter how casual or brief it might have been.

Such had been his life after losing Dana.

Sony didn't talk much about her, probably for fear of reminding Devlin of his loss. Dana's mother certainly didn't, except to complain every so often that Dana would have done something differently from how he did it, which might have been true, but Dana wasn't here, and he did what he thought best.

This time, AnnaBeth reached out, just touching his wrist. "I assume she was beautiful, because you're so gorgeous, and Mia is a doll. I'm sure she was wonderful, too, and that's why it's hard for you to talk about her. I didn't mean to pressure you."

"You didn't." She hadn't, not once in the year he'd known her. She'd been nothing but supportive and helpful, and now interested.

His heart took up an uneven rhythm. Other parts of him were also on high alert. Energized, primed, and hungry.

Because AnnaBeth was unlike anyone else he knew, talking about his wife with her seemed the most natural thing in the world. "Mia got Dana's blond hair."

He heard the smile in her tone when she replied, "I wondered about that. Yours is so dark, but she's a fair little pipsqueak. Did Dana have dark eyes, too?"

"No." He studied her face. "She had blue eyes, lighter than yours, without the mix of shades that your eyes have." The observation stalled her for a moment, but she quickly rallied. "So Mia has your eyes and her mama's hair. It's a pretty combo. Like a little bit of each of you." She continued, asking, "You have photos around your home so Mia can see her mother?"

"No, but I printed several and put them into an album. Sometimes Mia likes to go through it, and she'll ask questions."

"Which of course you answer," she said decisively, as if she didn't have a single doubt. "You'd want her to know all about her mama."

Emotion left him solemn, but it wasn't talking about losing Dana that caused it. It was AnnaBeth's faith in him. She trusted him to make the best decisions—and God knew, that's what he wanted to do.

"Sometimes, it isn't easy to know what the right thing is. I answer Mia's questions the best I can, and there are some favorite stories I share with her. But when she asks about the wreck and how her mother died, I skim over that part. It was . . . horrible. Dana had a small, sporty car that she drove when she was alone, and it didn't fare well in the wreck." Such an understatement. Her car, with her inside it, had been demolished. No, he never discussed those details with his daughter.

"No one else died?" AnnaBeth asked.

"No, though there were some serious injuries." And now he drove a large, sturdy SUV, as did Mia's grandmother.

"Thank God, Mia wasn't with her."

"I've thought that a million times." Often, just because Mia did something new, or changed in any small way. "She's only five. She doesn't need details. Plus, I'm afraid she might say something to Cindy—Grandma Olsen," he explained. "My mother-in-law is a good grandma, despite the over-indulgences, but she's also emotional about the loss still. I don't want her crying with Mia."

"What about Mia's grandpa?"

He shook his head. "Cindy got divorced when Dana wasn't much older than Mia is now. He took off, so Dana never really knew him, and Mia has never met him."

"Cindy hasn't remarried?"

"No. Says she isn't interested, and she does just fine on her own. She's a little too clingy with Mia, but I understand that. While Cindy has her friends and her activities, Mia is the only family she has left."

"She has you." AnnaBeth waited for confirmation.

"Yes, she has me." It wasn't always easy, but he tried to ensure that the relationship continued.

AnnaBeth drifted her fingertips over his wrist. "You're an amazing guy; you know that, right? You're selective in what you say to protect Mia. It's important to keep what you share age appropriate, so you do. And even though your mother-in-law oversteps a little here and there, you still make sure that she and Mia stay close. I admire that so much." Her hand closed warmly over his. "I admire you."

Giving her words back to her, he said, "I like how you see me. It's nice."

Pleasure brightened her eyes. "Well, then, I should also tell you how great it is that you and Sony are still so close. You help him even more than you realize."

"I help Uncle Sony when I can, but he helps me, too. When I have business calls I have to make, he sits with Mia." Given Sony's age, Devlin didn't leave him alone to babysit, but when they were all in the same house, his uncle was terrific about keeping her occupied. "He advises me, too. And he's a great sounding board when I'm trying to work out a problem."

"Family, right?" She gave a whimsical sigh, as if such a

thing were a fairy tale. "That's how I always imagined it would be. Good and bad times, there for you no matter what."

"In a nutshell." It was family that had kept him together after losing Dana. Family that had been by his side through funeral arrangements and sleepless nights and the heavy grief.

Only AnnaBeth didn't have any family. He found that so hard to imagine. She was a beautiful person, inside and out. He hoped her friendly outlook on life and her giving nature meant her upbringing hadn't been too rough. AB Positive. It could be a really cute, complimentary nickname—if used for the right reasons.

She said, "You've gotten quiet."

"Just thinking." *About you.* "Sony's eighty-eight now. When my mom and dad moved to Florida, Mom tried to get him to go along, but he wouldn't leave this house. They visit several times a year, and they came for two months after we lost Dana." He'd had family surrounding him, doing what they could, but he'd known he had to get it together for his daughter. "Mia and I go there for two weeks on vacation each winter, and I invite Sony along, but he won't budge. He says he's rooted here."

With empathy in her eyes, she looked around the kitchen. "His Evelyn is here."

"And all his memories of her." Devlin understood why Sony wouldn't leave. What years he had left, he wanted to spend in the home he loved. "He's as healthy as a man that age can be, but I still worry, so I try to be with him as much as I can, whether he's helping me or I'm helping him, or we're just sitting together sharing a meal or a movie or playing cards."

"He's a card shark," she said with a gentle grin.

"Is that firsthand experience talking?" Sony hadn't mentioned playing cards with AnnaBeth, but it seemed probable. TV, talking, and cards were his favorite activities.

"I try to keep an eye on him, too," AnnaBeth said. "In the morning, I watch for his kitchen light to come on and the porch light to go off. That's how I know he's up and about so I don't have to worry. Then I check on him in the afternoon, after I've finished my morning work." She made a face. "He always offers me tea."

Devlin laughed. Obviously she drank it, just to keep Sony happy.

Shifting, she pointed to a business card held on the fridge with a magnet. "That's my number, but I also put it in his contacts. I mean, I know he'd call you if he really needed anything, but I'm right here, so . . ." She lifted her shoulders with uncertainty. "I'm convenient in case there's an emergency. I hope you don't mind."

Amazing. He could see that she didn't think anything of going above and beyond for a neighbor, but to him, her kindness was exceptional, making her even more appealing—if such a thing were possible. After all, he was aware that he came with family attached. He wasn't just himself. Any woman he dated would have to understand that his family would always be a priority, not just his young daughter, but an elderly uncle, as well. "Thank you."

"Hundred percent my pleasure. Honest. Sony is a super-likeable guy. Funny and sometimes snarky. And as you said, he's pushing ninety. I'm glad he has such a set routine so he never keeps me guessing. His kitchen light comes on; then a few minutes later, his porch light goes off, and not long after that, he opens the blinds and waves at me." Her gaze softened, and she said, "He makes me feel needed. I like it."

It was one thing for him to take such an interest in his uncle; he loved the man dearly. It was another thing—a *wonderful* thing—for her to spend so much of her time looking in on him.

Sony talked about AnnaBeth often, and Devlin had seen the casual, familiar way they interacted, but it still hadn't registered exactly how close they'd gotten.

"Would it be okay if I gave you my number, too? As you said, you're close, and since you don't mind checking on him, I'd want to know right away if you noticed anything that worried you."

"Sure." She lifted a hip, withdrew her phone from her back pocket, opened her contacts, and said, "Go."

Bemused at how easily she'd accepted his offer, Devlin recited his number and then got out his own phone. "Mind if I have yours?" He waited to see how she'd react.

"Makes sense." She shared her number.

They stared at each other as an invisible spark ignited between them. Did she feel it? Deciding to test the boundaries just a little, he asked, "Would you mind if I called you when it had nothing to do with Sony?"

She started to smile, but then hesitated, as if she wasn't sure how he meant the question. "Feel free."

That blasé answer told him nothing. Devlin studied her, and damn, the more he thought about it, the more he wanted her. Right now, here with AnnaBeth, he felt reinvigorated, more like himself than he had in years. "What if I called to invite you out?"

"To where?"

Her confusion got the better of him, and he grinned. It seemed clear to him that AnnaBeth didn't do a lot of flirting. "During the week, Mia has morning kindergarten. Twice a week, she's with her grandmother. I think we could sneak in lunch or a movie." *And maybe more.*

Her brows went up, and she asked carefully, "You mean . . . like a date?"

"Is that a problem?"

She went comically still. "A date-date?"

His ego was starting to sting. "You said you aren't seeing anyone."

"I'm not," she was quick to say. Then she added, "And yes, I'd love to have lunch with you, or see a movie, or whatever."

The *whatever* interested him the most.

She gave him a smile that faltered just a little. "As long as I'm not pressuring you."

"The opposite. I may be pressuring you."

"No," she denied, shaking her head. "Not at all." She gave him another happy smile. "Actually, I'm flattered. Big time."

"Big time, huh?" She was so funny, and so plainspoken, that his ego rejoiced. "I'm out of practice, but I'm enjoying this." He gestured between them. "As a man and a woman, not just as neighbors." He frowned. "And not just any woman. You, AnnaBeth. Because I like you." He needed her to understand that. He'd had other opportunities, other women showing interest, but no one had broken through his self-imposed single status.

By not even trying, by just being herself, an involved neighbor and a caring friend, she'd affected him as no one else had.

"I like you, too. I always have. The thing is, I want to make sure I understand." She bit her lower lip. "Is it because I asked about your wife?"

Devlin shook his head. "For the longest time, I've been focused on getting through each day. On being the best dad I could be for Mia. On watching over my uncle and trying to help my mother-in-law through a really bad time. Assuring my parents that I'm doing fine, and setting up video visits for them to talk with Mia."

Maintaining the house, working full time, getting as involved in Mia's school as he could. . . . There hadn't been many minutes left for him to think about himself, and that had probably been a good thing.

Until now.

Folding her arms on the table, AnnaBeth said, "You're important, too, you know. You can't just take care of everyone else; you have to take care of yourself, as well."

"I do."

"I don't think so. Do you even know what you want? Personally, I mean. For yourself as a man."

It was sweet, but also sexy, to have her look at him like that. "I haven't given it much thought." Actually, he hadn't given any thought to what he needed or wanted in a personal sense.

"I have," she said. "Thought about you as a man, I mean. A lot."

There went his ego again. "I'd like to kiss you, Anna-Beth." He wanted to kiss her and so much more. Damn, it was nice to *feel* again. "What do you think of that?"

"Anytime I thought about kissing you, I always reminded myself: *Single dad, single dad, single dad.*" She emphasized that by lightly bumping her palm on her forehead. "Anyone could see that being a dad was your focus, but it wasn't easy for me to remember. So I made it a mantra in my head to keep from doing anything dumb, like coming on strong." She wrinkled her nose. "Sort of like I am now."

He gave a shake of his head. "I had no idea. You hid it well." So many times, he'd been attracted to her and hadn't known she was sharing similar feelings. Now that he did know, temptation was riding him hard.

She teased him with a flirty once-over. "You seriously thought I could be around you without thinking . . . *things.* No way. You're just that kind of guy."

He'd love more details on what *things* specifically, but instead he asked, "What kind of guy is that?"

"You know, super good-looking, calm. and in control." She gave a little shiver. "All buff and stuff. Plus the way you care for Mia just tugs at the old heartstrings. You're the whole package, dude. Except I know you aren't looking for a girlfriend, and even if you were, you wouldn't be looking at me. So I've tried to just be a no-pressure neighbor."

"There's no 'just' to you, AnnaBeth." And he *was* damn well looking at her, only her.

As if the flattery made her uncomfortable, she teased, "You haven't dated for a long time, so you're not a good judge."

"The hell I'm not. I might have other priorities, but I'm still a man." The part of him that had gone dormant when Dana died was wide awake now.

"I agree with you there." She gave the tea a nasty look and pushed the cup aside. "I can't imagine all the things you had to be feeling."

"And missing," he said, without thinking. "Not that we need to talk about that."

"Why not? Seems to me that the things you're missing would be the hardest part of losing someone. The big stuff and all the little stuff, too." Her eyes, far too understanding, didn't shy away. "Talking about things sometimes helps."

"I haven't talked about Dana with anyone."

She nodded; then, with soft encouragement, said, "You can talk about her with me if you want."

"That wouldn't seem weird to you?" Immediately, he said, "And no, don't say you're weird."

"Okay, I won't." She gave him a crooked smile. "You know Sony likes to talk about Evelyn, so I assume you'd like to talk about Dana. Except Mia is only five years old, and she probably doesn't remember much about her mother. And Sony is almost ninety, so I'm betting you don't like to burden him. From the tiny bit I gathered from Mia, her grandma is still struggling over losing her daughter, so you can't share much with her, either. Since you haven't dated, I'm guessing there hasn't been an opportunity to talk about someone who was super-important to your life."

So astute. "I wouldn't talk about Dana on a date with another woman."

"Well, why not? You had an amazing little daughter with her, so Dana will always be a part of your life."

See, that. That was what made AnnaBeth so special.

"True," he agreed softly.

She sat forward, again reaching out, this time clasping his hand. "I mean it, Devlin. You can talk to me. I'm interested, in you and Mia and Uncle Sony. If it's still too painful, you can tell me that, too. Whatever you need."

Whatever I need. Funny, but now that she said it, what he needed most was her. Probably too soon to tell her that, though.

He knew what she expected, for him to focus on himself. That didn't quite feel right, but maybe if he shared a little, she would, too.

"It was a running joke in our marriage that I had to be in charge of paying the bills or we'd be living on the street. Don't get me wrong. Dana more than carried her fair share. She did the majority of chores around the house— cooking and laundry and so many things I hadn't realized were a part of her daily routine until she was gone. Sometimes I worry that I didn't show her enough appreciation."

AnnaBeth gave a quiet huff of disbelief. "Unless you've changed completely, I'll never believe that."

He hoped she was right. "In so many ways, Dana was perfect, but before we married, she'd run up a lot of debt, so she insisted that I keep track of our accounts."

"Smart."

"Yeah, she was. She worked with me to get it all paid off, and then we both stuck to our budget."

AnnaBeth encouraged him with a smile. "You were a team."

Yes, they had been. "She loved decorating." He brushed his thumb over AnnaBeth's knuckles, thinking this conversation shouldn't be so comfortable, so easy. Yet it was. "The house reflected her in a lot of ways, and I struggled with that after she was gone. With seeing her everywhere I looked. I ended up changing it all, especially in the bedroom."

"I imagine sleeping was difficult enough for a while."

"Not like Mia let me sleep much anyway." God, that had been a terrible time, one he usually refused to revisit, because the memories were grueling. Now though, with AnnaBeth . . . "She'd just turned two, and she wanted her mommy so badly."

Squeezing his fingers, she whispered, "Heartbreaking."

"So many nights, I sat in a rocking chair with her, and we'd rock and rock until she finally wore herself out crying and dozed off."

"Bet you were afraid to move even a tiny bit."

She had that right. "I didn't dare blink. I just held her and hoped she'd get some rest." He remembered her red eyes and cheeks, her breaths uneven, and how his heart would ache so badly, he didn't know how he'd survive it. But he had, and now his daughter was a happy little girl.

With a quiet sniff, AnnaBeth said, "You must be a really strong person to have gotten through something like that."

He heard it in her words, in the gruffness of her voice, that she really got how devastating it had been. "You don't get a choice, really. You do what you can do, however you can do it, until the new reality starts to settle in.

It was months before I figured out that reading to Mia in her bed made it easier for me to slip away once she fell asleep. Then after a while, that became the routine."

"Is it still a bedtime ritual?"

"Most nights." It was something they both enjoyed. "Sometimes she wants to read to me, which means she repeats back a favorite story she has memorized while we turn the pages. Occasionally, she falls asleep before we can even get started."

With a teasing smile, AnnaBeth said, "She told me her grandma thinks she's special and gives her anything she wants."

"True enough. I've tried to be patient with the situation."

"But then your daughter comes back puking because she's eaten way too much junk."

"That's about it. It's not just the sweets, though. Her grandma also promised to buy her a parrot—then I was the bad guy when I had to say no."

"A parrot? Wow." AnnaBeth subdued a laugh. "Did she offer to keep it at *her* house?"

"I suggested it, but no. She argued with me that it was for Mia. And of course, Mia kicked up a fuss, but at least I can control *her.*"

Tipping her head again, AnnaBeth asked, "What did you do?"

"I told her I wouldn't let her play with Ruby if she didn't behave."

"Ha! Genius dad move." She offered her other hand for a high-five.

With a grin, he complied. Her mood affected his own, making him more lighthearted. "Dana loved her mom, of course, and they were actually close, but they butted heads a lot, too."

"Both individuals," AnnaBeth surmised aloud. "With

their own interests, priorities, and opinions, but still with that mother/daughter dynamic. I'm guessing that happens a lot with adult children."

So intuitive. "My mom and I have always gotten along great—even before she moved to Florida." They both laughed. "You said you didn't have any close family, so how are you so smart about all this?"

Instead of taking his comment as the compliment he intended, she flushed in embarrassment. "I overstepped again, didn't I? I didn't mean to sound like a know-it-all."

"AnnaBeth," he murmured, wondering why she so readily assumed the worst. "I was being sincere. You have incredible understanding of the situation."

Wearing a smile of doubt, she said, "Well, then, thanks."

"You're welcome." Devlin decided to let it go. Now that they were getting closer, he'd have the opportunity to interact with her, and in the process, he'd show her all the ways she was appreciated.

Which was funny, because before now, he hadn't realized how much she actually did for his uncle, for Mia—and yes, for him. AnnaBeth had been paying close attention to his family for a while now, but he'd been so mired in duty, in keeping it all together, he'd been oblivious.

"You mentioned mother/daughter dynamics. I think it's often different for sons than daughters."

"And from family to family," she said.

He guessed she'd had experience with different families—none of them her own. "After Dana had Mia, she gained some weight. Totally natural, and she still looked great, but her mom kept offering her dieting advice and making subtle comments on the size of her thighs. Drove me nuts. I had to grit my teeth a lot."

"I'm sure you lavished Dana with compliments to counter the negativity, right?"

"I did. You know how it is, though. Compliments fade,

but insults stick." Like AB Positive. He had a feeling that hadn't been a kind nickname.

"Yeah." Her gaze turned away from his. "Insults have a nasty way of digging deep."

It bothered him, seeing her like this. "We've talked a lot about me." Far too much, really. "Will you tell me more about you?"

"Eh, there's nothing much to tell." She tried a grin that didn't quite reach her eyes. "I'm just me."

He thought she was pretty damned special. "You told me once that you're a social media manager?" He wasn't sure what that entailed. "You work from home?"

"That's the cool part of the job. I don't have to go anywhere."

But if she didn't date, either, then was she always alone? "What exactly does a social media manager do?"

"Hmm, well, a bunch of stuff, actually. I have a lot of accounts, some small and some large. I oversee the social media presence, so my clients are freed up for other stuff. I do campaigns, create content, and then analyze the success of stuff already in place, things like that."

"What kind of campaigns?"

She seemed nonplussed by his interest, but gamely explained anyway. "So campaigns differ, depending on what the client wants. Some are after more reach, some want more followers, or they just want to drive traffic to their site. Maybe they have a new product to introduce, and they're hoping to get it out there. Or they're pushing a big sale, maybe a new feature."

Fascinated, he asked, "You said you create content? What kind?" It was amazing to see the difference in her, a sort of animated surprise that she'd get to talk about her work.

"I *love* making videos. All kinds. Goofy or serious, really detailed or simple. I do most of it in a program using stock images or footage that I alter, but sometimes I get to stage the whole thing. It's awesome when I go on-site, like to a factory or an office, and I can use the content there. Polls are always fun, and contests often work well if they get enough reach." She gave the question some thought. "I recently did this big interactive campaign for a local business here. It was loads of fun and really got the community involved."

"It sounds incredible. Very artsy."

"I got a degree in marketing and graphic design. I wanted something I could use to be my own boss." She wrinkled her nose again. "I don't really mesh in the office environment."

"Who says?"

Again, she looked nonplussed. "Well . . . I don't know. I guess I've always been the odd duck that didn't fit in. Growing up, I mean."

Had that been her experience with her foster families? "Will you tell me something, AnnaBeth?"

Wary now, she said, "If I can."

Apparently, *he* was pushy, because he wanted to know everything about her, not just the traits easily observed, the things he'd learned in day-to-day encounters, but her secrets, her hurts and expectations, any and every detail that made up AnnaBeth Posey Sanders.

He'd start with a simple question. "How many foster homes were you in?"

Her face flushed, and she quickly looked down at her tea. "Let's just say a lot."

"Hey." He reached out, taking both her hands in his. "You realize that's not on you, right?"

"Of course it's on me." Her chest lifted with a deep breath. "I mean, I know a lot of foster parents give up after a year, so I was just part of the statistics and all that. But it's still personal, because I tried so hard."

Had she been shuffled from one home to another *every year*? He couldn't even begin to imagine what that would do to a kid. Of course, his thoughts darted to Mia, and fierce protectiveness swelled within him. He'd take on the world to make sure she felt loved and secure, yet Anna-Beth had been utterly alone.

She let out a short breath. "Maybe if I'd been . . ."

"Different?" Less herself? God, no, he couldn't imagine that. "Don't think that way, okay? I happen to like who you are."

Her fingertips drifted idly over the grain in the tabletop. "With some people, less is more, you know? I'm okay in small doses, but too much of me?" She shook her head. "I start to get annoying."

Had someone actually told her that? "AnnaBeth, listen to me. Kids—*all* kids—are a challenge. It's not easy for any parent. There are good times, and hellish times, and those times that rip out your heart."

"I tried not to do that, though. Not to create anything hellish or hurtful." Her mouth flattened. "Seemed it always happened anyway. And then I got the nickname."

His heart ached. "AB Positive?"

"Guess trying to make everyone happy is as annoying as misbehaving." Breath left her in a sigh. "I figured that out a little too late."

Devlin wasn't quite sure how it happened, but he was out of his chair and circling the table before he thought it through.

Lips parting in surprise, AnnaBeth stared up at him— until he caught her upper arms, gently drew her out of her seat, and brought her against his chest. The body-to-body contact was both startling and bolstering, like a hot drink on a wintery day. Parts of him thawed that he hadn't known were frozen. She was a gift—truly a gift—but she didn't seem to realize it.

Closing his arms around her, he enfolded her in a hug that he needed, whether she did or not. "Parents have good and bad days like everyone else. They get short-tempered and say hurtful things they don't mean."

"They weren't my parents, though—and I'm pretty sure they meant what they said."

He seriously wanted to go back in time and somehow shield her from all the hurt. "I love your positive attitude. I hope you go on being AB Positive forever." Somehow, he'd get her to see that nickname in a whole new way. "But when you aren't feeling so upbeat, when things bother you or worry you, that's okay, too. I promise."

Slowly, her arms came up, and her hands opened on his back. Tentatively resting her cheek against his chest, she whispered, "I don't know how to be any other way, at least not for long. Whenever I get down about something, I don't like it, so I cheer myself up."

I cheer myself up. It was such an AnnaBeth thing to say. How many times over the years had she needed to do that?

Likely, far too often—because she didn't have family to help her with it.

Devlin leaned back to take in her earnest expression, then cupped his hands over her cheeks. "Great attitude." As she started to smile, he kissed her—just a soft, two-second touching of lips, in case she objected. "You amaze me, AnnaBeth. Everything about you."

Her eyes were wide, staring into his before dropping to his mouth. She tilted closer, maybe with the intent of another kiss . . .

Lightning cracked across the sky, sending a bright flash into the kitchen, followed a mere second later by a bellow of thunder. With a slight jump, she breathed, "Wow."

The electricity died, filling the house with an eerie silence. Before either of them could comment on it, Mia shouted, "*Dad!*" with a tinge of panic.

Chapter Three

Four days later, AnnaBeth breezed through her work, all the while wearing a smile. *Devlin Connely kissed me.*

Too bad the storm had interrupted, but the second Mia had called out, they'd both been on the move, practically running into each other to reach her. It wasn't really AnnaBeth's place, but hey, she knew what it was to be a little girl, suddenly feeling alone and afraid. Never, not in a million years, did she want Mia to feel that way.

She shouldn't have worried, though. The second she'd seen Mia jump into her daddy's arms, she'd known he would move heaven and earth to protect her. He'd held his daughter close while calmly explaining to her that it was just a storm. Simultaneously, he checked on Sony, who'd come awake with a start.

Devlin was a world-class multitasker.

With Ruby yapping in startled excitement, AnnaBeth had scooped up the little dog and watched them all interact. Sony spoke too loudly, Mia demanded attention, and Devlin had sent her a look of apology while dealing with it all.

And she'd stood there, knowing she was in love.

Not just with Devlin, who'd bowled her over from the moment he'd introduced himself a year ago, but with the whole family. With each of them as individuals, and as a unit.

They didn't know it, and she could never say so, but they were everything she'd ever wanted while growing up alone.

Only better. More real.

Perfectly imperfect in a way she'd never been able to imagine. Oh, she'd read about storybook families in which every piece of advice was sage and well-received. The kids were always angelic and wise beyond their years. Parents were like saints who never made mistakes or lost their tempers.

Devlin and Mia and Sony were *not* that. Mia had her moments of bossiness and five-year-old fits, and the girl could be totally whiny when she was sleepy or sick. Sony sometimes grumbled, often intruded, and the man had the subtlety of a runaway semi—especially when he forgot his hearing aids and shouted every word.

Then there was Devlin. . . . When she'd first met him, it had been like talking to a warm mannequin. Polite smile pinned in place. Every reaction practiced and precise. To her, it had seemed Devlin went through life by rote, doing the expected—and doing it well—without fully experiencing every wonderful moment life had to offer.

It was truly tragic that he'd lost his wife, but he still had Mia and Sony, and he had his health. He had family and love.

So many reasons to be grateful, to celebrate . . . yet he never celebrated for himself, only for others.

Her heart usually hurt around him, because she'd so badly wanted to break through his polite façade, to truly reach him so he understood that while the future he'd wanted had changed, he was still very much alive.

Alive and wonderful.

Naturally, she hadn't. How could she advise someone else on how to live when she'd made such a muck of her own life? After alienating so many people, she hoped she had enough sense to keep her thoughts to herself. Mostly, anyway.

Instead, she'd limited herself to being neighborly. Well, her version of neighborly, which granted, was about as intrusive as it got.

She'd loved them all for so long that it had saddened her to stand there in the room and yet be apart from them. So she'd cuddled little Ruby, who hated storms, and made her excuses about needing to get home.

Her expectation had been that Devlin would forget all about their conversation in the kitchen. For him, it probably hadn't meant much. Same with the kiss.

Only he hadn't forgotten.

He'd called her that night, and every day since, just to talk.

Being considerate, he always asked if he was interrupting her work, or her day, or . . . anything. Of course, he wasn't. Her time was largely open. She rarely got behind on her schedule, so taking a break here and there wasn't a problem. Since it was only her and Ruby, she had more free time than she wanted or needed.

Today they were supposed to have lunch together. She glanced at the clock. One more hour, but it felt like an eternity.

She finished her current project, saved her work, and then glanced out the window. By design, her desk faced the side of Sony's house. Not so she could snoop on him—she'd arranged the furniture before she ever met him—but because he had big, mature trees in both his front and backyard, and in between tasks, she enjoyed watching the squirrels and birds.

When Sony came to the side of his front porch railing, she waved at him through the window. He waved back, then waited, still looking toward her, so she hustled out of her chair and headed to the door.

Ruby looked up from her nap on the couch cushions, yawned, and used her doggy stairs to climb down.

To get next door more quickly, AnnaBeth lifted the little dog and hurried out.

It was another overcast spring day, but everything was starting to smell clean and fresh, if a little brisk still. Crocuses and daffodils were showing up in her landscaping, and she inhaled the scent of grape hyacinth. Life felt full of possibilities.

Going to her own railing, she called out, "Hey, Sony. What's up?"

"You busy?" he shouted back, a little louder than necessary, which told her he hadn't put in his hearing aids, or they needed adjusting again.

For answer, she lifted one finger in the universal sign for "just a second," and ran back in to shove her feet into her sneakers. She grabbed Ruby's leash, a zip-up sweatshirt for herself, and hurried back out. In less than half a minute, she was striding up his porch steps.

Sony was still there waiting. With his bushy white eyebrows beetled together, he looked apologetic.

"Hey, you okay?" Tucking the dog into one arm, she laced the other around Sony and led him to his door. "What's up? What can I do?"

"I dropped my damn pills. The blasted things went everywhere. They're tiny enough that I can barely see them, and I can't get down on the floor to look for them."

Relieved that the problem was something so minor, she brought Sony inside while saying, "Well, of course you shouldn't be down on the floor. I'd have a heart attack if I saw you there. You did the right thing, waving me over."

"I was going to call, but I didn't know if you were busy."
He shot her a look. "You're the type of girl who'd come
running even if you were in the middle of things. You're always helping me, but I can't ever do anything for you."
"What? Don't be silly." She smoothed down a wild tuft
of white hair sticking out on the side of his head, probably
where he'd rested during a nap. "I love visiting you, Sony.
You share your tea with me all the time, and you tell me
about your wife."

"Aw, that's just an old man sharing memories."

"I love your memories," she said, meaning it. "It's almost like I knew your Evelyn, you paint such a vivid picture of her. Besides, we're friends. Friends always come
running when needed."

"We are friends, aren't we? And that's why I didn't want
to bother you if you were in the middle of things. When
you waved, though, I thought maybe you'd have time—"

"Sony." She faced him with a smile, then couldn't resist
a quick hug. At one time, he'd probably been as tall as
Devlin, but now he was only a few inches taller than her
five feet, seven inches. "I promise you, I am never, *not ever*,
too busy for my favorite neighbor and friend. Okay?"

He patted her shoulder. "You're a good girl. I keep
telling Devlin so."

AnnaBeth grinned. "Thank you for the endorsement."
Unwilling to discuss Devlin too much, she looked around.
"So where did you drop them?"

"In my bedroom. Was a fresh bottle, too, so there should
be thirty pills." He put a hand to his stomach. "They help
my heartburn."

Concerned, she turned back to him. "Why don't you sit
down, and as soon as I find one, I'll bring it to you."

"Take your little dog out first so she can piddle. Then
she can sit with me."

Knowing he liked Ruby almost as much as Mia did, she

agreed. A few minutes later, she got Sony settled in his recliner with a knit throw over his legs and Ruby curled against his side, and she headed off for the pill hunt.

It took her no time at all to locate a few, so she made tea for Sony and took him a pill. Good timing, too, because he looked ready to nod off. At her interruption, Ruby did her best to lick AnnaBeth's face. When she leaned out of reach, the dog huffed, and then tucked herself under the throw near Sony's hip.

Smiling, Sony patted the dog. "Thank you, AnnaBeth. It was my lucky day when you moved in next door."

She inhaled the appreciation, touched by his sincerity. "I feel the same." Sony wasn't her family, but he was better than any family she'd ever had, like a kind grandpa and a favorite uncle combined. With him, she always felt truly valued.

"Why don't you rest?" He was already half asleep. "I'll let you know before I leave." She moved the tea away from his elbow, gave his shoulder a soft squeeze, and went back to work.

The pills had literally gone everywhere. Beneath the bed and the dresser. Behind a nightstand. A few had even rolled into an open closet. She counted what she had, but there were still some missing.

Crawling half under the low bed, she found two more. She was awkwardly wiggling out when she heard a deep, amused voice say, "This is unexpected."

AnnaBeth froze. She twisted to look back, but all she could see was a pair of dark sneakers. "Devlin?"

"You can keep wiggling like that if you want. I don't mind."

Keep wiggling? Did that mean he liked seeing her wiggle? She was tempted . . . but no. Now that he'd said it, she'd feel silly doing it. "I don't have much room to maneuver."

"How about I tug you out?" Warm hands clasped her bare ankles beneath the hem of her jeans. He drifted his thumbs across her skin. "Yeah, that's what I'll do. Nice and easy. Ready?"

Not really, but she said, "I have pills in my hand."

"You can explain that in a minute." Gently, he dragged her out until her head had cleared the bed frame. Pretty sure she had dust stuck to her hair and her dark sweater, but oh well.

Immediately, she rolled to her back and stared up at him. Every time she saw Devlin, he took her breath away. His dark hair was a little mussed, maybe by the wind, and his brown eyes were filled with humor.

Kneeling beside her, he said, "Hi, AnnaBeth."

He looked . . . well, he looked really happy to see her.

"Hi." She thought about sitting up, but he was super-close, so instead she stayed flat and asked, "What are you doing here?"

A smile played over his mouth. "You weren't at home, so I came here and found my uncle conked out with Ruby. I figured with the dog here, you had to be around somewhere, too, but I didn't expect to find you under the bed."

"I have a good explanation." She came up on one elbow and handed him the pills she'd retrieved. "We have around five more missing. Sony dropped the bottle, and they went everywhere. I don't even know where else to look."

Neither of them stood. Or even really moved. Mostly they just looked at each other. She felt her breath hitching a bit.

Devlin set the pills on the mattress, then reached out to tuck back a hank of hair that had escaped her ponytail. "You're dusty."

Yup, that was her heart lodging in her throat. The way he watched her, spoke to her, and touched her, it was all so new. "I never thought to clean under your uncle's bed. Herds of dust bunnies have taken over."

"I don't think bunnies come in herds. More like . . ." He thought about it a moment, then drew out his phone.

"You're looking it up?" They were on the floor in his uncle's bedroom. She hadn't expected them to hang out.

"Yeah." Then with a smile, he announced, "A group of bunnies is a fluffle."

"Oh, well, that's cute." God, she liked the way he grinned, how it showed in his eyes and put a little crease in his cheek. "They still gotta go."

"It's not your job to clean out the dust fluffle. Uncle Sony has a woman who comes every other week to do a thorough cleaning. I'll make sure to tell her to get under the bed."

Good plan, but AnnaBeth knew she'd check that it was done right. She didn't want anyone taking advantage of Sony, and at his age, he shouldn't be breathing all that dust. "Want to help me on the pill search? Then I can run home and clean up real quick before lunch." She looked down at her body in the now rumpled, oversized black sweater and her softest, most worn and faded jeans. "I'd planned to change clothes and do something with my hair, but then I saw Sony through the window and—"

Leaning down and putting his mouth to hers, Devlin silenced her. She liked his method. At the moment, she had no interest in talking.

She could totally get used to this impromptu kissing stuff. His lips were warm, skimming over hers, sort of teasing her bottom lip, then the corner of her mouth before he pulled away. His eyes looked into hers, and with a soft sound, he came back for two more kisses, both a little firmer.

"Your mouth is irresistible."

Since he said it against her lips, she wasn't sure if she

should reply or not, but then decided another kiss was in order. She caught the back of his neck with one hand and deepened the kiss.

He couldn't just tease like that. No way.

She parted her lips, his tongue touched hers . . . but then he quickly pulled away. "No more of that." After standing, he reached down and assisted her up. "Not in my uncle's bedroom."

Disappointment hit with the first sentence, and embarrassment with the second. Yeah, Uncle Sony's room. How could she have forgotten? "I guess that would be kind of awkward."

"I don't want to think about it." Glancing around, he said, "Let's find the pills, head to your house, and pick up where we left off." He paused. "Unless you want to run right out for food."

Ha! Fat chance. She'd spent a year imagining multiple scenarios of her and Devlin getting together. None of them involved pill hunting in his uncle's house, but she could roll with it. Plus, no one had ever accused her of being shy. "If you want my honest preference, then I vote we order pizza to be delivered. I'll throw together a salad, open a few colas, and we can hang out with more time for the fun stuff."

"I like the way you think." He checked the time on his phone. "Let's get to it."

Unfortunately, by the time they located the last of the pills—two of which were somehow under Sony's pillow—Sony had awakened. He showed up in the doorway, Ruby beside him, and smiled at them. "Devlin. I didn't know you were here."

Devlin winced. "We seriously need to get your hearing aids checked."

"What's that?"

With an exasperated smile, Devlin slid his arm around

her waist and drew her forward. She stepped stiffly beside him, mostly because he'd taken her by surprise, showing affection in front of his uncle. Felt like her legs locked up a little there, and she couldn't seem to manage a blink.

Took Sony by surprise, too, judging by the way his suddenly astute gaze zeroed in on them. Then he slowly grinned, making it clear he was pleased by Devlin's more familiar touch.

Loudly, so his uncle could hear, Devlin said, "Let's find your ears, Uncle Sony."

Sony just kept on grinning, so much so that AnnaBeth shook off her surprised stupor and started to grin, too.

Near her ear, so only she would hear, Devlin said, "Good thing we weren't still on the floor together."

Devlin would never say or do anything to hurt his uncle, but when Sony suggested ordering a pizza to thank Anna-Beth for her help, he nearly groaned in disappointment.

He wanted to kiss her again—without restraint. He wanted to touch her, to feel her body against his. So many wants bombarded him, they left his blood burning and his muscles primed. He hadn't felt like this in far too long.

Sony looked hopeful for company, so Devlin immediately caved. "Sounds good. AnnaBeth?"

Expecting her to show some frustration, he was surprised when she only said, "Great idea. And I have stuff for salad next door. I can grab it."

"I'll help." At least he'd get a small bit of time alone with her. In so many ways, AnnaBeth intrigued him. Always had, but now, it was different. Sharper edged.

Personal and intimate.

He was used to putting his own wants and needs last. Until this new hunger for AnnaBeth, it hadn't been an issue. Everything he'd wanted had been wrapped up in family, in his closeness with Uncle Sony and his daughter's happiness. In the day-to-day survival of heartbreak and learning to be just himself, when for so long he'd been part of a couple.

There were times when he'd thought he'd always feel that way, like half of a whole, with a vital part missing. To some extent, he did still; the awareness of what he'd lost remained. But the loss no longer felt overwhelming, as if it dominated his life. It was just there, like other memories of things now gone. Tempered by his feelings for AnnaBeth.

With an understanding look, she acknowledged that they'd missed their opportunity to enjoy a brief, casual date.

Thanks to her quick thinking, he could still get her alone for a few minutes.

After calling in the order, they walked over to her house. Ruby, who was happy to stick with Uncle Sony, had no interest in joining them.

On her front porch, AnnaBeth said, "I might have left things a little messy." She opened the door and stepped in. "When your uncle waved at me, I'd just finished working, so I—"

Close behind her, Devlin crowded in, pushed the door shut, and turned her all in one move. "Mind if we get to this first?" He saw the question in her eyes, saw her lips part to voice it, and he covered her mouth with his. Better still, he gathered her close, relishing her soft curves, the scent of her hair and skin.

He *loved* her hair, the silky weight of it and how it framed her face. Loved her skin, too, so warm to the touch.

He made a rough sound as her slender arms came up and around his neck. She opened her lips more, tacit permission for his tongue to sink in, tasting her, stroking and inciting.

Going up in flames, he pressed her back to the door and feasted on her. *This.* He needed this. With *her.*

Tilting his head, aligning it for the best advantage, he deepened the kiss until he couldn't tell where his breath ended and hers began.

Her hands roamed restlessly over his shoulders, down to his upper arms, where she stroked his biceps. Liking that, he did his own fair share of touching—but for him, it was difficult to stick to shoulders and arms. He could feel her breasts cushioned against his chest and he wanted, *needed*, to touch her.

Leaving her mouth, he kissed her throat. "AnnaBeth?"

She replied with, "I wish we had time for sex."

That disclosure hit him like a heat bomb, stealing his breath. He pulled back to see her heavy eyes, flushed cheeks, and a smile of willingness. "I should have told Sony we had other plans."

AnnaBeth touched his cheek. "He's eighty-eight years old. We can't ever disappoint him, not for any reason."

God love her, she made him feel things he'd never felt before—and what a realization *that* was. In some ways, he felt a decade younger, falling into his first serious infatuation. But he was thirty years old, and he knew his own mind. This was a far deeper, more serious emotion, and it was hitting him hard.

"Does that annoy you?" she asked. "I'm sorry. We'll have other days and opportunities, right? At least I hope we will." She tilted in for another kiss. "Tell me we will."

"Most definitely."

"But with Sony, sturdy as he may seem, age is an issue."

"I agree—and you didn't disappoint me. Not even close."

"Good." She traced her fingertips over his jaw. "I want you to know, Devlin. I don't have any plans where you're concerned."

Because he had plenty of plans, his brows went up. "What does that mean?"

"This is going to sound blunt, but I don't want to leave Sony alone too long, so I'm just going to toss it out there." Something in her tone put him on edge. He braced himself. "Yeah, do that."

"Just as Sony loves his house, I love mine. It's the first real home I've ever had, and I'll never leave it. Since I know you would never uproot Mia or leave the home you shared with your wife, you don't have to worry that I'll start planning a future for us."

"Is that so?" She was telling him not to look ahead— when he was already doing exactly that. *With her.*

"Not for anything permanent, I mean." Frowning, she continued in a rush. "I didn't become friends with Sony as a way to get to you. I wouldn't use him like that. He's the sweetest guy, and not to make it weird, he's the closest thing I've ever had to family. I care about him, and about Mia. She's a doll." Nervously, AnnaBeth licked her lips. "None of that is to get closer to you, though. If you want to have sex, I'd love it. I've thought about you a lot, but I know it'd just be that. Sex. Not a relationship or anything."

Knowing she was waiting for him to say something, though he had no idea what, Devlin just stood there.

Great, we can keep it casual. Hardly. He was already invested. Until she'd pulled back, he hadn't realized how much, but he knew it mattered.

That works perfectly for me. No, it damn well didn't. Relationships weren't play for him, not at his age, and not with his daughter taking up the majority of his time.

Thanks for clearing it up. He wasn't about to let her off the hook that easily.

To stall, he turned to take in her living room, surprised to see that it was decorated in a neutral palette, picture perfect, but obviously lived in and comfortable.

A short, overstuffed couch in light tan fabric was flanked by two slightly darker corduroy padded chairs. Plush pillows and a knitted throw blanket added homey touches. Ruby had her own little comfy bed on the floor that matched, but also very pretty, dainty stairs so she could get up on the couch.

On the white wooden coffee table were magazines, a book about digital design, a stack of cork coasters, and a lush plant. In fact, she had a lot of plants, in baskets on the floor and a few on stands. It was nice.

She shifted nervously beside him until he asked, "Who decorated?"

"Me." She looked around, too, as if seeking the flaws in her style. "I read a book on interior design and looked through a bunch of magazines, then sat on a *lot* of furniture. Over the years, I lived in houses that had really worn furniture and some stuff that was so formal we weren't allowed to use it. Traditional, early American, contemporary, farmhouse . . . so many different styles, but they were all nice for different reasons. I guess my taste in furniture is eclectic, based on what looks good to me, but also feels good because I use it."

"That makes perfect sense to me. It looks great. Super professional, but also like you live here."

"Well . . . I do. Ruby and me, I mean. I made sure the material on the couch was easy to clean. Same with the rug and the curtains." She gestured toward the couch. "That's Ruby's blanket. When I'm working, she'll yap at me until I get it exactly right for her, then she burrows in and sleeps."

Devlin bent to lift a squeaky bone, then a ball that rattled. "Her toys?"

Defensively, AnnaBeth took the toys from him and tossed them into an overflowing basket in the corner. "She lives here, too. She has a right to her things."

"I agree." He kissed her again, then made an obvious connection. "It's the same with Mia and her stuff. I try to keep the house organized, but she has her favorites that rarely get put away. A stuffed giraffe that she likes to snuggle with on the couch, an old doll she's had forever that she sleeps with every night. Like the basket for the dog's toys, I have a hamper in the living room where Mia puts away the things she plays with most often."

AnnaBeth smiled in relief. "I love that. Houses are to be lived in, right? They should look nice, but no one should feel like they're walking into a museum. They should feel comfortable and welcomed."

Had she felt that way before? In the many foster homes she'd lived in, she'd probably faced every scenario imaginable. Tenderness, protectiveness, and good old-fashioned lust all warred inside him.

Yet she'd already laid out the ground rules for a temporary relationship between them.

He nodded toward a big desk. "That's where you work?" It took up a lot of space in her modest-sized living room, and he noticed how it faced his uncle's house.

"Most of the time. Sometimes in bed or on the couch, but that's usually when I already have things nailed down and I'm just reviewing or tweaking, or if I've got emails from clients to read."

Her desk chair was oversized, padded, and looked as comfortable as the rest of her furniture.

"Do you think we have time for me to show you the rest of the house?" she asked. "Or would you rather I just get the salad together?"

"I'd love to see it. We should have time if we make it quick."

She grabbed his hand and hauled him toward the hallway. "The house is laid out a lot like your uncle's, but it's been updated more than his has." Pushing open a door, she showed him her main-floor bathroom, which was so clean he assumed she rarely used it. Next was a bedroom that she'd set up like a library, with shelves everywhere and a worn recliner with a single table and lamp.

"You like to read."

"A lot," she confirmed, as she quickly tugged him back out of the room before he could make out more than a few titles. He noticed mysteries, romance, and a few biographies. "Down here is the guest bedroom. It's big, but it's basically empty. Just a twin bed and a nightstand." She lifted her shoulders. "I don't have family to visit, so I mostly just use it for storage."

Another painful dart to his heart. "You never know, so it's good to have a bed there just in case."

"I guess. Mostly I just set it up that way because it's expected." She trotted him out and up the stairs. "Sorry to run you, but I think the pizza guy could be here soon, so . . . ta da, my upstairs bathroom."

"Wow, nice." The standard tub had been replaced with a whirlpool bath, and the room was done in light gray and white.

"The previous owners redid the room, and I love it. I do most of my reading in that tub."

He noticed a book sitting on the ledge, along with a book light, and in one corner was a fat white candle. "Scented?"

"Gardenia. I do love my leisurely baths. That white pillow on the floor is for Ruby. Usually, wherever I go in the house, she goes, too."

Except for when his daughter—or this time, his uncle—took her pet from her.

"Down here is my room." She led him along the hall to a third bedroom, this one done in all natural materials. A rattan headboard, light wood nightstands, a chunky knitted spread, and too many pillows for him to count. More books were stacked on the left nightstand, so he assumed that was the side she slept on.

"It's beautiful, but now I'm imagining you in that bed, and that's making me think of things other than houses, or design, or even pizzas and my uncle."

She grinned at him. "Seems fair, since I've often imagined you in that bed with me."

Before he could react to that comment, other than with a low groan, she grabbed his hand again.

"Now that we've decided, our time will come. But we need to hustle before Sony thinks we've abandoned him."

Devlin stopped her at the bottom of the stairs, brought her around, and kissed her thoroughly. "I hear the pizza delivery guy. Why don't you throw together the salad stuff, and I'll go next door in case Sony is sleeping again."

She touched her lips, then squeaked, "I'll only be a minute."

"Soon, AnnaBeth." He back-stepped away from her. "It has to be really soon."

Chapter Four

Two weeks passed in a haze of semi-happiness. Life was good, and she enjoyed plenty of attention from Devlin, but the "soon" he'd promised hadn't yet happened. Not his fault. She knew he was trying.

They'd arranged three "dates" to finally get together, but fate had other plans.

On their first attempt, Mia's school called to say she wasn't feeling well. She had a fever, and that nixed any extracurricular activities. Poor Devlin had his hands full for four days until Mia was finally over her bug.

AnnaBeth helped as she could, dropping off a care package of popsicles, a coloring book and fresh box of crayons, and a silly "get well" card for Mia. She'd also included a big serving of stew and bakery bread for Devlin, with a "miss you" note.

Devlin had insisted he didn't want her or Sony to get sick, so neither of them could visit in person. She'd put all the goodies in a pretty basket on their porch, then texted him to let him know it was there. From the doorway, he'd waved. Feeling a little more daring, she'd texted him a series of kissing emojis, which had made him laugh, and he texted back, promising again: *Soon.*

On the day of their next attempt, she got an offer for a big project promoting a new amusement park, but the manager wanted to meet her in person first. She had to drive two hours to the park, then spent most of the day touring the facility, making notes and taking photos of all the activities. By the time she got home, it was late. She was just thankful that the spring weather, while windy, had been dry and mostly sunny.

Then on their third attempt, Sony tripped and bruised half his body. Literally *half*. It was awful. The worst of the bruising was on his shoulder, where he'd landed first against the wall, but his hip had bumped a table on his way down, and the poor leg and side where he'd landed were far too colorful. Even the arm he'd attempted to brace himself on was now myriad shades of purple and olive green. It nearly made AnnaBeth cry to see it, which had amused Sony even as he'd assured her he was fine.

Their "date" ended up being at the emergency room, where she sat with Mia in the cafeteria while Devlin stayed at Sony's side. Thankfully, his uncle hadn't broken anything or suffered a concussion, but it was a long day of tests to make sure. By the time they'd gotten home, everyone was beat. Devlin spent the night with his uncle, and AnnaBeth had gone home alone—again.

Seriously, she was starting to feel jinxed.

Early the next morning, she was sitting at her desk, sipping coffee and going through emails, when a text dinged on her phone. Already smiling, she lifted it and read the message from Devlin:

b at your door in 2 mins FYI

At her door? She glanced out the window and saw

plenty of lights on at Sony's house. Were they all up then? She hoped Sony was okay.

But good grief, she hadn't even brushed her teeth yet! She'd awakened, stumbled down the steps, fixed her coffee, and gotten online. It was her usual routine, the way she liked to prep for her day. She never had company, definitely not while she looked like the walking dead.

Racing from her desk, which startled Ruby, she bolted up the stairs two at a time, then slid into the bathroom, thanks to her socks. She looked in the mirror and groaned—but priorities won out. Forget her messy hair and sleep-puffy eyes. Teeth first.

She brushed with a vengeance, gargled and rinsed, then splashed her face and dried it. She reached for the tie keeping her hair in a sloppy knot at the top of her head . . .

And the knock sounded on her door.

Ruby yapped in excitement, and AnnaBeth, wishing she wasn't such a slug in the morning, headed quickly back down the stairs. "Coming," she called out, while her brain scrambled for ways that she might be able to improve her appearance in the fifteen seconds she had left.

Regrettably, not a single good idea came to her.

Giving up, she snagged Ruby's leash, clipped it on the dog's collar, and opened the door.

Devlin stood there with one shoulder propped on the doorframe, a sexy smile in place. With morning whiskers and messy hair, his shirt and shorts wrinkled, his feet shoved into sneakers, he looked rumpled and irresistible.

Already a little turned on, AnnaBeth said, "Hi."

His gaze dipped over her; then he murmured, "Hi," in a super-hot way and, curving one big hand around her neck, drew her in for a kiss.

Yes, that was definitely a better kick to her morning than caffeine.

He went on kissing her until Ruby pulled at her leash.

"You look amazing," he whispered, while taking the leash from her and going out to sit on her porch step. "And I've always thought you had gorgeous legs."

Completely dazed, AnnaBeth joined him. "We're coming through a long winter. You've never seen my legs." Around him, she'd mostly worn lined leggings or jeans.

"The first time I met you, a little over a year ago, you were in shorts. Trust me, I noticed."

Her heartbeat tripped. He'd noticed her legs? *A year ago?* Odd, because he'd barely seemed to acknowledge her at all way back then. He'd been busy with family, as she recalled.

As if he understood her confusion, he said, "I've always noticed every little thing about you, AnnaBeth. First how you look, because honey, you are incredibly attractive in a 'not-trying' way."

His rough, sexy voice seemed to sink into her—and she had no idea what to say. "Um, thanks."

"I mean it. You have incredible hair, no matter how you wear it."

She touched a hand to her currently tangled updo. "Not so much now."

"Definitely now." He kept his attention on the little dog as she investigated the yard, a flower bud, and a bug. "Seeing the back of your neck makes me want to put my open mouth there—and my tongue."

Her breathing deepened. "Yeah."

He turned to her, searched her gaze, and smiled. Lightly, he grazed a finger over her nape, down along the side of her neck, then her shoulder, easing aside the loose fabric of her shirt as he went.

Breathlessly, she said, "No fair seducing me on the porch steps when neighbors might come out of their houses any minute."

Reluctantly, he drew his hand away but said, "If a few

words count as seduction, I predict we're going to have a lot of fun once I get you alone for two solid hours."

"Two hours?" AnnaBeth shivered, getting far too warm at what he was suggesting. "Seriously, *no fair*, Devlin."

Giving her another slow, carnal smile, he countered, "But it's fair for you to be flaunting all this bare skin when I've been hungry for you for so long?"

He had a point. "Two weeks *is* a long time."

"Honey, I've been wanting you for much, much longer. I just didn't do anything about it until recently."

Whoa, what an admission. Liking the sound of that, she stretched out her legs, displayed beneath her shorts but with thick, white, oversized socks on her feet, now slouching around her ankles. Wiggling her toes, she said, "The socks are a bit much."

"They're cute. Like fetish wear." For a brief moment, he rested his left hand, the palm large, warm, and a little rough, just above her knee, while his thumb played leisurely over her skin. "I like them. Feel free to wear them to bed if you want."

Much more of that, and she wouldn't be able to breathe at all. "I figured I looked pretty ridiculous."

"Adorably sexy," he countered. "As always." He slipped his arm around her, and for a minute, they sat quietly while Ruby chose three different spots to do her business.

When the little dog finished, she stretched out on the walkway to enjoy the warm morning sunrise.

"It's already a gorgeous day."

"A day I'll need to spend with Sony. He's fine," Devlin said, knowing she was about to ask.

"But?"

"I don't want to leave him alone."

"Of course not. If there's anything you need to do,

please let me know." She looked toward the house. "In fact—"

"Don't worry. He's awake, stiff, and feeling it, you know? It makes me cringe to see how bruised he is. I convinced him to spend the day in bed, resting. He has a TV in his room, and I told him I'd be around to fix his meals and help him to the bathroom or whatever. He can get there on his own steam, but he's sore."

"I'm surprised you were able to talk him into staying in bed."

"It helped that Mia curled up on top of the covers next to him. She knows I'll be here on your porch, and she should come get me if there's any problem, but for now they're watching Ninja Turtles." He nudged her a little. "She's explaining the history of it all to Sony, how they were regular turtles that got splashed with ooze by an evil guy, and that turned them into talking teenage turtles who love pizza and were taught by a rat."

His explanation made her smile. "Sounds like a riveting story."

"Like most kids, Mia has her moments. Today should have been a school day, but after everything yesterday, I let her take the day off."

"What about you? You're able to take a day off?"

"You know I'm a personal banker, right?"

She did, but she wasn't sure exactly what that entailed. They'd only talked about his work a few times. "You can work remotely?"

He nodded. "Especially when I don't have any face-to-face meetings lined up. I do have some business calls to make, and a little financial research to do for a client, but it shouldn't be too tough to juggle."

"I have a light day today. Want me to come over when I'm done so you won't get interrupted? I could take care of lunch, and even dinner. Plus, Ruby could visit with Mia, and vice versa."

For several heartbeats, he just gazed down at her, warm emotion in his eyes. "I was thinking . . ." Devlin said.

Wondering if she'd overstepped by inviting herself over, she gave a nervous laugh. "The way you're looking at me, should I be worried?"

"No. You should never be worried with me, because I would never hurt you."

AnnaBeth blinked. "I know that. I was just joking." Sort of.

"No, I don't think you do." He hugged her to his side. "I care about you. Far more than I think you realize. We're good together, but right now it feels one-sided, because you're the one giving everything."

"That's not true." How could she explain to him how much she loved being included? If she just threw that out there, he might think she only wanted him for his family. True, she loved Uncle Sony and Mia, but they were bonuses to . . . loving Devlin.

Oh, crap. She loved him. She was *in love* with him.

And had been for a while. Now that she'd acknowledged it, the truth worried her.

Tentatively, she said, "So you've noticed how well we work as a team?"

"With you doing all the work."

She sought words that wouldn't spook him, and settled on saying, "Being with you, being with Sony and Mia, it's special to me. Not at all like work. More like being accepted, like I'm part of it all." *Like having a family of my own.* Of course, she didn't say that part aloud.

Hugging her a little closer, he kissed her temple and said, "We love having you be part of us."

Love. That word seemed to be ringing in her head right now, then echoing in her heart.

"That's what I wanted to talk about. Keeping you a part of us."

Her shocked heart skipped a beat, then seemed to stumble while trying to catch up. Slowly she turned to face him. "Meaning?"

"Meaning I want my uncle and daughter to know I'm seeing you. I want to be able to explain to Sony that we're a couple, so when we want time alone, he'll understand."

Her lips parted for a slow breath. A couple.

"I wouldn't hurt you, AnnaBeth, not you or your feelings, and I would never deliberately do anything to disappoint you."

She nodded. "Okay." Then added, "Same," for reassurance. Her thoughts seemed to be as jumbled as her breathing at the moment.

One side of his mouth curled. "Perfect. Then maybe we'll be able to figure out that alone time fairly soon. Understand, though, I'm not talking about a temporary thing."

She nodded again, and started to say, "Okay," but she'd already said that, so she switched to, "Works for me."

"Love how agreeable you are."

So they were going to keep exchanging that word? Playing along, she quipped, "I love that you care so much about Sony and Mia."

"And you."

Yup, that was her heart, trying to leave her body. As if to contain it, she pressed a hand to her chest. "Back atcha."

"I know we're on your porch." His gaze dropped to her mouth. "Pretty sure some neighbors might be up."

"Probably."

"I'm going to kiss you anyway."

Nodding, she managed to say, "Go for it."

With another crooked grin, he teased his mouth over

hers, softly at first, then with more pressure, and more heat, until she felt his tongue.

She clutched at his shoulders, need suffusing her, and—

"Dad."

They broke apart so quickly, AnnaBeth nearly slid off the step.

Holding her close, Devlin leaned forward to look past the railing to his uncle's porch, from which Mia had called to him. "What is it, honey?"

"Can I play with Ruby? Uncle Sony said she can get in the bed with us."

Completely discombobulated, AnnaBeth stood and did what she always did—she took charge. "Of course you can. I'll walk her over to you. Then after I change clothes and answer a few more emails, how about we make breakfast? Do you like waffles?"

Mia's gaze went back and forth between the adults; then she smiled real big. "I love waffles."

Apparently, *love* was the word of the day. "Perfect. I have everything here. While we're doing that, your dad can get some work done."

Devlin said, "AnnaBeth."

Realizing what she'd just done, how she'd taken over, she cringed a bit and asked, "Hmm?"

Cupping a hand to her jaw, he lightly kissed her lips. "Thank you."

Over the next week, they worked out a near-perfect routine. Or at least it felt so to Devlin, except that he'd never wanted a woman more, and so far, he and AnnaBeth hadn't found the right opportunity.

They spent plenty of time together, shared many heated kisses and enough prolonged touching that he felt tortured—in the most sensual way.

He and Mia had stayed with his uncle, him on the couch

and Mia "camping out" in a pillow fort on the floor, something she considered great fun. The upstairs bedroom was available, but until Sony was back one hundred percent, he wanted to stick close enough to hear him.

Each day he drove Mia to and from preschool and to her visits with her grandma, and while he was away, Anna-Beth happily made sure that Sony wasn't alone for more than a few minutes at a time.

What Devlin really noticed was how much Sony enjoyed her visits, and how more and more, Mia grew closer to her. Several times his daughter had started out at Anna-Beth's side, only to end up largely in her lap. Once, he'd even found the two of them conked out together. Sony had explained that they'd been reading.

He remembered standing there beside his uncle's chair, both of them staring at AnnaBeth and Mia, with Ruby piled on top. For once his uncle had managed a mere whisper when he said, "Does my heart good to see them like that."

"Yeah, mine as well."

Sony had eyed him sharply, and then his mouth lifted in a satisfied grin. " 'Bout damn time."

"I agree." He'd lightly patted Sony's shoulder. "She hasn't yet agreed, though, so don't pressure her, okay?"

With a not-so-quiet snort, Sony had turned his gaze back to the sleeping huddle on the couch. "I know my girl. She's been in love with you forever."

It was the snort that had caused AnnaBeth to stir, cutting short any further conversations on love. They'd both watched in amazement as AnnaBeth had expertly extricated herself from the couch without waking Mia or disturbing the dog. It was the sweet, lingering touch she'd put on Mia's cheek that had really gotten to him.

Even his uncle had murmured a quiet, "Aww." Then to Devlin, "Wrap it up, before she gets away from you."

AnnaBeth hadn't understood that, but Devlin certainly did—and he intended to heed his uncle's advice, at least to the extent he could. To gain everything he wanted, he'd definitely need AnnaBeth's cooperation.

The days that followed gave him a glimpse of how his future could be. AnnaBeth included Mia in everything, from fixing meals to planting flowers, to dusting the house, as well as playtime with dolls and dinosaurs. Several times, Devlin insisted on doing meals *and* cleanup, much to AnnaBeth's consternation. It was clear to him that she enjoyed feeling useful, but he also wanted her to feel appreciated.

And loved.

They all fit so perfectly at Sony's house that Devlin had no real urge to return to his own home—except that he planned to get AnnaBeth there soon, for obvious reasons.

Yesterday, he'd overheard Mia asking why AnnaBeth had a stake in her front yard, and she'd explained that she was going to plant a lilac tree there but hadn't bought it yet. Without making a big deal of it, she'd said she was waiting until she had time and funds to take care of more landscaping.

In an effort to do something for her, he'd picked up Mia from school and then taken her to a nursery, where they'd found a large, healthy lilac tree ready to be planted. They returned home to find AnnaBeth and Sony in her yard together, his uncle in a lawn chair holding Ruby's leash, and AnnaBeth on her knees, removing some weeds from around the early spring blooms in her landscaping.

The second he helped Mia from the SUV, she ran over, announcing to AnnaBeth, "We got you something!"

"You did?" AnnaBeth started to stand but Mia leaped against her for an exuberant hug. Even while keeping her dirty gloves from touching Mia, AnnaBeth managed to return the embrace with a laugh. Ruby wanted in on that action, so the little dog started running circles around them until she got tangled in her leash. Sony, who felt much improved, reached out to give the leash to Mia.

Once again, Devlin found himself watching them laugh together and smiling from the inside out. AnnaBeth hadn't seemed to realize it yet, but she was a part of this family— a very special part.

She'd added so much to their lives.

Whether she accepted his plans for the future or not, that wouldn't change. But he wanted to do everything he could to cement their relationship in the best possible way.

After getting a wheelbarrow from his uncle's garage, he loaded the ornamental tree, along with a shovel, and called out to her, "Where do you want it?"

Her eyes rounded and she started to put one mulch-covered glove up to her mouth.

Sony caught her, saying, "Here now, take those off first, or you'll be eating dirt."

She blinked at him, then at Mia, who grinned hugely, and then back to Devlin. Quickly she stripped off the gloves and dropped them to the grass. "Is that for me?"

"It's not for me," Sony said. "I don't need any more trees."

As Devlin wheeled it forward, she moved excitedly to the right spot. "I have to dig the hole! It'll go right here, and the ground is mostly prepped but—"

"I'll dig it," he said. "That's part of the gift."

"It's purple," Mia announced. "I knew you'd want purple."

Devlin whispered, "But we can exchange it for white if you'd prefer."

"Purple is *perfect*." She clutched her hands together. "I've been wanting to get it, but I haven't had time."

"Because you've been taking care of us," Sony said, looking every bit as pleased as Mia.

Tears welled in her eyes, and she reached out for Sony, drawing him in for a gentle hug. "That's not true," she said. "We're friends spending time together. I've enjoyed it so, so much."

"We're not friends."

She leaned back, her face aghast. "But I thought—"

"We're *family*," Sony declared, pulling her back in for a tighter hug. "And you've done a lot."

"Family!" Mia seconded, wrapping herself around AnnaBeth's legs. Ruby yapped happily.

"Oh, but . . ." Freeing herself, AnnaBeth turned to Devlin, her expression both hopeful and wary.

His heart filled with emotions he'd never felt before, a special kind of contentment he'd never expected to find. "Family," he agreed softly.

Her lips trembled; she sniffled, then gave a quick nod. "I really do love you guys." She scooped up the dog, hiding her face against Ruby's scruff. Concerned, Ruby licked her cheek while her skinny tail went wild.

"Here now," Sony said. "Mia, you're going to get your school clothes dirty. I'll walk in with you so you can put away your backpack and change. Then we'll join them again."

Mia asked, "Can I take Ruby with me?"

Lifting her head with a happy smile and damp eyes, AnnaBeth said, "I'm betting Ruby would insist." She subtly used her shoulder to wipe away a tear, then set the dog back on the ground and returned the leash handle to Mia. "Are you sure you don't need any help, Uncle Sony?"

"I might still have a few colorful bruises, but I'm feeling good as new," he declared. "Now go thank my nephew properly."

Her gaze skipped over to Devlin. "I'll see what I can do."

Devlin waited until his daughter and uncle were out of

sight, then he caught her hand and pulled her in close. "I have a plan."

"To bowl me over, apparently. Seriously, dude, thanks for the beautiful tree. It's beyond awesome."

"It's nothing at all compared to everything you've done, but I'm glad you like it."

"I love it." She drew a shuddering breath and stared up at him. "I love that you got it for me."

Her eyes said even more than the words she spoke. "I love that a tree makes you happy."

She laughed. "*You* make me happy."

Perfect. "So here's my plan. Tomorrow, if you can spare the time away from your work, you could come with me to take Mia to school, and then we'll head to my house, where we'll finally be alone."

Her beautiful blue eyes grew brighter. "Okay, wow, *love* that plan—if you're sure Sony will be okay alone."

"I'll get his lunch together for him before I leave, but he really is doing fine now." Devlin smoothed back a long, silky hank of her hair that had escaped her untidy top-knot. God, she was beautiful to him—inside and out. "Tomorrow is one of the days Mia visits her grandma, but instead of me dropping her off there, Cindy asked if she could pick Mia up from school. Something about a salon day for girls."

"Sounds like fun," AnnaBeth murmured while staring at his mouth, her breath coming a little quicker.

"I think they'll get their nails done or something. Cindy's done that with her before, and she's on the school's list of approved people to pick up Mia." He traced his fingertips over her jaw, brushing away a smudge of dirt. "Would it be okay if I added you to that list, as well?"

Her gaze popped up to his. "For real?"

"In the case of an emergency. I wouldn't just impose on you—"

Shooting to her tiptoes, she clasped his face in her hands and smooched him soundly. "No joke, you can seriously impose on me anytime. I'm honored."

In so many ways, usually just by being herself, she made him laugh. Hopefully, she would be just as enthusiastic once they were in bed. "So tomorrow. Are you able to take the time off your work?"

"You kidding? For what you have planned, I've already rearranged my schedule in my head."

"You make me happy, AnnaBeth." This time, he kissed her before he turned away to pick up the shovel.

Tomorrow, he'd make sure she knew everything he felt.

AnnaBeth fidgeted as she and Devlin left his SUV. This was the first time she'd seen his house, and she didn't know what she'd expected, but the tidy mid-sized brick ranch with the barest, old-fashioned landscaping just didn't fit with the Devlin she knew.

And as soon as she thought it, she felt guilty. This was the home he'd shared with Dana. Surely, he had to love it.

With a hand on the small of her back, he guided her up the sidewalk to the front door. A plain door, she noticed, painted in a color that blended with the bricks. The black, utilitarian doormat didn't add anything to the curb appeal.

Casting her a surreptitious glance, he unlocked the door and pushed it open. As they entered, he said, "This place has never really felt like home, not like Uncle Sony's house does to him, or your house does to you." He secured the door behind them.

"It's nice," she replied. And it was, the bones of it anyway. "I guess Mia has a lot of friends here?"

"Not really. She's made friends with kids at school, but none of them live close by. A few live nearer to Sony's house, though."

Hmm. She'd just assumed . . .

"AnnaBeth." He turned her, cupped her face, and asked, "Are you nervous?"

"What?" She huffed. "No, why?"

"You're frowning a lot."

Damn. She immediately gave him a blinding smile. "I was distracted by seeing your house, but now that you've taken a roundabout way of reminding me why we're here, what do you say we make a beeline to . . ." Damn again. Did he want to use his bedroom? Would that room have special memories for him? She honestly hadn't thought that far ahead, so she quickly amended the end of her sentence to, ". . . wherever it is we're doing this." Then she bobbed her eyebrows—and felt ridiculous.

His gaze softened. "How about instead, I kiss you?"

"Solid plan." She threw her arms around his neck and took the lead, which had him first laughing through the kiss, then pinning her to the wall and taking control.

Mmm, nice. Devlin in control mode was a special treat. Especially when his hands roved over her back, then went low to her hips and drew her closer still. He left her mouth to kiss a damp, heated path to her throat.

"Seriously," she whispered, "I'm not the patient sort on a good day, but I've been waiting a year for you, so—"

He dropped his forehead to her shoulder and laughed. "Want me to get the show on the road, huh? Fine, I can do that." Taking her by surprise, he scooped her up and headed down a long, carpeted hall.

"Hey, I'm impressed, but I could have raced you there."

"You don't know where we're going." He entered a room, then pushed the door shut with his foot.

Curiosity took her gaze on a quick trip from one side of the room to the other, but it was as uninspiring as the rest of the house. Clean, neat, and pretty much as utilitarian as the doormat.

"I told you," he said, as he stood her on her feet by the bed. "It's never felt that much like home."

"It's a great house."

His mouth twisted to the side. "Honey, Dana has been gone for three years. She was a decorator, but I purged most everything in those first few months while I was trying to cope, and I've never really gotten around to redoing anything other than Mia's room."

Relief lifted her spirit. "So her room is different?"

"As she's grown from a toddler to a little girl, she's made her preferences known. Her room is pretty much how she wants it. Colorful, convenient, eclectic, and often a little messy." He brushed a kiss over her mouth. "Nothing that Dana bought, because she long ago outgrew the baby stuff."

"So there are dolls and dinosaurs, Ninja Turtles and My Little Ponies?"

"Exactly. I'll show it to you later if you want. *Much* later. For now, I want you to put everything and everyone else from your mind. It's just you and me, and I've also been waiting a year."

"Fibber," she teased. "You only got interested over the last month."

He said, "I realized I was in love over the last month, but I've wanted you from the day I saw you."

Her breath snagged, thoughts scattering in a chaotic whirl before slamming back together with a resounding clap of acknowledgment. She could hear her own heart beating, her eyes going damp.

Barely above a whisper, she asked, "You love me?"

This time, when he framed her face and kissed her, it was enough to melt her bones. "I love you so much, I can't imagine life without you."

"Devlin . . ." She had a million things to think about, but at the moment, all she could do was feel.

His eyes darkened even more. "We'll work it all out, AnnaBeth. I promise. Every concern you have right now. Anything that's worrying you."

She wanted to believe him, but life had taught her to mistrust good fortune.

"Shh," he murmured, kissing her forehead, her cheek, the corner of her lips. "Just you and me. Can we concentrate on that for now?"

Pretty sure that was all she could concentrate on. "Consider it done." She stepped back up against him, and this time when he kissed her, her entire heart was ready.

Chapter Five

When he'd mentioned love, Devlin had seen the joy in her eyes, followed by a flash of doubt, and worse, fear. AnnaBeth could give love so freely, but she didn't trust it when it came her way. She'd been hurt so badly in the past, but she was still kind and generous, and her resilience only made him love her more.

Determined to show her how much she meant to him, he countered her every move to take over—and he slowed her down, a feat that wasn't easy. Especially when he pulled off his shirt.

"*This,*" she said with dramatic enthusiasm. "I've been wanting this since that peek you gave me in your uncle's bathroom." Her hands were all over his, down his abdomen, and then at the snap of his jeans.

He caught her wrists. "I like an even playing field," he said, right before he tugged her shirt up and over her head. She tried to press herself against him, but he held her away, soaking up the sight of her. "You're not shy."

"Well, not usually."

Forcing his attention from her body, he saw the bright

color in her face. She was not a delicate blusher, but he hid his smile. "You are so sexy."

"Glad you think so." This time when she crushed herself against him, he let her, but he also got busy removing the rest of her clothes. As with everything else, they seemed to be in perfect sync. From touches to intent, they were evenly matched.

Hoping to keep the momentum going, he quickly set his cell phone, keys, and a small jeweler's box on the nightstand.

Matching him, she pulled her cell phone from her pocket, then unclipped her keys from a belt loop.

She didn't seem to notice the box, which was fine by him, since he wanted to address that later. He was hoping that once she realized how good they were together, in *all* ways, the rest would come more easily.

He'd had every intention of taking his time, savoring the experience, but the temptation of her nearness proved to be too much. Especially with her bold demands—which, yeah, were just one more thing that made her perfect.

"I love you." He said it with every touch, every kiss. He wanted to go on saying it every day for the rest of his life.

"Yes." She tangled her fingers in his hair, drawing his mouth back to hers. "Love . . ."

How much time had passed, Devlin wasn't sure. He could finally draw a deep breath again, and when he did, he inhaled AnnaBeth's fragrance. She stirred slightly, snuggling closer and releasing a satisfied sigh.

Feeling the soft thumping of her heart, Devlin said, "Now, for the rest of my plans."

"Mmm," she teased, moving sensually against him. "I'll just need a couple more minutes to finish recovering."

Life with her would never be boring. "I do love you, AnnaBeth."

She stilled, but then rallied with a big hug. "Love ya back."

Not exactly a romantic endorsement, but he'd learned AnnaBeth's moods, and he knew she felt uncertain.

He coasted his hand up and down her spine, relishing the silky warmth of her skin. "Do you love me enough to share a life with me?" Before she could answer, he said, "Keep in mind that it's not just me. It's Uncle Sony, who I hope to have around for another decade at least, and my daughter, who I think is beyond amazing, but she's still a rambunctious, inquisitive, ever-talkative little girl."

She reared up to brace her arms on his chest, then gave him a frown. "Uncle Sony is healthy, you've said so yourself, and of course he'll be with us for a long, long time yet."

Us. He liked the sound of that. Whether she acknowledged it yet or not, she was already thinking of them as a family unit—together.

"I love you," he said again.

That smoothed her frown. "Love you, too." Then she moved on, saying, "Mia *is* amazing. Yes, she's curious, but that's a good thing. Only a really happy, healthy, secure kid could totally be herself—and let's face it, that is pretty perfect, right? She knows she's loved, and that's what's most important."

"She loves you, too."

Again, that hint of panic showed in her expression. "I love her more. Who wouldn't?"

"Uncle Sony loves you. Mia loves you. But I wouldn't want to plan a life with you if *I* didn't love you."

Her lips parted, then compressed, and she looked away without saying anything.

"AnnaBeth?" Gently holding her face, he brought her

gaze back to his. "If you don't love me, it's okay. I'll still want you in our lives—"

"I *do* love you." Breathing a little faster, she whispered, "I have for so long."

"Then would planning our future together be so hard?"

"Plans with other people never go right for me."

Silently, Devlin vowed he'd give her so much love for the rest of her life that it would somehow make up for the past. "Maybe when you were a child, plans didn't go right because you didn't have control." And she was still living with the hurt in a little girl's heart. "This is different. You're a successful woman with her own home and a job she loves. You're independent, and you can do whatever you want, however you want. My family and I will go on loving you, regardless. You need to believe that."

"The thing is . . . my house is my *home*, the only home I've ever had." She hurried on, assuring him, "I love you so much, but I can't imagine living anywhere else."

"I want us to be together—where doesn't matter to me. In fact, I think your house is perfect, and it's right next door to Uncle Sony's."

Her gaze widened on his. "You don't want to keep this house?"

Finally, some of the worry left her expression. "I was already thinking of selling it and moving closer to Uncle Sony. When I mentioned it to him, he said I could live in his house."

"Right next door to me."

"Yes, and I can still go that route if that's what you want. Like I said, you're in control."

She leaned down and kissed him. "It would be torturous to have to say good night, knowing you were so close."

Tension coiled into his neck and shoulders, but he was determined not to pressure her. If she didn't say yes now, he believed she would eventually. *Patience*, he reminded himself.

Keeping his tone as light and sincere as he could make it, he said, "If you'd prefer I not do that, then I won't."

"I'd prefer you just move in with me—if you're sure you don't mind leaving your house."

Relief hit him in a tidal wave, and he hugged her tight, then couldn't seem to make himself let her go. "It might take some rearranging at your place to make it work."

She laughed. "I have an empty room, remember? Two bathrooms. An office I don't really use that often . . . and just think how happy Ruby will be."

Devlin laughed, too. "We can use the equity from the sale of this house for any remodeling that needs to be done."

She worked herself out of his arms, but when he saw her face, she was grinning. "This is getting exciting." Raising a fist, she said, "Go us!"

That deserved another kiss; then he reached out and snagged the box on the nightstand.

AnnaBeth bit her lip. "I was wondering about that."

"So you noticed it? You didn't let on."

"Dude, we were about to have sex. I was a little distracted."

Grinning, he said, "It's for you." Taking his time, he scooted up against the headboard and then helped her to get comfortable beside him.

"You seriously don't need to build the suspense," she grumbled with a mock frown. "Stop teasing."

"I look forward to teasing you for the rest of our lives."

Just like that, her expression melted, and she said in a soft voice, "Devlin."

He allowed only a brief kiss so they didn't get off track. "Just a second." The lid of the box lifted off easily, and he took out the square, black velvet case. Loving the excitement in her eyes, he whispered, "Open it."

Trying and failing to temper her smile, she eased up the edge, then gasped and snapped it shut again. "Devlin!"

"If you don't like it—"

"Get real! I *love* it." Opening it again, not so slowly this time, she pulled out the single, oval-cut diamond mounted on a gold band and stared at it with awe. "It's the most beautiful thing ever."

"No. That honor belongs to you." He took it from her, then slid it onto her finger, finding the fit nearly perfect.

"First a tree and now this. I'm feeling spoiled." She held out her hand to admire the ring. "When did you know this was what you wanted?"

"I think I've known for a while, but then that day Mia was sick, you were so good with her, it was like a kick in the heart."

"That sounds painful."

"Actually, it felt pretty good. Like priming a motor to run again."

She touched his face. "Had your heart stopped doing its job?"

"Not with Mia or Sony—but yes, it wasn't running like it should have been, not until you." He pulled her down beside him once more. "Things started adding up in my head, like how much you love your dog, but you share her with Mia anyway. How protective you are of Sony. The way you go above and beyond for everyone."

She nudged him. "Don't forget my biggest sacrifice."

Honestly, she gave so much, he wasn't sure what she meant. "Let's hear it."

"I drink that disgusting tea with Sony."

"So noble of you," he said with a grin. "Staying with Uncle Sony, and seeing you so often, I realized that you both understood 'home' far better than I did."

"It's not so much where you are," she said, "but who you're with."

"I want to be with you."

"I want that, too." After a moment, she asked, "Do we need a long engagement?"

"I'll marry you tonight if you're up for it."

Laughing, she lightly bit his chest, then kissed the spot.

"I'm pretty sure you want your uncle and daughter there."

"And my parents will insist."

"Your parents," she breathed, as if the idea overwhelmed her.

"They're going to adore you." Soon, she'd have so many people loving her, she would never again feel alone.

She bit her lip, then let out a breath. "I was thinking, spring weddings are perfect. Sony certainly thinks so."

"Uncle Sony married in the spring, so he's biased." He tipped up her face. "But I like the idea—as long as you mean *this* spring." Yes, he'd wait if she needed him to, but knowing what he wanted, he'd prefer to marry sooner than later.

"The weather is perfect right now, flowers are blooming, and it wouldn't be too hard to plan."

"I'm with you so far."

"Do you need fancy? Because I'm not a fancy kind of person, but if that's what you want, I can try to figure it out."

"I want you. Casual works great for me, and it means my parents would only need a little notice." He tucked back the long length of her hair. "My mother will make it work no matter what, but it'll be easier if she doesn't have to shop for a special dress."

She threw her arms around him. "Awesome. How about a few weeks?" Lifting her face up to his, she said, "Now that I know we're doing this, I don't want to wait."

Surprised, he slowly sat forward. "That's what you want?"

For once, she didn't look unsure. Instead, she glowed with happiness. "Positive. Unless you need more time?"

Not about to wait, he shook his head. "I'll tell Sony when we get back, Mia as soon as she gets home, then I'll call Mom and Dad tonight."

"And your mother-in-law," she reminded him. "You'll want to tell her before Mia does. And we should invite her to join us. After all, you and Mia are all the family she has now."

He paused, knowing she was right but wondering how Cindy would take the news. "I'll talk to her soon, but understand, AnnaBeth—I love you. As long as you feel the same, nothing else matters."

The way she hugged him told him that she agreed.

AnnaBeth couldn't remember ever being so happy. She'd seen it in Devlin's eyes, the love he felt and the desire to spend his life with her. Not only would she have Devlin for her own, but she'd gain a bonus family, too. Score!

During the drive home, they discussed everything: when to get the marriage license, how to rearrange things in her house to fit in an active little girl, even a family vacation to Florida. It all sounded too wonderful to be real, but she reminded herself that Devlin had always been rock steady. She believed if he said it would happen, then it would.

Unfortunately, when they got to Sony's house, there was an SUV parked at the curb that she didn't recognize. She could tell by Devlin's expression that he wasn't exactly pleased.

"Who is it?" she asked.

"My mother-in-law, and now I'm wondering if she's early because Mia is sick again." He parked in the driveway. "I was looking forward to sharing our news with Sony and Mia." He glanced at her. "But not in front of Cindy."

"It'll be a slight delay. I'm happy enough that I can wait." In fact, AnnaBeth felt as if she were floating. She started to tell him that, but then a movement drew her eyes to Sony's porch.

Holding Ruby in her arms, Mia stood there—with much shorter hair. "Um . . ."

Devlin noticed it at the same time. "What the hell?" He opened his door and got out.

AnnaBeth got out, too, and hurried around to him, saying low, "Smile, Devlin. You'll hurt her feelings."

Catching himself, he nodded, drew a long breath, and then drummed up a friendly greeting. "Hey, sweetheart."

Mia hugged Ruby until the dog wiggled in protest. Readjusting her hold, she kissed Ruby's head, rubbed her cheek against the dog's ears, and said glumly, "Grandma got me a haircut."

"So I see." His gaze moved over her.

"It's too short," Mia complained, her face downcast.

AnnaBeth nudged Devlin, then said, "You're cute as a button, Buttercup, but then you always are."

"Very cute," Devlin said, lightly stroking his hand over Mia's crown, where long curls used to bounce.

Glancing behind her into the house, then back to Devlin, Mia whispered, "I don't think I like it."

"Well, why not?" Trying to give Devlin a moment, Anna-Beth said, "We girls need to change up our looks every now and then, am I right?"

"I look like a boy."

"Not even!" Crouching down, AnnaBeth pretended to share a secret. "I've tried a few different cuts, some I liked, some I didn't. But the great thing about our hair is that it always grows back."

An older woman stepped into the doorway, her hands clasped tightly together. She was probably in her mid-fifties or very early sixties. Her honey-colored hair was cut in a bob, and her gaze was defiantly direct. On the slim side, dressed in stretchy slacks and a sedate tunic top, she looked pretty, and a little unsure.

No one said anything.

Even as AnnaBeth told herself to head home and let Devlin handle his family matters, she knew she couldn't do it. In awkward and uncomfortable situations, she always felt compelled to fix things—it was how she'd gotten the horrid nickname of AB Positive.

Stepping forward, she extended her hand. "I bet you're Mia's grandma. I've heard so much about you. I'm Anna-Beth Sanders, a neighbor."

Cindy eyed her critically but accepted her hand. "Yes, I'm Cindy Olsen. Nice to meet you."

"AnnaBeth is family," Uncle Sony said from behind the woman, edging his way around her to the porch. "Isn't that right, Devlin?"

"Definitely family," Devlin agreed. Again, he touched a gentle hand to his daughter's hair. "When did you decide to do this, Mia? You didn't say anything to me."

Narrow shoulders lifted. "I didn't really want to, but Grandma said it was time I had style." Ruby whined, then licked Mia's cheek in doggy commiseration.

Kneeling down, Devlin touched Mia's chin, turning her face this way and that before stating, "As AnnaBeth said, you're as cute as ever." He tousled her hair, messing up the new 'do. "But honey, you never have to cut your hair if you don't want to."

That seemed to galvanize Cindy, who stepped farther onto the porch. "Dana would have kept her styled."

"You don't know that, and it's beside the point." He came back to his feet, tension radiating from him. "Anna-

Beth and Sony, could you take Mia inside? I want to talk to Cindy just a moment."

With that statement out there, Cindy stiffened.

Sony held out his hand to Mia. "Come on, honey. We'll get Ruby a few doggy treats." The two of them went aside, Mia still carrying Ruby.

AnnaBeth smiled and hooked her arm through Devlin's. "I think we should all go in." And maybe she could cool tempers a little. "I can make some tea."

"You don't like tea," Devlin reminded her.

"Still," she persisted, giving him a quick frown. "It's the polite thing to do."

For her part, Cindy glanced at each of them accusingly, then said to AnnaBeth, "You're obviously more than just a neighbor."

Oh, shoot. AnnaBeth hadn't even considered how it'd look for her to latch onto Devlin; she'd just acted on instinct. Quickly, she tried to disengage, but Devlin didn't let her. Instead, he slid his hand down to hers and laced their fingers together.

Cindy's gaze dropped to their hands, and her eyes widened. "Is that an engagement ring?"

AnnaBeth almost cringed.

However, Devlin said simply, "I was going to call you tomorrow."

Voice dropping to an agonized rasp, Cindy asked, "You're telling me you're *engaged?*"

"Yes." His voice softened. "But this wasn't how I intended for you to find out."

Guilt nearly crushed AnnaBeth. Of course this wasn't how he would have told his mother-in-law. She'd messed up everything with her interference and caused an unnecessary conflict. "I'm so sorry—"

He smoothly cut off her apology. "AnnaBeth just agreed today. I'd planned to talk to Mia and Sony now, then call my parents." Still in that calm, controlled tone, he added, "You and I can discuss the engagement later."

"I don't see that there's anything to discuss. You've obviously made up your mind."

"Yes, I have." Despite her condemning tone, Devlin forged on. "For now, I want to make something perfectly clear."

"Devlin . . ." AnnaBeth tried, but she wasn't sure what to say. He hadn't raised his voice, but he'd most definitely dug in, and she couldn't help the clench of her stomach or the nervous tripping of her heart. Confrontations like this always made her uneasy, especially because she'd blundered her way into causing it. "Maybe . . ."

He released her but put a possessive hand at the small of her back. "Mia loves you, Cindy. She loves spending time with you. But you can't keep overstepping."

"I'm her grandmother! I have a right to—"

"See her," he specified firmly. "To love her."

Cindy said, "I *do* love her."

"I know it. More importantly, she knows it. That won't change, but you can't repeatedly go against my wishes by overindulging her after I've asked you not to, and you definitely can't coerce her into a haircut."

"You haven't been fixing her hair!"

AnnaBeth nearly gasped. Devlin was a *wonderful* father. No one could suggest otherwise. It worried her, because this was an insult that could bring tensions to the boiling point.

To her amazement, he still kept his cool. Honest to God, she was so proud of him, it made her love him even more.

"I wash her hair every night in her bath, and it's brushed every morning before she starts her day."

"She's a little girl." Cindy flung the words out there, her voice rising. "She should be wearing ribbons and braids and—"

"It's too short for braids now, isn't it?" Devlin remarked.

Cindy clamped her mouth shut.

"Also," he continued, "she doesn't like ribbons, and I'm not going to force her to wear them. If you wanted to have her hair cut, you should have spoken to me about it first."

With all those reasonable statements out there, Cindy deflated. AnnaBeth suspected the woman had only wished to share something special with her granddaughter—not cause strife. She couldn't help but feel bad for her. "Maybe I can talk to Mia, tell her how cool ribbons are or—"

Cindy shot her a look of antagonism. "No offense," she said, which of course meant offensive comments were on their way. "I don't need your help." Then to Devlin, "I can see where your attention is now."

"On my daughter, as it always is, but also with my parents, Uncle Sony, *you* . . . and yes, AnnaBeth."

Raising her chin, Cindy said, "I suppose I won't be seeing her as often?"

He seemed resigned to her continuing the disagreement. "If you can respect my wishes as her father, then we can continue as we always have. All I'm asking is that you—"

Cindy didn't give him a chance to finish. "I'll just get my purse and go."

He narrowed his eyes at her abrupt rudeness, then gave a short nod. "That's probably best." Taking AnnaBeth's hand, he brought her with him as he followed Cindy inside.

More slowly now, Cindy went into the living room, picked up her purse, and put the strap over her shoulder. She adjusted and readjusted, basically stalling, before slowly making her way toward the open front door, her every step reluctant.

AnnaBeth couldn't bear it. The situation was unraveling right in front of her, and she didn't know what to do to make it better.

Devlin said nothing. He would let Cindy leave in a snit—and honestly, AnnaBeth couldn't blame him. Not after Cindy had pushed things so far.

Yet she was family, Mia's grandma, and sometimes people couldn't change who they were. AnnaBeth was living proof of that.

"I'm sorry," she said abruptly, because she knew was about to overstep again. "Cindy, please don't go like this." Then to Devlin, she said, "Please, don't let this happen."

Cindy looked at her in surprise, but Devlin shook his head. "I'll talk with Cindy tomorrow."

"It's my fault—"

"No," Devlin said, his fingers lifting her chin. "It absolutely is not."

"If I'd left—"

"You're not going anywhere," Sony interjected in his booming voice, as he and Mia stepped out of the kitchen.

"No, she's not," Devlin assured him.

It felt so good to have ties to this family. She knew Cindy had to feel the same. How could she not? They were all wonderful, and anyone near them could feel the love.

Drawing him to the side, and lowering her voice, she whispered, "Devlin, don't you see? You're stronger than her."

"I'm less dramatic," he replied just as quietly. "Less stubborn." He blew out a breath. "And it's been three years."

AnnaBeth looked into his dark eyes—eyes that really saw her—and she breathed, "She'll be alone." Emotion tried to close her throat, making her voice crack. "You don't know what that's like."

His gaze softened, then went to Cindy, who lingered at the door. "No, thankfully I don't." He touched his forehead to hers. "You are the most amazing woman I've ever met."

"AnnaBeth." Mia came running to her, with Ruby keeping pace. "Are you upset?"

Quickly kneeling, she caught Mia close while Ruby jumped around her. "I'm fine, Squirt. I promise."

"We love you, AnnaBeth."

She choked on a tearful laugh. "You guys." She swiped at her eyes. "Now I'm a mess."

"A pretty mess," Sony said, and that made Mia grin.

Cindy stoically waited. If the woman had really wanted to leave, she would have by now, right? So maybe all she needed was one more nudge. "Devlin?"

As if he understood what she was asking, he sighed, but nodded.

Mia called out, "Bye, Grandma. I mostly had fun today."

A startled sound, part humor, part relief, came from Cindy while she nodded vigorously. "Me, too, honey."

The tea kettle started to whistle, so with a wave, Sony and Mia returned to the kitchen.

Smiling in relief, sensing that it'd be okay, AnnaBeth said, "I'll go with them," knowing she really had to get out of the middle of things.

Cindy said, "Wait."

Uh-oh. She'd probably tried to make her exit too late. Cautiously, she turned, but Cindy's expression had warmed a bit.

"If we could talk, just briefly . . ."

"Sure." She was super proud of Devlin for smiling at Cindy as he walked with AnnaBeth to meet her halfway. Before anyone could speak, AnnaBeth said, "I really am sorry for taking you by surprise."

Cindy graciously accepted the olive branch. "It was a bit of a shock."

"I can only imagine. Boom, engaged to a neighbor you knew nothing about." She tried a laugh that didn't sound too forced. "I feel like I know you, though, because Mia talks about you a lot, all of it wonderful."

"I adore her," Cindy said with a grin; then she flicked a glance at Devlin. "I guess that's why I go overboard sometimes."

On impulse, AnnaBeth touched her arm. "I hope you don't mind me saying this, but I'm so glad you and Mia have each other. I mean, Devlin is an *amazing* dad."

"Yes, he is," Cindy agreed firmly.

Huh. Score one for grandma. "And Sony is awesome, too. Loads of fun."

"He's always seemed very nice to me."

"He's the best." AnnaBeth smiled. "But you're Mia's grandma, and that's really special."

"Thank you." Cindy warmed another few degrees. "I bet you're close with your grandparents."

"Actually, I didn't have a grandma, and now I know what I was missing."

"Oh, I'm sorry." Cindy faltered. "They've passed?"

Trying to play it off as unimportant, AnnaBeth lifted a shoulder. "It's a long story, but I was raised in foster care. I never really knew any family."

"Because of that," Devlin said, "family is especially important to AnnaBeth."

She loved that Devlin understood her so well. "And this is like, the *greatest* family ever, right? Devlin, Mia, Sony, you . . . I'm so excited to be a part of it."

"It seems you're already well-loved." Wearing a gentle expression, Cindy asked, "How long have you known Devlin?"

"I moved in a year ago. With Sony being my neighbor, I got to know him first. Then Devlin and Mia were often over, and Mia fell in love with my little dog—who's basically Mia's dog now." She bit her lip. "Will you forgive me for blundering in on a family matter?"

"You're family now, too," Devlin reminded her. He turned to Cindy. "We're hoping to marry in just a few weeks, and if you're able, we'd love to have you there. It'll be small, just my parents, Uncle Sony, and Mia."

"And . . . you're inviting me?"

"Please say you'll come." AnnaBeth badly wanted her to take part. "It won't be fancy or anything, but I'll spiff up a little, and I'm hoping to find Mia something really pretty to wear. You could shop with us! That is, if you wouldn't mind." She leaned in and whispered, "And maybe if you and I wore ribbons, we could sway Mia to the idea."

"But not coerce her," Devlin said.

"I would never," AnnaBeth countered theatrically, making his mouth twitch.

"I shouldn't have, either," Cindy admitted, with her own crooked grin. "Poor little thing looked so upset when they took the first snip, and then it was too late." She looked at Devlin with apology. "I wasn't sure what to do."

"As AnnaBeth said, it'll grow back. Going forward, though, it really would be easier if you—"

"Discuss it with you first." She sighed. "I honestly thought she'd love it and that we'd surprise you."

He said, deadpan, "I was surprised."

They each laughed. And that was such a great turnaround from the earlier tension, that AnnaBeth was back to floating on happiness. Oh, how she loved these people. Plus she had a feeling she and Cindy could become friends. She wouldn't push it, but she'd definitely remain open and hope for the best.

Devlin reached out, his hand on his mother-in-law's shoulder. "It will never be my intent to keep her from you.

You're far too important to her, and she loves visiting you. I just think we need to work out a few issues."

Somewhat humbled by all that, Cindy said, "Thank you."

AnnaBeth beamed at them both. "It would mean a lot to Mia to have her grandma at our wedding."

Clearly touched, Cindy nodded. "I'd love that. Thank you." She lifted her chin again. "We can talk soon, but tonight you have other things to do, and you need to call your parents right away. They'll be thrilled."

Those words relieved AnnaBeth's heart greatly—especially when Devlin embraced the older woman, and then walked her out to her car.

She knew there would still be the occasional conflict, but for now, she couldn't have been happier.

It was the last day of spring, the sun shining, the breeze warm, and the second lilac tree they'd planted in Anna-Beth's backyard barely had any fragrant blooms left. Didn't matter. She'd planted flowers everywhere, including her window boxes.

It was a Saturday, so everyone was off work—although AnnaBeth sometimes played catchup on the weekends. Today, with Cindy and Sony both visiting for a cookout, she'd put her work aside.

The large umbrella table on her patio offered shade to Sony and Cindy while Devlin grilled and Mia played with two school friends on a newly installed swing set.

After pouring more lemonade for everyone, AnnaBeth carried a glass out to him.

"Thanks." He guzzled down half of it, peered up at the bright sun, and asked, "Do you think Mia needs more sunscreen?"

"I sprayed her again just an hour ago." She took the glass from him and set it aside. "The pink in her cheeks is just from running around with her friends. She's fine."

"Thank you." He pressed a quick kiss to her mouth.

"For the sunscreen?" she asked. "The lemonade?"

"For loving us. For making life so wonderful."

Smiling, she put her head on his shoulder and said, "This is all so incredibly perfect. Everything I ever wanted—but even better than I ever imagined, because it's you."

"You know what I think, AB Positive?" Now that she enjoyed the nickname, he used it often to reinforce it as a wonderful compliment. "It's because we're together, and that's as good as it gets."

THE MEMORY CABIN

CAROLYN BROWN

Chapter One

Jenna Stewart had a lot of regrets.

The first one was not spending more time with her mother before she passed away ten years ago. If only life had the expiration date stamped on the birth certificate, then there could be more preparation for what comes between the beginning and the end. Marsha Jenene Stewart was supposed to at least live as long as her own mother—Jenna's maternal grandmother—who didn't pass away until she was ninety. But that didn't happen. She was brushing her teeth one second, and the aneurysm that had been hiding in her brain decided that it was time for her to step away from the earth and into eternity in the blink of an eye.

Second on her list of regrets: Bryce Johnson, Jenna's ex-husband. She should have listened to her mother when she said something felt wrong about the man. But she fancied herself so much in love that she wouldn't have listened to what angels had to say—not even if they had wings, a halo, and were playing harps while they told her to steer clear of men like Bryce. So she vowed to love him until death parted them. Eleven months after the wedding, she learned that her mother had been right, and that natural death couldn't be more painful than the death of a marriage.

Both came on the same day. Bryce came into the art gallery where Jenna worked, handed her divorce papers, and told her that he had fallen in love with another woman. She was too numb to do anything but call her mother, and had the phone in her hand when it rang. Her mother's picture popped up on the screen, and she answered it. Her mother's housekeeper told her that Marsha was gone before she even hit the floor.

Stop thinking depressing thoughts. Her mother's scolding voice seemed so real that for just a split second, Jenna thought she was sitting in the Adirondack chair beside her.

I wish you were really sitting there, Jenna thought. *I would love to spend just one more day together here on the lake.*

The one thing she did *not* regret was moving to the cabin after her mother's death. She and her parents had shared happy memories there every summer, and her honeymoon with Bryce had been one of the few good times in their marriage. From day one, when she arrived at the cabin to live permanently, she had never had a single doubt that this was where she belonged.

A gentle night breeze blended the smell of freshly mowed grass, the earthy, musty odor of lake water, and the aroma of the rosebushes blooming beside her back porch. The sunsets over the water were always gorgeous, but that night, Mother Nature put on an especially beautiful show for her. Orange, yellow, purple, and pink streaks that swished through the sky like artists' strokes were reflected in the water for a double show. A little group of rogue bluebonnets out at the edge of the lake added their own slice of color to the picture as the sun dropped below the horizon, and dusk settled in.

"Beautiful evening," Carson Makay said.

His deep drawl startled Jenna and jerked her back into reality in a flash. "Yes, it is. There's nothing like a Texas sunset over the water. Have a seat?" She motioned toward one of the empty chairs circled around a firepit. "Want a beer or a bottle of water?"

"Beer would be great, but I'm on duty," he answered.

Carson was one of the new park rangers at Lake Livingston and would be taking over for Victor, who had been there as long as Jenna could remember. Carson was at least six feet tall, had brown eyes and dark hair that had finally grown out from the military haircut he had had when he first came to the area. His shoulders were broad, and he carried himself like a retired soldier. He had filled out a lot from the first time Jenna laid eyes on him, twenty years ago. Of course, he didn't know that she'd seen him back when she was fifteen and still had braces, or that through the years, she had dreamed about him.

Back then, Victor told her that Carson was right out of high school and headed off to basic training when he and his folks left the cabin right next to her house. Even though she hadn't formally met him until two months ago, she knew him from the stories Victor told her through the last ten years.

Jenna reached into a cooler and brought out an icy cold bottle of water. "How are things on the home front tonight?"

Carson took the water from her, twisted the lid off, and took a drink. "Pretty quiet for Memorial Day weekend. Uncle Victor has told some wild stories about holidays on the lake, so I was prepared for more." He eased into a chair and set his bottle on the arm. "I'm not complaining. I'll take quiet over rambunctious any day of the year. I had enough of that as a military policeman."

"Hey! Got another one of those?" Victor waved from a few yards away.

"Sure do." Jenna pointed toward the cooler. "Come on over and take a load off for a few minutes."

Victor pulled a bottle of water from the cooler and plopped down into an empty chair. No one would ever believe that the short, round man with a rim of gray hair around his otherwise bald head could possibly be related to Carson. A couple of months ago, he had brought his nephew around to introduce him to the permanent folks living around the lake, and let everyone know that Carson would be taking his place as park ranger when he retired on the first of June.

"Is Dorena counting the days?" Jenna asked. "I haven't seen her in a couple of weeks. I can remember having to clean out the house in Beaumont when my mama passed away. I didn't realize that a person could gather up so much stuff in thirty years."

"We've been here twenty years, but she's so ready to leave that she's had the house packed up for a month. She's so ready to get on the road to Virginia. The movers will be here bright and early on Saturday morning, and me and Dorena will be in our RV and headed east at daybreak on Sunday morning."

"I bet your daughter is counting the days until you are living close to her."

Jenna thought of her mother and wished that she'd lived closer to her after getting married to Bryce. One more regret, but Bryce insisted that they live in Lufkin, close to her job. When they were dating, he told her that he owned a roofing company and traveled a lot. A couple of months into the marriage, he quit that job and sold used cars. By the time they divorced, he had had six jobs in eleven months.

She blinked a couple of times to shut out unpleasant thoughts and listened to Victor.

"Dorena is very excited, and our daughter is over the moon. But then so are our three grandsons," Victor answered. "Carson can have my job and my cabin for the next twenty years or until he's ready to retire. Then he'll have a double retirement. Out with the old, and in with the new. And, honey, these old knees of mine are glad that they are getting to retire."

"I imagine when that time comes, I'll be glad to turn it over to someone else," Carson said with a chuckle. "But I'm going to miss you and Aunt Dorena. That woman could make a meal out of cardboard and glue."

"Yep, she could," Victor agreed. "Hey, isn't this about the time of the year that all your friends come around for a week?"

"Yes, it is," Jenna replied. "They both get here tomorrow about noon. Seems like a hundred years since they visited the last time, and I'm so excited to see them."

"I remember them coming around for the last several years," Victor said. "Maybe we can all get together for a breakfast over at the marina café we all like. Got your plans all lined up?"

"I've been cooking for weeks so that we don't have to do anything but visit and talk about our memories." Jenna turned up her beer and finished it off.

"They call her house the memory cabin," Victor explained to Carson.

"Why's that?" Carson asked.

"Because the three of us met at grief counseling ten years ago, became friends, and the next year we decided to get together right here for a week," Jenna answered. "We talk about our memories, both good and bad."

Victor stood up. "It's kind of like a once-a-year therapy session, isn't it?"

"Absolutely, but we try our best to keep it balanced. If

we talk about a bad memory, then we have to remember a good one and talk about it," Jenna explained.

"Be careful," Carson said in a serious tone, but his eyes sparkled like he was kidding. "If folks find out what's going on, you might have to hang out a shingle."

"He's right. The permanent residents around the lake would keep you so busy, you wouldn't even have time to paint." Victor stood up. "We should be going to finish up the rest of our rounds. Even if it is a fairly quiet holiday weekend, we need folks to know that the park rangers are out checking on things."

"See you later," Carson said, as he got to his feet and followed his uncle out into the darkness.

A splash took Jenna's attention to the dock on the left, where a bunch of bikini- and Speedo-clad teenagers did cannonball jumps out into the lake. She remembered back when she was that age and doing the same thing when she and her folks came to the lake for the summer. She might not have worn a skimpy bathing suit—her mother would never have allowed that—but she did make a few transient friends among those who only came for a week, and not for the whole summer like she and her folks did.

She heard voices to her right and turned her head to look at the dock a hundred yards on down the lake from the other side of her property. She couldn't make out what they were saying, but one girl did a perfect swan dive from the end of the dock out into the water. Not to be outdone, the young fellow with her did one just as beautiful.

"Hey, you two newlyweds!" Someone called out from the dock. "Don't forget we're going out to dinner in an hour."

"Thank you," the woman yelled.

Jenna wiped away a tear. Ten years ago, *she* was a new bride, and she and Byrce had spent their honeymoon at her folks' cabin. They had dived off the docks and swam in the lake every evening, and she thought she would be married to him forever. Who would have thought that eleven months later, he would walk in and tell her that he wanted a divorce? Or that when the story came out, he would admit that he'd only married her for the fifty grand that the prenup guaranteed when he divorced her.

"Thank God for prenups," she muttered, as she picked up the cooler and headed back to the house. "If Mama hadn't insisted on one, he would have gotten half of my trust fund."

The only sounds that Carson heard as he and Victor made their way back to his uncle's house were the occasional rumble of a boat coming to shore or the laughter of folks gathered around a firepit. In comparison to the bomb and missile alerts he heard when hc was deployed, the noise of folks having a good time was downright peaceful.

"You've been pretty quiet since we left Jenna's place," Victor said. "I can guess that you are remembering being somewhere that didn't involve a lake. When I first got out of the Army and took the position as a park ranger here at the lake, it took me a while to get used to the fact that Dorena and I were putting down roots. Mary Beth was grown and living in Virginia, and we missed getting to be around the grandchildren more, but Dorena's mama was still alive and living south of Lufkin. This was the perfect place and the perfect job to let us spend a lot of time with her before she passed away two years ago."

"And now you get to enjoy time with Mary Beth and her family," Carson said.

"Yep," Victor agreed, "and in just another week, we'll trade places with you. You get the cabin that comes with the job, and Dorena and I will take the motor home on our road trip to Virginia and get settled in our new home a couple of miles from Mary Beth. Think you are ready?"

Carson stopped by the steps leading up to the front door of the trailer that had been his home for the past several weeks. "It's been an adjustment for sure, but I'm finally settling into it. It's a lot slower paced than what I was used to."

"That's a good thing, right?" Victor asked.

"I believe it is." A visual of Jenna popped into Carson's head. He didn't believe in all that bunk about love at first sight. Still, there was something about her that seemed to draw him to her backyard almost every evening.

Victor took a step toward the house. "Good night, and we'll see you at breakfast tomorrow morning."

Carson opened the door into the RV. "I'm going to miss Aunt Dorena's cooking."

Victor wiggled his eyebrows. "Maybe you can get Jenna to invite you over to her house for a few meals when you get tired of bologna sandwiches and canned soup."

"Or I can go into town and get a pizza," Carson threw over his shoulder.

Victor chuckled and waved.

What Carson had called home for the past couple of months was a loft-type bed above the cab of the motor home, and a suitcase to hold a couple of changes of clothing. The rest of his things were stored in the spare bedroom of the cabin. Dorena had turned that room into a craft area when they moved in all those years ago. Now, when Mary Beth came back to the lake every few months, Victor rented one of the many cabins around the lake for her and her family to stay in.

Carson and his parents had visited his aunt and uncle at the lake twice in the past. Once just after he'd graduated from high school, and then again just before he deployed for six months—that turned into two tours of duty and lasted over a year—to the Middle East. Both times, they had stayed in the cabin right next door to where Jenna now lived. He hadn't actually met her until two months ago when his uncle introduced them, but that didn't mean he didn't remember her, or that she even noticed him. The first time, he would have guessed her to be about fifteen, a beautiful woman in the making. The second time, she spent most of her time on the back porch, concentrating on a painting she was working on. A lovely woman had emerged, but from a distance, she seemed distracted and sad. Victor had told him that she had just recently moved to the lake as a permanent resident, and that she had lost her mother.

His uncle often said that life was a circle. He slipped a pastry into the toaster for a night snack and pondered that idea while it cooked. If the saying were true, then where was he on that sphere, and where would the next step take him?

The toaster popped and threw his pastry out onto the cabinet. He grabbed it and played a one-person game of hot potato, shifting it from hand to hand until it cooled. Then he sat down at the small table and wondered what had happened to Jenna Stewart in the last twenty years. If he had met the tall brunette back when they were just teenagers, or later when they were in their twenties, would that have changed the course of their lives?

"It is what it is, and no one has invented a time machine yet so we could go back and see what would happen if we'd met then," he muttered as he took a bite of the brown sugar and cinnamon pastry.

Chapter Two

Jenna tried to paint, but she was too antsy. Finally, she gave up and made a batch of brownies, because she knew how much Kelly liked them. While they cooled, she waited for her friends on the wide front porch. The texts she had gotten from both Amber and Kelly said that they should be there at noon. Everything was ready for them. Now it was just a matter of waiting.

"Wait is a four-letter word," she muttered.

"Well, good morning!" Carson rounded the end of the porch.

"No, it's a *great* morning," Jenna answered. "My friends that I only see once a year will be here in a couple of hours. Patience is not one of my strong points." She motioned toward a second rocking chair. "Have a seat. Want a glass of sweet tea?"

"Don't have time for either," Carson said. "Do your friends come from a distance?"

"Kelly drives from Sweetwater, and Amber from Texarkana. We all lived in Lufkin ten years ago. That's where we became friends," Jenna answered.

"If they're that close, why don't you see them more often?" Carson asked.

"We all have lives and responsibilities, but once a year, we meet here for a week. It's hard to explain, but . . ."

Carson raised a palm. "I didn't mean to pry."

"You weren't," Jenna said. "I guess none of us have really found closure, so this week is what helps us find enough peace to keep us going through another year. I just hope the weather is good while they are here."

"Uncle Victor and I check the weather every morning. So far, so good for today and tomorrow. There's a chance of rain on Wednesday, but it's only like forty percent. If we're optimistic, that means there's a sixty percent chance that it won't rain. From the looks of all the vehicles leaving the area, I'll predict that things will be pretty quiet the next few days."

"That's what I saw when I checked things out this morning, too." Jenna couldn't remember the last time she was comfortable around a man. Comfort came with trust, and Bryce had taken that away from her.

"So, y'all all met at grief group therapy? Victor told me about your mother. I'm sorry for your loss."

"Thank you for that. The three of us met at grief counseling. I had been served with divorce papers, and my mother died the same day—actually within the same hour. Kelly's twin sister had passed away of a drug overdose. Amber had had a stillborn child and had complications that resulted in a complete hysterectomy. We bonded, and we still have all these feelings and memories that not many people would understand after a decade. So, we spend a week together every year to remember good times and bad, and then go back home refreshed."

"That is pretty awesome," Carson said. "I know a lot of soldiers with PTSD that gather with their old buddies like this whenever they can. Only folks who've shared in the same experiences and have endured can understand how it affects a person."

"That's the gospel truth in a nutshell," Jenna said with a nod.

"I should be going," Carson said. "I'm picking up a vehicle at the ranger station and driving all the way around the lake without Uncle Victor today. My first solo trip."

"Good luck. Stop by the Seashell Marina for one of their shrimp po' boys if you haven't had lunch," she said. "They are pretty fantastic."

"I had planned on doing just that. Great minds must really think alike. Why don't you come with me? You could ride with me, and we would have some lunch. By the time we finished the trip, it would be time for your friends." He flashed a grin.

"That sounds like a wonderful idea." She grabbed her purse and walked with him toward the range station. Back when she was fifteen, he and his folks had stayed in the cabin next door to her place, and then again some years later, right after she had moved to the lake permanently. That first time she had noticed him, she had made excuses to sit on the back porch and pretend to read a book while she watched him jog along the shore every morning. She hadn't learned until he'd already left that he was joining the Army that summer. The second time was years later, and he looked a lot like he did these days—only his hair was a lot shorter and didn't have a little bit of gray in the temples. Victor told her after he left that he was being deployed for at least six months, but in those days, she was battling with too much guilt and anger to make friends with anyone.

"What are you thinking about so hard?" he asked when they reached the station and went inside to get keys to a vehicle.

"Just a couple of summers from long ago," she answered. "I haven't driven all the way around the lake in months or had a shrimp po' boy, either. Thank you for curing my impatience."

He ushered her back outside with his hand on her lower back and opened the truck door for her. She was a little breathless but attributed it to a case of nerves because Kelly and Amber were on the way.

"Shall we roll up the windows and turn on the AC?" he asked.

"No, let's get the fresh air flowing through." Jenna stuck her arm out the open window and opened her hand, like she had done when she was a child.

Jenna sat in the truck while Carson made half a dozen stops to do a check on empty cabins, but that only took a few minutes. After the last one, Carson said, "I'm ready to eat. How about you?"

"Impatience breeds hunger," she said with half a giggle.

"Then let's have lunch." He started up the truck and drove to the café. "Shall we eat outside on the patio or go in?"

"Outside, please, at that table closest to the lake," she answered.

"Okay, then, I'll go inside and order," he said, as he snagged a parking place close to the door.

Jenna pulled a bill from her purse. "I'll treat today, since you rescued me from pacing the floor."

Carson shook his head. "Aunt Dorena would take a peach tree switch to me if I let a lady pay for dinner."

"But . . ." she started to argue.

"No buts." Carson grinned and got out of the truck. "You can grab that table, and I'll bring out the food. What are you drinking?"

"Sweet tea, please, and thank you, but . . ."

"No buts," he repeated, as he jogged around the vehicle and opened the door for her.

This is not a date. This is not a date, she told herself as she waited. *It's two new acquaintances having lunch together.*

Two cars slowed down and then turned into the driveway to park behind her SUV. Jenna met her friends in the middle of the yard for a three-way hug.

"I'm so happy y'all are here. Did you have a good trip? Come on inside and . . ." She took a step back and studied both of the women. Kelly's hair had been prematurely gray ten years ago, but she had always had what her mother called a peaches-and-cream complexion. Today she was absolutely glowing, and her blue eyes danced with excitement. Something was definitely going on, and Jenna couldn't wait to hear all about it.

Kelly patted her on the back. "Honey, this is our escape, and we look forward to it as much as you do. And I had an uneventful trip. How about you, Amber?"

Amber, the youngest of the trio, opened the back door of her car and took out a suitcase. Like Kelly, she was smiling so big that there was no doubt in Jenna's mind that she was hiding a big secret. What could both of them be so excited about, and why had they kept it from her when they talked last month?

"Just open road and a lot of country music," Amber said, as she rolled her suitcase across the yard. "But I was so excited that the two hundred and fifty miles from my place to yours seemed like a thousand today, and bittersweet. I cried the first half hour, because I had to leave Ian and Lisa behind, and then I got excited as ever that I was getting to spend a week here on the lake. I already feel peace settling over me, and we haven't even gone inside the cabin yet."

"Me, too," Kelly agreed.

Amber sniffed the air when she made it to the porch. "Is that soup I smell? I hope it is. Can we eat on the back porch? I've envisioned the lake for the last couple of hours, but I'm starving. We could kill two birds with one stone if we take our lunch to the porch."

"That's not soup." Kelly started up the stairs with her suitcase. "That is chocolate for sure."

"It's both. I made it for supper, but nothing says we can't have some right now." Jenna opened the door to let them enter the house ahead of her. "Y'all toss your suitcases in your rooms, and we'll have a mid-afternoon early supper out on the porch. Amber is right. The day is too lovely to spend in the house."

Amber parked her luggage beside the credenza in the foyer and headed for the kitchen. "I'm not even taking mine up until later. I've saved some big news for weeks, and I can't wait to share it with y'all while we have our first lunch together."

"Me, too!" Kelly yelled as she hurried back downstairs.

"Shotgun!" Amber said. "I get to go first."

Jenna didn't have any big news, but she loved all the excitement bouncing around in the cabin. She pulled a plate of assorted cheeses and relishes from the refrigerator and carried it to the picnic table on the back porch. When she returned, Amber was filling three glasses with ice and tea, and Kelly was ladling soup into three bowls.

"This must be something really, really big that you two are keeping from me," Jenna said. "You are both absolutely glowing with excitement. Have you both bought a cabin on the lake? Are you about to tell me you are moving here permanently?"

Kelly put the bowls on a tray and carried them out to the porch. "That would be good news, and it might happen later when I'm ready to retire. I love the view from here, and the fresh smell of the water and the roses all mixed up together. I'm glad that you came back here to live. This has been the perfect place for our girls' week every year."

"Thank you." Jenna really wanted to kick off the visit with whatever wonderful news that her friends wanted to share, but they seemed to be procrastinating. That could only mean that it was wonderful news for each of them, but maybe it wasn't going to be something she would love to hear. And she had not missed the past tense in that last sentence that Kelly said. This *has been*, not *this is.*

All good things come to an end, but when one door closes, another opens.

She saw that on a wall plaque at the craft fair in Lufkin a few years before and still wished that she had bought it to hang above the credenza in the foyer. "Now, you've both teased me long enough. Spit it out."

Amber raised a finger, swallowed a mouthful of soup, and took a sip of tea. "I'm getting married, and I get two kids, age two and four with the marriage license. I've told you all about Ian and Lisa, the two children that I've been a nanny for the past year and a half. Well, their father and I finally gave up fighting what we felt in our hearts, and he has proposed. I said yes without even a split second's hesitation."

Jenna's spoon rattled against the wooden picnic table when she dropped it. "We have a conference call once a month, and you didn't share something this big with us?" She gasped.

"Shame on you, and congratulations at the same time. When . . . how . . ." Kelly stammered, "We need details! You don't just drop something like that and then go back to eating lunch."

"His name is Ethan Massey, and he is thirty-five years old. He works in technology for a big company, and . . ."

she started, and then ate a couple more bites. "I really am hungry. So, anyway . . ."

"Ethan?" Jenna whispered, and then remembered, "He's the one that adopted those two little kids when his sister and brother-in-law died in a car wreck, right? We knew you worked for him, but you never said you had feelings for him."

"Yep," Amber answered. "Lisa was just six months old, and Ian was two when that happened. Ethan and I finally gave in and admitted we had feelings for each other about six months ago. The kids are spending this week at their grandmother's, and we're getting married as soon as I get back to Texarkana. I didn't want to get married until after we spent our week together, and I wanted to tell y'all my news in person. We're just having a simple courthouse wedding, and then the next week, we will be moving to Germany, where Ethan will be CEO of the tech firm there."

A couple of doves cooed off in the distance, and the laughter of two small children taking a walk with their parents down by the water's edge finally broke the eerie silence that suddenly filled the whole back porch. Jenna had known for a long time that someday life would get in the way of the week that she got to spend with her two friends, but she had truly hoped that wouldn't be until they were a lot older. Silence hung over the porch like a heavy wet blanket on a cold winter night. Jenna felt the need to say something, and she opened her mouth, but no words came out.

Amber wiped away a tear with a paper napkin. "Someone say something . . . anything. Do you think I'm just marrying Ethan to get to be a mother? Are you about to tell me I'm doing the wrong thing?"

"I'm shocked and happy for you at the same time," Kelly finally broke the silence. "If you love Ethan, then listen to your heart. You talk so much about those children that there's no doubt about the love you have for them."

"I visit my daughter Gloria's grave every Sunday," Amber said. "She would have been ten years old this week. I imagine her talking to all her friends and wanting to put pink streaks in her blond hair. I felt guilty for loving Lisa at first, as if Gloria would feel like I was forgetting her. But . . ." She dabbed at her eyes again.

Kelly laid a hand on Amber's shoulder. "If Gloria had lived, she would have wanted you to be happy. We all have to believe that. Remember what we learned in grief counseling? We have to push back the gray skies of guilt, and let the sunshine in."

"But what about my weekly visits to her?" Amber's voice caught in her throat. "She'll think I have deserted her."

"She understands, and honey, it's time to let her go so she can rest in peace," Kelly said. "At least you had the foresight to bury her in your hometown instead of Lufkin, where you were living with your boyfriend at the time of her birth."

Jenna thought of her own situation. Was she holding so tightly onto her mother that Marsha couldn't fly away to a peaceful eternity?

"Thank you," Amber said. "My mama says that she'll keep flowers on the grave for me. It will probably be a couple of years before I get back to the States. The kids' grandparents have promised to fly over to Germany every three months to visit. My mother will try to come for Christmas every year."

Jenna felt Kelly and Amber staring at her. She needed to say something, but the words still wouldn't come.

Stop feeling sorry for yourself because life is changing, and be happy for Amber, the pesky voice in her head scolded.

"I'm speechless, but I am so, so happy for you," Jenna

said. "What Kelly said about letting go so our loved ones can rest in peace struck a chord. I realize that I've been doing just that with my mama. But we'll talk about that later. Right now, I want to see pictures of Ian and Lisa. I know you have a gazillion on your phone, and why haven't you sent more of them to us before now? We'll expect weekly photos from now on."

Amber slipped her phone out of the back pocket of her jeans. "I think I was their mommy the minute I laid eyes on them. The nanny job was only supposed to be for a few weeks while I applied for other jobs, but . . ." She shrugged as she passed the phone across the table.

"Oh, no, you don't!" Kelly moved around to sit beside Jenna. "I want to see them, too."

"They are precious, and they both have blond hair," Jenna said, as she flipped through the pictures. So, this would be the last year that Amber would be at the memory cabin for a week. Her good friend was going to have the family she thought would never be possible. Still, she couldn't help but feel sad that the dynamics of their gathering would change when it was just her and Kelly.

"When I take them to the park to play or to the grocery store, folks often tell me that they can sure tell that I'm their mama," Amber said, beaming.

"I would probably say the same thing," Kelly said. "Oh . . . and here's one with you and Ethan with the kids. He's one good lookin' feller. If I was younger, I might steal him from you."

Amber shook a finger at Kelly. "You could try, but I'd fight a forest fire with a cup of water if anyone tries to get between us."

Jenna handed the phone back to her. "I'm glad that you've found closure for the baby you lost. Now you can have peace and happiness, but I'm going to miss you being here for our week every year."

"We'll still talk every month, right?" Amber asked, and then went on without waiting for an answer. "There is a six-hour time difference, so we'll have to figure everything out, but we will make it work."

Kelly took a long drink of her tea. "It's eight hours from here to Africa, and two from there to Germany."

"Is that your news?" Jenna whispered. "Are you leaving Texas, too?"

"You are going to Africa?" Amber's eyes widened.

"I've leased my house, packed what I need, shipped the rest over to the apartment that the company has ready for me, and am leaving from here. I'll drive down to the Houston airport next Sunday afternoon, check my rental car in, and meet the rest of my team. Y'all be happy for me, please." Kelly's eyes darted from Amber to Jenna.

"What will you be doing?" Amber asked.

"I'll be the nurse in charge of a new hospital there. We will disperse medical staff to small clinics around the area periodically," Kelly answered, "and right now, I plan to be there until they force me to retire. I couldn't make a difference in my sister's life no matter how hard I tried. But this is my chance to be a help to other folks in need."

"So this is the last year for our memory cabin visit?" Jenna blinked back tears.

"Don't be sad," Amber's voice quivered.

"I can't help it, but at the same time, I'm so happy for both of you that I could dance a jig right here on the table," Jenna said. "Maybe I can learn from your experiences, and finally make peace with my own situation."

Kelly swiped a tear from her cheek. "I'm going to miss y'all, but we'll manage to talk every month, and if y'all can ever manage the time, come to Africa. From the pictures I've seen of the small area where I'll be working, it's a beautiful place."

"Or Germany," Amber said.

"Who knows?" Jenna forced a smile. "The future might hold all kinds of wonderful things for us."

"Well, if all the memories we've talked about and made right here is a foretaste of the future, then bring it on," Kelly said. "I heard a car door slam. Are we expecting someone?"

"Hey, don't mean to intrude, but I found this on your front porch." Carson held up a yellow-striped kitten. "Does it belong to one of y'all?"

"It's not mine, but it's a cutie," Amber said.

"Mine, either," Kelly answered. "I'm allergic to cats, so keep it over there."

"Carson, this is Kelly"—Jenna nodded across the table— "and . . ."

"And I'm Amber," she butted in and introduced herself. "And from your shirt, I'm guessing you are the new park ranger that Jenna told us about?"

"Pleased to meet you both," Carson said, "and yes, Amber, I'm going to be the new resident park ranger. I take over next Monday morning when my uncle leaves."

"Victor is your uncle?" Kelly asked. "He's just the sweetest guy ever. He and Dorena usually come over for a little visit while we are here."

Seems like everything is changing, Jenna thought.

"Well, I'll leave you to your visiting and take this little guy home with me. If you hear of anyone losing him, just give me a call," Carson said, "and again, it was nice to meet y'all. Jenna has really looked forward to y'all coming for a visit."

"So have we," Kelly said.

"If you can't find a home for the kitty cat, let me know," Jenna said. "I could be forced to take him in."

Carson shook his head and slid a sly wink her way. "I've already promised him that I would adopt him if no one comes around to claim him. He seems to like me, and

I'll need something to keep me company when Uncle Victor and Aunt Dorena are gone."

"What are you going to name him?" Jenna asked.

"Bubba, after my buddy in the service, who lost his life on our last deployment," Carson answered.

"Sounds like a good Texas name to me." Jenna was still trying to digest what her two friends had told her without being sad—or maybe a little jealous of their happiness.

"Well, then, y'all enjoy your afternoon. See you around." He whipped around and disappeared around the corner of the house.

"That is one sexy park ranger," Amber whispered. "I bet the little old ladies that live here permanently will need his services real often. You should ask him out."

Kelly fanned her face with the back of her hand. "I would beat your time if I lived here. How long have you known him?"

"Known him, a couple of months," Jenna answered. "Seen him, twice in years past. His folks stayed in that cabin over there"—she pointed to her right—"for a week when I was fifteen, and then he showed up again right after I moved here permanently. We had lunch together today, but it was not a date."

"Did he kiss you at the door?" Kelly teased.

"He did not!" Jenna protested.

"Then this one was just friends. When he kisses you at the door, then it's a date," Amber said with a smile. "But all joking aside, did he look like that when you were a teenager?"

"Did he have that deep Sam Elliott drawl back then?" Kelly asked.

"He was twenty years younger, but his looks haven't changed all that much, and I never even spoke to him, so I don't know about his voice."

"Well, honey"—Kelly stopped fanning and went back to eating—"you might have been too shy to make a move on him when you were young, and too heartbroken a little later on, but it's time to move in now before someone else snatches him up. That's saying that he's still single. Is he married, or engaged, or in a serious relationship?"

"None of the above, according to Victor," Jenna answered.

"Then what are you waiting for?" Amber asked.

"Let's talk about Germany and Africa," Jenna answered.

"We can do that, but remember, we share everything and we are here for a week, so you might as well get ready to 'fess up," Kelly told her.

Chapter Three

"Well, Bubba, unless someone comes around saying that you belong to them, I guess it's me and you, just like it was over there in the sand pit," Carson said as he walked back to his vehicle, got in, and drove up the road to Victor and Dorena's cabin. The kitten curled up in his lap and purred until he parked the Jeep; then he climbed from Carson's lap to his shoulder and perched there.

"You aren't afraid of riding, so you'll make a good partner."

"Who are you talking to?" Victor asked from the front porch.

Carson held up the kitten. "Meet Bubba, my new partner."

Victor pushed up out of the rocking chair. "Looks like a good partner to me."

"Since the rental cabins have a no-pet rule, he could belong to one of the permanent residents. I should probably put a picture of him up in the ranger station," Carson said.

Victor chuckled and reached for the kitten. "He's tame, so that means he's been with people and not one of the feral cats that we see occasionally. Mamie Duvall is the only permanent resident that has a cat, and he's got to be fifteen years old. I would imagine this little fellow got thrown out. Folks who treat animals like that should be jailed." He petted the little guy for a couple of minutes and then handed him back. "I'd bet dollars to doughnuts that Bubba is yours now, unless you can pawn him off on Jenna. A pet might do her good."

"She offered, but one of her houseguests is allergic, and in a week's time, I figure I'll be too attached to him to give him away." Carson held the kitten close to his chest. "He'll be company when you and Aunt Dorena are gone."

"Yep," Victor said with a smile. "I reckon Jenna could be better company, but Bubba will do until you figure that out on your own. I don't meddle in other folks' lives."

"Yeah, right," Carson chuckled.

The time that Jenna and her friends had together every year was flexible, but if it wasn't raining, the first evening after dark was the hot dog roast at the firepit. All the fixings, including condiments, chili, and sauerkraut, had been laid out on one end of the picnic table, ready to build whatever anyone wanted. Chips and two kinds of dip, plus the stuff for s'mores, were on the other end. Wood was ready to light in the fireplace, and the weather was cooperating.

A few dark clouds danced back and forth across the western sky as the sun dropped behind the horizon, but they didn't look threatening and seemed to be moving to the west.

"I'm going to miss all this, but . . ." Amber said.

"But what?" Jenna asked.

"This door closes for a while, and the one that opens is so wonderful that I can't wait to see the life behind it. I guess this is what you call bittersweet."

"No wonder you like to paint here. The light is fantastic," Kelly said.

"It's always been an escape, and it gives me something to occupy my mind," Jenna said. "At the end of a day in front of a computer, I need to be outside and create something beautiful—even if the beauty is only in the eyes of the beholder. Mama told me that when I would whine about being disappointed in something I finished."

"She was and still is right," Kelly said. "Just like my mama was when she told me that I was enabling my sister. She used to tell both of us that when you find yourself in a hole, you quit digging."

Jenna thought of the hole she had dug for herself right there at the lake. "The rut I've carved out for myself right here is pretty comfortable."

"You've adopted that old *I don't need anyone* attitude, and maybe that's good, but honey, we all need friends, and I don't just mean two that show up for a week once a year. I couldn't have made it through the grief, the regrets, or the guilt without y'all, and the group therapy," Kelly said.

Amber raised her beer. "Amen to that."

"I've got y'all," Jenna argued, "and I've had Victor and Dorena, and I know most of the permanent residents on this side of the lake."

"In what capacity?" Amber asked. "Do you confide in them?"

"Of course not." Jenna shook her head. "I only tell y'all my secrets."

"Then they are acquaintances, not real friends," Kelly said. "Have you scattered your mama's ashes yet?"

"I haven't been able to do that. It seems so final," Jenna answered.

"You'll know when it's the right time, but you need to set a date and do it. Then you can begin to have some closure," Amber said.

"Are you speaking from experience?" Jenna asked.

"Yes, I am. When I finally got a little measure of closure about my baby girl, it freed me to be able to fall in love with Ethan and to be a real mama to Lisa and Ian."

Jenna glanced over at Kelly. "Think you will ever fall in love?"

"I did twice, and neither time worked out," Kelly answered. "So, now I'm happy with my job and the fact that I help people."

Jenna made a mental note to find out what hospital her friend would be working at, and to make yearly donations to that place. For the past ten years, she had split the profit from each painting that she sold between three research facilities: drug and alcohol rehabilitation, brain aneurysm research, and stillborn and miscarriage treatment. She had revamped the trust fund left to her by her folks and made women's shelters for abused women.

Amber nudged Jenna on the arm. "Your brain is somewhere between here and the moon."

"Earth to Jenna," Kelly teased. "You are supposed to share your memories with us this week, good or bad."

"Bryce never hit me, or even threatened to, but I suffered from mental abuse," she blurted out.

"I can sympathize with that," Amber said. "Frankie was one of those mean men who was verbally abusive when he was sober and then physically when he was drunk. I've never told anyone that he beat me the week before I had the baby," Amber whispered. "I thought it was my fault. He said my fried chicken wasn't like what his mama made, and I told him to go back to Texarkana and eat his mama's food."

"You never told us that or mentioned it in group sessions," Kelly said.

"I was too ashamed. If I hadn't upset him, then he wouldn't have hit me, and Gloria wouldn't have died, so I blamed myself. I couldn't admit that to anyone until I fell in love with Ethan and we talked about everything. Now, I'm telling y'all, because he helped me see that it wasn't my fault," Amber said.

"In my opinion, mental and physical abuse go hand in hand," Kelly said. "I'm glad you are realizing that no man has the right to hit a woman, or vice versa. When my sister got drunk or high, she was meaner than a rattlesnake. I felt sorry for whatever boyfriend she had at the time. If she didn't get her way, she threw things. Big things like chairs and lamps. I have no idea what kind of mother she would have been, but it's probably good that she never had children."

"Do you regret not having kids?" Jenna asked.

Kelly shook her head. "Not one bit. My mama divorced my father because of his drinking and temper. Then when we were teenagers, I saw my sister fall into the same addiction, and she always had my dad's temper. I was always afraid I might pass that kind of thing down if I had kids."

All three women turned to the window when they heard a familiar voice calling to them from outside.

"Hey, how are things at the Stewart cabin this evening?" Victor asked, as he and Carson made their way across the yard.

"We're good," Jenna answered. "How's everything around the lake?"

"Just finer than frog hair split three ways," Victor answered, and then chuckled.

"We're just about to roast hot dogs and make s'mores,"

Kelly said. "Y'all want to join us? Jenna has enough to feed an army back there on the table."

"If you don't help us out, she'll make us eat them for breakfast," Amber added.

"Can't waste good food!" Jenna was glad that the mood had lightened around the firepit.

"We've had supper," Carson said.

"But that was more than an hour ago, and we're on our way home to call it a day," Victor said. "I'd love a couple of kraut dogs for a night snack, and I never turn down s'mores."

Jenna got up and headed for the table, with Victor right behind her. "It's a roast-your-own hot dogs and marsh-mallows and all-you-can-eat buffet. Skewers are right here, and the lantern throws off enough light so you can see how to build your own."

Carson hung back, but Victor was the first one to stick two hot dogs on a long metal stick and carry them over to the firepit. "There's this little hot dog wagon that will be coming around the lake area pretty soon, and the folks serve up kraut dogs and chili dogs so good they'd make you kiss the devil's pitchfork."

"Now that's a saying I've never heard before," Jenna said, and laughed out loud. "Just how good is that, Victor?"

"You'll just have to order one when they park their food truck up by the ranger station and figure it out for yourself," he told her. "When these get roasted to a nice brown color, I'm going to load them up with mustard, onions, and kraut. Dorena, bless her heart, won't give me a good night kiss, but missin' one will be worth it. Carson, you better take advantage of this. Not many of the residents offer to feed us when we stop for a visit."

"Are you sure we aren't intruding?" Carson whispered for Jenna's ears only.

"Not one bit. We're glad to have you sit and visit a little

while. Our conversation was getting dark, and needed some light," she said out of the corner of her mouth.

"Then we are glad to help out however we can," Carson said. "Ladies first."

"Kelly and Amber are already . . ." she started.

"You are the lady I'm talking about," Carson said.

Could he be flirting, or was his military training just showing up in full force? She didn't have an answer, but it did feel good to have someone call her a lady. Even when Bryce was first dating her, he had never been very romantic. She scolded herself for even comparing her ex with Carson. The devil himself would look good if he was standing beside Bryce.

She smiled when she thought about what Victor had said about the hot dog vendor and wondered if those words had brought on the idea of Bryce and the devil.

"How's Bubba doing?" she asked, as they both prepared their hot dogs for roasting.

"Adapting well to the travel trailer," Carson answered. "I drove up to the store and got what he needed in the way of a litter box and some kitten food."

"The offer still goes to take him if . . ."

Carson shook his head. "I'm already attached to the little guy, and once Uncle Victor and Aunt Dorena are gone, he'll be company for me. I've never had a pet of any kind before, so I'm liking the idea."

The picture of him—a big military man—holding that tiny little kitten, had stayed with her all afternoon. It showed that he had a good heart and a gentle nature, and that spoke volumes.

They had just stuck their hot dogs out over the blaze when Victor, Kelly, and Amber finished cooking theirs. They met them coming back to slip them off onto buns and load them up. Amber raised an eyebrow and shot a smile over her way. It didn't take a rocket scientist to know what she meant by either or both.

Yes, Carson was sexy. Yes, he seemed to be a good man. But that did not mean he was available for anything other than friendship.

"Have you ever been married?" she blurted out, then blushed, then stammered, "I'm sorry. That's personal."

"I don't mind answering," Carson replied. "I was engaged once. It didn't work out, and we parted ways on good terms. I'm not in a relationship, either. Why do you ask? Kelly seems to be a little old for me. Amber is a little young. Should I steer clear of this place until they are gone?"

"No, you do not need to stay away," Jenna answered. "Kelly is going to Africa to be head nurse at a new hospital. Amber is getting married and going to Germany. That makes me sad that this will be our last memory cabin week together."

"Life is full of changes. I've learned that we just have to roll with the punches," Carson said.

Victor sat down in one of the lawn chairs and balanced his plate on his knees. "Did I hear something about Africa? I've always wanted to go on a safari, but Dorena says that she's not going to be a lion's breakfast."

"I'm going to work in a hospital over there," Kelly said, "and I'm very excited about the job."

Victor bit into his hot dog and made appreciative noises. "This is as good as that wagon serves up. You ladies should forget whatever jobs you've been doing and put up a café."

"Not me," Amber protested. "I might be cooking, but it will be for my family in Germany."

Jenna was thinking about what Carson had said about life being full of changes, when she looked up and realized that everyone was staring at her. "I'm sorry. Did I miss something?"

"I was saying that y'all need to put in a café or maybe buy a food wagon. You could make a mint during the summer months," Victor said.

"Thank you for the compliment. Roasting them over an open fire is what gives them all that flavor. It's nothing I do."

"You were spacing out again, Jenna," Kelly fussed at her. "Your hot dogs are about to burn, and you hate them when they turn black."

"She's a hermit," Amber said. "She lives inside her head with her paintings and the banking business that she does from home on the computer."

"That's right," Jenna agreed, and pulled her skewer out of the fire.

Her computer business involved working with the various art gallery CEOs that she hired to operate her Texas art galleries. No one, not even Amber or Kelly, knew anything about her financial situation. Things like that didn't come up in group therapy, and she was happy to just let her friends think that she had inherited the cabin and worked from home.

Bryce had thought she worked in acquisitions for a gallery in Lufkin when he signed the prenup stating he would get fifty thousand dollars if he divorced her. When she cried the day he had told her he didn't want to be married to her anymore, he had laughed and said she had a right to cry, because she would have to go to the bank and borrow the money to fulfill her prenup duties.

"Then I guess since this is probably the last night I'll ever get to have a hot dog right here, I had better have another one," Victor declared. "Seems to me that working from home wouldn't make any more than selling hot dogs."

"I like my job. It gives me purpose and something to

do," Jenna answered. "Let's talk about that safari you want to go on, Victor."

Anything to shift the conversation away from me, she thought.

When her father died, her mother had sold most of their assets, but oil royalties and interest on the other money built up yearly. She didn't care so much about the money, but she did care that she was able to sponsor several scholarships—like Miz Ramona had done for her—with some of it.

"Carson, have you ever wanted to go on a safari?" Kelly asked.

"No, ma'am," Carson answered without hesitation. "I don't know what Africa is like. I wasn't ever there, but I've spent time in the sand, and I'll take this nice green grass and that lake out there any day of the week over that heat. Sand did not stay outside where it belonged. It got into everything, and you haven't lived until you get a dose of sand fleas."

Jenna listened to the conversation as it went from one subject to the next, and wondered how Carson would feel if he knew that her job was more than a simple banking job from home.

Victor finished off his last bite and was on his way to the table when his phone rang. He pulled it out of his back pocket and listened for a minute, then turned around. "Dorena said that the show we watch together on Monday night is coming on in ten minutes. I'll have to get on back to the house. You kids have fun." He waved and disappeared into the darkness.

"I should be going, too." Carson started to get to his feet.

"Nonsense," Kelly said. "You haven't even had a s'more yet, and the night is young."

"Bubba will wait up for you," Amber teased.

He glanced over at Jenna.

"You are welcome to be our newest member to our group therapy session," she said in the best authoritative voice she could muster, but she couldn't keep the smile off her face. "Would you like to share with us this evening?"

He settled back in his chair. "Hello, everyone. I am Carson Makay, recently retired after twenty years in the military, and the new park ranger here at Lake Livingston."

"Hello, Carson," all three women chimed in together.

"I'm glad to be here at this session, but I don't have much to share, other than I still have not found closure for losing my best friend, Bubba Benoit, last year. Thank you all for inviting me to your session," Carson said. "And y'all serve better food than the other groups I went to before my enlistment was over. The doughnuts were a little stale there, and the coffee tasted like motor oil mixed with mud."

Kelly giggled and then laughed out loud. "We are glad to have you, and we will never serve bad coffee or unsweetened tea. That's just bad southern manners."

Amber laid the back of her hand over her forehead in a dramatic gesture. "My mama would disown me for such a thing."

"Tell us more about Bubba," Jenna said. "I bet you've got a good memory there, right?"

"Lots of them," Carson said with a bit of a smile. "His given name was Benjamin Benoit. We rode the bus together with a bunch of other recruits up to Fort Sill, Oklahoma. It was one of those scalding hot days in the middle of July when we deboarded. When we all complained about the heat, Bubba called us sissies, and said that it was so hot where he came from that the weather there felt like air-conditioning. He was a little short guy with black hair that he pulled back in a ponytail, before they sent us all to the barber. His eyes were every bit as dark as his hair, and

from day one, I could tell that we were going to be ene-
mies. When they lined us up, we were side by side. When
we marched from one place to the other, we were side by
side. He was put on the bottom bunk, and me on the top
in the barracks. We had an instant dislike of each other."
He stopped and took a long drink of his tea.

"How did you get to be friends, then?" Jenna asked.

"I've never been real coordinated, but Bubba ..."—
Carson paused—"that boy could have kept time when we
were marching, read a book, and scratched his head, all at
the same time. And he would deliberately throw my count
off so that I'd stumble. I finally had enough of it and went
to the drill sergeant, only to find Bubba already there,
standing at attention in front of the drill sergeant's desk.
Sarge let me go first, and I told him that I just flat-out
didn't like Bubba, and he was always the cause of me always getting yelled at. Bubba went next and accused me
of looking down on him because he was short and had a
southern accent."

"Is that the way you both said it?" Kelly asked.

"No, ma'am, our language was much more colorful.
Bubba said that he wouldn't even carry a sorry son-of-a-
bitch like me in his pirogue to a doctor if I was bleeding
out, and that's just a taste of his southern temper. I said he
had short man's syndrome, and I would rather spend basic
in hell than have to deal with him." Carson paused and
downed the rest of the tea in his bottle.

"Go on," Amber said. "I want to know how y'all got to
be friends after that."

"Sarge said that we both needed to learn to be part of a
team," Carson answered, "so for the rest of basic, if there
was more than ten feet between us, we would have to go
back to week one of our training. And we would do it together, so if one of us broke the rule, then the other one
was punished, too. We had to sit at the same table when

we ate. I had to stand right outside the bathroom when he showered—or did other things. The first week was pure misery, and we hated each other more than ever."

"And then?" Kelly asked.

"Then one night I woke up, and he wasn't in his bunk right below me. I just knew the sorry SOB was about to get me sent back to week one just for spite. I hopped out of bed and went looking for him. I couldn't call out his name for fear of waking someone and having them tattle on us. I found him curled up a corner of the shower room, his shoulders shaking and crying so hard he couldn't talk," Carson said. "He just handed me the letter he was holding. The ink was blurred in spots from his tears. It was a Dear John letter from his fiancée. They were supposed to get married right after he got done with basic, but she had fallen in love with his best friend in the last three weeks."

"What did you do?" Jenna asked.

"I sat down beside him and cried with him," Carson answered, "and we were best friends after that. The ten-foot rule became a joke, and we each carried a tape measure in our pockets to be sure we didn't even push things by one inch. We finished basic and were sent to MP training at Fort Leonard Wood, Missouri, for the next twenty weeks. Then we were assigned to different posts, and it was only in the last deployment that we were together again. I guess I was bad luck, because I lost him then."

"No, that was the universe giving y'all one last time to be together to relive all those old memories and good times," Kelly told him. "You'll find closure for your friend eventually, but don't ever lay blame on yourself for what someone else did. That's not your burden to carry."

"Easier said than done," Carson said, "but thanks for the encouragement. Anyone else in the mood to share this evening?"

Jenna raised her hand. "Since Carson shared a good

memory, I think we should all dig down and find one. Mine comes from the summer I was fifteen. Miz Ramona Andrews lived two cabins down that way from right here"—she pointed to her left—"and she was a retired art teacher. Mama talked her into giving me some basic lessons in oil painting. That's what set me on the path I'm on now. Miz Ramona said she saw raw talent in my work, and she mentored me that summer and the next two, as well. I had hoped she would teach me more, but she passed away during my senior year of high school. She willed me all of her art books and supplies and left me a full-ride scholarship to the University of Texas in Austin. After undergraduate work, her will stated that I was to spend six months in Paris. After that, I came home to work in a small gallery in Lufkin."

"So, your happy memory was painting in Paris?" Amber asked.

"I enjoyed my time there, but my happy memory was working with Miz Ramona right here at the lake," Jenna answered.

"Ramona . . . Mona Gallery in Houston . . . I wonder if there's a connection?" Kelly frowned. "I haven't been to many galleries and wouldn't know trash from treasure, but still . . ."

"If you go there sometime, you will see her picture and name in the lobby. She was the inspiration for that gallery," Jenna said.

"Okay, my turn." Amber held up her hand. "Since we're remembering happy memories from before the bad ones sent us to therapy, mine is my graduation gift from my mama. She raised me as a single mother, and her job was cleaning offices for a big corporation at night. We lived with my grandmother, so she could put me to bed and read a story to me while Mama was gone. So, anyway, Mama saved for years and years to take me on a cruise for my graduation present. Granny had passed away my sopho-more year, or she would have gone with us. That explained, now for my happy memory. The first night of the cruise, Mama sat down on the edge of my bed, opened up my fa-vorite children's book, and read all of *The Velveteen Rab-bit* to me."

Kelly wiped at the tear rolling down her cheek. "That is beautiful, Amber. Hang on to that and never let it go."

"Mama gave me the book, and it's now one of Ian and Lisa's favorite stories. I've read it so often that the pages are worn," Amber said. "Now, it's your turn, Kelly. A happy memory."

"I have one that I can think of," Kelly said. "My sister and I were not identical twins. She was the pretty one who got all the boys in high school, and I was the one with my nose in a book. We didn't see eye-to-eye on anything. But when we had our junior prom, she went shopping with me, and we chose the same color dresses. She did my hair and makeup, and since she didn't have a date, she and I went together. For that one night, I felt as pretty as she was, and we were best friends. When I start to think negative thoughts, I hang onto the feeling that I had for that evening like a bulldog with a bone."

Jenna nodded. "According to the self-help books, if we keep the good memories alive, the bad ones will eventually fade. Group session is officially over, and now it's time to make s'mores. We don't want Carson to have to go back to bad coffee and stale doughnuts."

Carson pushed up out of his chair, and for a few min-utes, Jenna thought he might be leaving. "I'm going to fol-low in Uncle Victor's example and have another hot dog before I make a s'more. I haven't had one roasted over an open fire since Bubba and I built a small one a week or two before he died. We made hot dogs and s'mores and drank contraband whiskey that his brother mailed to him in mouthwash bottles. So, this one is for Bubba."

"And my s'more is for my sister, who loved anything chocolate," Kelly said.

"Mine will be for Miz Ramona," Jenna added.

"And mine is for Mama and all the support she's given me, even when I didn't listen to her words of wisdom." Amber stood up.

Carson held out a hand, and Jenna took it. There was definitely electricity between them. He just hoped that she had felt what he did.

"Thank you," Carson whispered.

"You are welcome anytime," she told him. "Group therapy, or even just sitting on the porch and visiting. It's a busy life here, but also a lonely one."

"I can see that, and I will take you up on that offer. Maybe we can have another lunch together sometime?"

"I'd like that very much."

Chapter Four

"I love that we do this every year." Amber covered a yawn with her hand. "I remember the first time you hauled us out of bed to go for a morning walk to see the sunrise, I thought you were out of your mind."

"And now?" Jenna asked.

"For crepes at that little marina café, I would get up at midnight for a long walk," she answered. "What were you and Carson whispering about last night?"

"I was rude and asked him if he was married."

Kelly plopped down on the grass. "We need details about the question you asked Carson while we rest for a second. I'm used to walking several hundred steps a day, but it's on level ground. While we're taking a breather, you can tell us all about what he said."

Jenna sat down beside her. "He's not married. He was engaged at one time, but he's not in a relationship now. I feel like a fifth grader talking about a new boy who's come to our school."

"Want me to make a note that says, 'check yes or no if you want to be my boyfriend'?" Kelly asked. "I can get it ready, and you can give it to him next time he pops by, or you could be real romantic and hide it under a plate of brownies."

"I don't think so," Jenna answered. "I'm not as far into the closure stage as y'all are. I'm not ready to trust anyone like Amber does Ethan. I haven't even been able to throw my mama's ashes out in the lake like she said to do in her will."

Kelly scooted over and gave her a sideways hug. "It will happen when it's supposed to, but until then, just enjoy having Carson for a friend if nothing else. Don't rush anything, or you might have regrets. We'll all be talking once a month like always, and we'll expect reports."

"With details," Amber said.

"And I will want details about your kids, Amber, and your job, Kelly, and everything else going on in your lives," Jenna told them. "We have to make the best of this week, since it's the last one we'll have for a few years. When y'all come back to the States for visits, please know you are welcome here anytime. I'll even rent an extra cabin if you want to bring family or friends."

"Thank you," Amber said. "And we can always have our morning sunrise walk with just us three, right?"

"Of course," Jenna said, past the lump in her throat, when she thought of not being able to look forward to their yearly visits anymore. "I am happy for y'all. I really am, but it's bittersweet. I don't know how I'm going to tell you goodbye when the week is up."

"Don't feel bad that we won't have our week every single year," Amber said. "Feel happy for all the good memories. You just need to find love, my friend."

"Does the pain from our grieving ever go away?" Jenna asked.

"We don't get over it, but we do get through it with a lot of help," Kelly answered.

Jenna shook her head slowly. "That's not reassuring."

"No, but it's the truth." Kelly gave her a weak smile. "The challenge is in not trying to make it go away but accepting it because that pain is what made us who we are today. Closure isn't in making it disappear, but it's in realizing that the experience has given us understanding of life and who we are. Living with the pain or the guilt is not easy, but it teaches us that if something of value is dropped into our lives in the future, then we should fight for it with all the energy that we have."

"And we daily, sometimes hourly, fight for what is better than what we had," Amber whispered.

"It's easier said than done," Jenna said.

"You've got to want closure, and you've got to put in the work to have it. I think that Carson might just be the answer," Kelly declared. "By the way, I read that in a romance book. I wrote it down and keep it in my Bible. It's not word for word, but you get the general idea."

Amber pointed at a bank of clouds gathering across the lake and moving toward the sliver of sun coming up. "That looks like rain. If we're going to get to the café for crepes before it hits, we might ought to get moving. Texas storms don't wait around for invitations. They just plow ahead with a force. But sometimes there's a rainbow at the end of a storm. Kelly and I have found our rainbows. Now, it's up to you, Jenna, to find yours."

"I'll try," Jenna said. "We should all start a daily journal. Nothing too elaborate, but just a few words so we don't forget anything when we visit."

"That's a great idea!" Kelly popped up on her feet. "I'm not a jogger, but as fast as those clouds are moving toward us, we better hustle walking to get to that café before the rain starts."

Jenna led the way and kept an eye on the clouds that really *were* moving fast. Could that be a sign that the dark clouds that still overshadowed her life on some days were moving away? That they would leave a rainbow in their wake, and she could truly find peace? Did true peace mean closure?

The rain came down in gray sheets on the other side of the lake right after they ducked into the café and claimed a table. Within five minutes, the wind was pelting rain against the windows so hard that Jenna felt like she was in a cocoon with her two friends inside the tiny little marina café.

"Looks like the weather is going to keep folks away until it passes," the waitress said as she brought three cups, three breakfast menus, and a full coffeepot to their table. "What can I get you ladies this morning? All of you want coffee?"

"Yes, for me," Jenna answered. "I don't even need to look at the menu. I'll have the strawberries and crème crepes."

"Same here," Amber said.

"And me, too, but I want the banana, not strawberry," Kelly added.

Jenna didn't recognize the woman, but she caught a glimpse of her name tag. "Thank you, Wanda. Did *you* make it to work before the storm hit?"

"Yes, but not with a lot of time to spare," Wanda answered. "I live on the other side of the lake, and when I left, it was raining cats and dogs and baby elephants— that's what my granny always said when it comes down in sheets like this. But I managed to get the café door unlocked before it hit. The cook was right behind me, but our busboy is going to get wet for sure when he gets here. If it's got to rain, I'd rather see it now than over the weekend, when all the vacationers are here. Rain keeps them inside. No gas for their boats. No beer sales. No one to get out for meals here in the café. I'll get these orders right in. Shouldn't be too long, since y'all are the only ones here."

"Thank you," Jenna said, and took a sip of her coffee. "Nothing like the first cup in the morning, and this is pretty good."

Amber twisted the back of her long, blond hair up into a messy bun and held it in place with a clip she pulled off of the tail of her T-shirt. Then she took a sip of her coffee and nodded. "I agree. Not as good as what you make at the cabin, but not bad at all. Ethan takes his with cream and two sugars, but my granny made me learn to drink it black. And that is another good memory."

"Want to share?" Kelly asked, as she opened three packages of sugar substitute and shook them into her cup. Then she peeled the top from three individual containers of half-and-half and added that before she took a sip. "Now *this* is good coffee. The fake sugar nullifies all the cream when it comes to counting calories."

"I like the way you think," Amber said.

"Thank you, but you were about to tell me that memory about coffee," Kelly said.

Amber pointed out the window. "I think I see a vehicle out there. We may not be the only ones in here in a few minutes."

The door flew open, and it seemed like a blast of wind literally blew Carson into the café. One second, they were alone, and the next, he had come inside and slammed the door shut behind him. He removed his yellow slicker, hung it on a coat rack, and then wiped his feet on the welcome mat right inside the café.

"Well, hello!" Kelly called out. "Come on over and join us. You are just in time to hear Amber tell us a story about her granny's views on coffee."

Carson didn't argue, but crossed over to the table, pulled

out the empty chair beside Jenna, and sat down. "I've already had breakfast, but I'd sure like a cup of coffee. That rain is cold, almost like it's coming off hail. I'm not complaining, though. Not after spending the better part of a year in hotter-'n-hell heat with no rain in sight for months and months on end."

Jenna was very aware of his shoulder brushing against hers, and of the heat that it stirred up inside her. *Dammit!* she thought. If Amber and Kelly hadn't talked about him being sexy, and having a voice like Sam Elliott, she wouldn't be thinking thoughts that shot desire through her body.

Just because you are a self-proclaimed hermit does not mean you don't have a woman's desires and needs, the voice that sounded a lot like her mother's whispered softly in her head. *Own them and embrace them. And there's nothing wrong with a little sexual attraction.*

Wanda brought out their orders and set the plates on the table. "Well, good mornin', handsome park ranger," she flirted. "Will you have the regular?"

"Not this morning. Just coffee," Carson answered.

She hurried back to the kitchen, brought out another cup, and then topped off the three ladies' coffee. "Anything else I can get y'all? How about you, Carson? Maybe just a small order of French toast? It'll be on the house to show how much we appreciate our park rangers."

"No, thanks," Carson said. "I'm good this morning."

"Well, honey"—she leaned down far enough to give him a good shot of her cleavage—"if you change your mind, you just holler."

She didn't wait for him to say anything, but rushed to the other side of the dining room when two customers came in and parked their umbrellas in the galvanized milk can right inside the door.

"She's flirting with you," Amber whispered.

"Yep," Carson agreed. "But I don't have to flirt back, especially when I'm sitting here with three lovely women. You were going to tell us a good memory, right?"

"Okay, here goes." Amber nodded. "I was fourteen that year and figured I should learn to drink coffee. After school, my friends and I would go to a little hole-in-the-wall café not far from the school. I would have a soda, but some of them would order coffee. That looked so grownup and cool that I decided to join them. So, the next morning, I told Granny that I wanted a cup of coffee instead of my usual glass of milk for breakfast. She didn't ask any questions, just poured me a mugful. Most folks used six scoops of coffee for twelve cups of water. Granny said that just made murdered water. She used twelve scoops. I took the first sip, shivered so bad that I thought my toenails had fallen off, and asked for milk and sugar. She shook her head and said, 'Oh, no, my child. Life does not come with sugar and milk to sweeten it up, and neither does my coffee.' I did not drink coffee for many years, not until I eloped with Frankie. Now I'm going to eat before these wonderful crepes get cold. Someone else can tell a story."

"Your granny was a smart woman," Jenna said. "Miz Ramona taught me to drink espresso when I was about that age. I think she was getting me ready for my Paris trip."

"Mama used to water down coffee and let me and my sister have it for tea parties," Kelly added. "She read somewhere that it would calm kids who were truly hyperactive. I think it was a bunch of bunk, because it just made my sister's ADHD worse."

Jenna turned to Carson. "How about you? When did you start drinking it?"

"At about age fifteen, when I got my first hangover," he said with a chuckle.

"I hear a good story," Kelly said.

Jenna remembered her first hangover, but she forgot about that story when a few hailstones hit the window right beside them. "Seems like the storm is stalling out right over the café."

"None of us have any other place to be right now, so we can enjoy our breakfast," Kelly said.

"In good company," Carson added with a nod.

For the next hour, the rain came down in sheets, and the wind gusts pounded against the windows. A few lightning streaks split their way through the downpour. Thunder followed and rumbled overhead.

"I need to get back on my rounds," Carson said. "Neither rain, nor snow, nor sleet keeps a park ranger from doing his job."

Wanda brought the check, and Carson pulled out his wallet. Jenna laid a hand on his arm. "I've got this. All you had was a cup of coffee."

"Thank you for the coffee, but even more for the company," Carson said. "I didn't see a vehicle out there. Can I give y'all a lift back to your cabin?"

"Yes!" Kelly said.

"Then you ladies wait by the door, and I'll drive the ranger Jeep up as close as I can get it so maybe you won't get soaked." He pushed back his chair, got to his feet, and put on the rain slicker and his hat.

"Talk about good fortune," Amber said. "Or maybe the universe is smiling down on you, Jenna, and putting Carson right in your sights."

"You need to open your eyes and see him, or you will hurt the universe's feelings," Kelly teased. "He's been flung down from the heavens to help you, but you have to do your part, or someone else is going to snatch him out from under you."

Jenna laid a couple of bills on the table. "I see him, but I'm not sure I'm ready to trust him. Or any other guy, for that matter."

Amber opened the door, waited a couple of minutes, then dashed outside with Kelly right behind her. Jenna had never been very graceful, so she chose her footing carefully as she went down the steps and out to the car. Carson had opened the passenger door for her with only a few big splotches of water on her denim jacket.

The windshield wipers couldn't keep up with the rain, so Carson drove so slowly that the five-minute drive back to her cabin took twice that long. Then as suddenly as the storm had begun, it stopped, and the sun came out just before he pulled into her driveway.

"Look!" Kelly pointed out the side window. "There's a double rainbow, and the end is right over the top of Jenna's house."

"Is there a pot of gold in there?" Carson teased.

"Could be." Jenna grabbed her phone from her purse and took half a dozen pictures of the rainbow. They wouldn't be as clear as she would like, but they would do as a reference for the picture that she would paint later.

"Thanks for the ride," Amber said. "I promised to Face-Time with Lisa and Ian every day, so I'm going to sneak upstairs and do that."

"And I've got a couple of calls to make to the team that will be flying with me. Just some last-minute details," Kelly added. "I'll be finished in ten or fifteen minutes."

"Want to come inside?" Jenna asked. "There's some brownies left from yesterday if you'd like a midmorning snack."

"I can't. I've got a list to fill for Aunt Dorena at the grocery store. You want to go with me?" Carson asked.

"Yes, she does. We'll be busy for an hour or more," Kelly answered for her.

"I can answer for myself," Jenna grumbled. "But, yes, I would like to go with you. I need milk and bread and a few other things."

Kelly and Amber got out of the vehicle and waved from the porch.

"The little snow cone stand beside the grocery store opened this week. We could get one when we are finished buying groceries," Carson said. "What's your favorite flavor?"

"Rainbow with orange, pineapple, and blue coconut. What's yours?"

"Strawberry, but I might try one like yours today. That sounds like a good mixture."

Jenna mentally listed the dozens of questions and the teasing she would get when she got back home. But, hey, both her friends had thought she should jump right into the deep water and move on. Besides, it was broad daylight. There wouldn't be any kissing at the door to make it a real date.

That did not mean that when he reached up to get the bread off the top shelf and his arm brushed against hers that she didn't feel electricity. Or that she wished the snow cone would do more than give her a brain freeze and cool down the heat in her body.

When they got back home, he insisted on taking her groceries in for her, and she had a brief moment of panic. She had not had a man in the house except for repairmen since she had moved in ten years ago. *Good God!* she thought. *I'm a grown damn woman. I need to get over this and tell him that I'm having feelings for him.*

He seemed to take in the whole area in one sweeping glance, and then came back to the painting above the credenza. "Is that one of yours?"

"Yes, it is," she answered, before she even thought. "Paris in the morning."

He tilted his head to one side. "It's beautiful, and I've seen it somewhere else." His brow furrowed, and finally he snapped his fingers. "I remember now. A friend of mine and Bubba's was married, and his wife had a reproduction of that above her sofa." He took a step closer to get a better look. "You *are* famous, aren't you?"

"Shhhh . . ." She put her fingers over her lips and pointed up the staircase. "Don't tell anyone. It's a highly classified secret."

"Do Amber and Kelly know?" he asked.

"They just know that I sell a few paintings every now and then," she answered. "I don't want recognition."

"But *you* are JayLee, the famous artist that no one has ever met," he argued, and pointed toward the signature in the corner.

Why had she let it slip? Was the universe truly trying to throw her and Carson together, and if so, why? But *in for a penny, in for a dollar*, as her father used to say.

"My name is Jenna Lee—my mother's middle name was Jenene. Lee after my father's middle name. Everyone called Mama by her first name, which was Marsha. Miz Ramona helped me decide on my professional signature." She was amazed that it felt so good to tell someone that little bit of news about her life.

"I don't know diddly-squat about art, but I do know that is beautiful, and my friend's wife said that her print was priceless to her," he said. "And Jenna, what you do isn't who you are."

"Who am I, Carson?" she asked. "I've been struggling with that question for years."

"From what I have seen in Kelly and Amber's eyes, you are the glue that has held your little group of best friends together for years. If I took a poll of the people here on the lake, they would tell me that you are a fantastic neighbor, willing to jump in and help whenever it's needed," he answered.

"And what about you?" she asked.

"In my eyes, you are a strong independent woman with a big heart," he answered. "One that I would love to get to know better in the coming days."

"I would like that, too," she said with a smile.

Chapter Five

Jenna had always promised herself that she would not paint the days that Amber and Kelly were there. In the past, a week without the brushes in her hands or her thumb tucked into a palette of paint had not been a problem. But that Wednesday night, after her friends had gone up to their rooms, she needed to escape into her world of blending oils and creating something. So much had been dropped on her in such a short time—both of her friends leaving the United States, and the feelings that Carson had woken up—that her emotions felt like they were on a roller coaster. She fought the battle and thought she had won when she went to bed, closed her eyes, and tried to make herself fall asleep. The harder she tried to blank out everything, the wider awake she became, until she finally got out of bed and paced the floor.

"This is ridiculous," she muttered, as she went out to the kitchen, grabbed a bottle of wine, and carried it outside. She eased down into one of her Adirondack chairs and popped the cork. She had started to pour some of the strawberry wine into the red plastic cup when she felt someone or something staring at her. She looked around to see if a raccoon or possum had come snooping around but found Amber sitting on the porch swing.

"So, you couldn't sleep either?" Amber asked.

"Nope," Jenna answered. "Wine?"

"Love some." Amber reached for the bottle and drank out of it. "I never pictured you for a cheap date," she said, as she handed the bottle back to Jenna.

"How did you picture me?" Jenna drank the little bit in the cup and took a long swig from the bottle.

"I figured that you had money until you said that about that lady, Miz Ramona, leaving you a scholarship and paying for you to go to Paris. If you came from a wealthy family, you wouldn't have needed that, and you wouldn't be living in a remote cabin like this," Amber answered.

"Life is complicated," Jenna said.

"I heard that last comment," Kelly said, as she came out onto the porch and sat down on the other end of the swing. "What makes life complicated, and why are y'all having a party without me?"

"We can't sleep, so we're sharing a bottle of cheap wine," Amber answered. "Evidently, all of us are having trouble sleeping tonight."

Jenna passed the bottle over to Kelly, and she turned it up. "I'm not sure one bottle is going to knock us all on our butts."

"There's plenty more where that one came from, but only one more is chilled," Jenna replied. "And life is complicated, at least for me, because I feel change in the air, and the rut I've carved out for myself these last ten years is so comfortable." She paused and took a deep breath. "I'm not sure I can leave it."

"Sure you can." Kelly handed the bottle off to Amber.

"It's easy. You just pack up the past and burn it, then you unpack the future and start living it."

"What's the first thing you did when you burned the past?" Jenna asked.

"My past and yours are different, but I finally accepted the fact that I was not responsible for my twin sister's death. Something I haven't told either of you is that I went to her grave and yelled at her for cheating me out of having her in my life, for having a friend, and maybe even a family. I was afraid to have a lasting relationship after seeing her fail at so many, or to have kids. After I threw my fit, I forgave her, because hate and love can't live in the same heart."

Amber passed the bottle to Jenna. "I miss my kids and Ethan. That's why I can't sleep. I want to be here with y'all. I need to be here for the final closure. But that doesn't keep me from missing having Ethan beside me when I wake up in the morning, or making breakfast for Lisa and Ian before we get dressed and go play in the park for an hour. Leaving behind my old rut for this new one is wonderful."

Jenna took a drink and then sighed. "I'm so glad you've both fully made it past all the stages of grief."

"What can we do to help *you* take that final step?" Kelly asked.

"We can just be here to support her," Amber answered for her. "That's one step that a person has to take on their own if it's going to work."

"Yep," Kelly said. "You got that right. Now pass me that wine and tell Jenna that we know that she's a famous artist."

Jenna almost choked on the swallow of wine she had just taken. "How . . . when . . . what . . ." she sputtered.

"We kind of figured it out years ago, but we didn't want to intrude on your privacy," Kelly answered. "We eavesdropped on your conversation with Carson, and that sealed the deal. Actually, we were hoping to see a makeout session, but we got disappointed on that."

"I don't go to galleries, and wouldn't know a Picasso from one of Ian's color sheets, but Ethan knows a little about art. His folks have a reproduction of one of your pieces hanging in their foyer. I recognized it from the one you were working on the first year we came here. That's the way I found out, and I told Kelly," Amber said.

"It was your secret to keep, but now it's out," Kelly said. "Is that what your banking job is all about?"

"No, it's . . ."—Jenna shook her head—"I own that Mona Gallery in Houston and a few others here in the state. I'm a trust-fund kid, and what I do on the computer is run those businesses."

Telling them was so liberating that it felt as if a weight had been lifted from her soul. Still, she liked her privacy and self-proclaimed hermit lifestyle so much that she didn't want to share that news with anyone else.

"We kind of figured you had an inheritance of some kind," Amber said.

"Money can't buy happiness," Jenna muttered.

"Amen to that," Kelly agreed, as she took a drink and passed the bottle over to Amber.

Amber finished off the wine, stood up, and headed across the porch. "I'll get the second bottle. I'm not sleepy yet, and we don't have to get up before the crack of dawn tomorrow to go for crepes. I'll make brunch when we are all up and around. I'm missing cooking for the family more than a little."

She returned in a few minutes and handed the bottle to Jenna. "I never can get the top off, whether it's a twist-off or a cork."

"I'm ready," Jenna said. "I've put it off long enough.

Let's go put Mama's ashes in the lake like she wanted me to do."

"Right now?" Amber asked.

"No!" Kelly reached for the bottle in Jenna's hands. "I want you to sleep on this tonight, Jenna. If you still want to do this tomorrow, we will, but your mother deserves respect. We should be dressed in something other than pajama bottoms and T-shirts, and we should have music and maybe say a few words."

"You are right," Jenna said, "but I'm ready to do this now, so let's plan it at sunrise. Mama loved to sit on the porch and watch the sun come up when we came to the lake for the summer. Tomorrow would be a perfect time, since the weekenders will start to arrive on Friday, and even in the early morning, things won't be quiet."

Amber stood up and took the bottle from Jenna. "This can go back in the fridge, and we really should get some sleep, since we'll be getting up in about five hours. Good night, my friends."

Kelly followed her into the house. "Good night. Shall we meet on the porch around six o'clock? And afterwards, we can talk more about Carson and the glow you get in your face when he's around."

"You are seeing what you want to see, not what is reality," Jenna said.

"We'll see about that." Amber blew her a kiss as she went into the house.

She waited until Kelly and Amber had gone upstairs, and heard the bedroom doors close before she went to the living room and took the urn from the fireplace mantel. She carried it into her bedroom on the ground floor and set it on the nightstand.

"Promise me that when your ashes have gone back to nature for good, you won't stop popping into my head with advice when I need it," she whispered.

My child, I will never forsake you. I will be in your heart forever. Marsha's calm voice whispered softly. *Let me go. Learn to truly live again, and most of all, learn to trust.*

Jenna laid a hand on the top of the urn. Kelly had been right. Her mother needed more than a trip to the lake in the middle of the night. It was past time to let her go, but it should be done with respect.

Chapter Six

Jenna held the urn to her chest as she and her friends walked together from the back porch, across the lawn, and to the edge of the lake. A soft breeze ruffled the leaves of the sweet gum tree at the edge of the firepit. She had no doubts that it was time to let her mother go, but she wasn't sure if she could really spread Marsha's ashes out over the water.

"This is your journey," Kelly whispered when they reached the edge of the lake. "If you have changed your mind and want to go back, then we will."

"I'll never be ready to let her go." Jenna kicked off her shoes and handed her phone to Amber. "When I open the urn, start the music."

She waded out into the cool water until it came up to her knees. A thousand memories flashed through her mind, beginning with one when she was about three years old. Her mother took her out into the water and sat down with Jenna in her lap. She sang a children's song, but Jenna could only remember the clear southern tone of her mother's voice. Tears dammed up behind her eyelids and finally spilled out to roll down her cheeks. Her breath caught in her chest, and her hands went so clammy that the urn began to slip from her fingers.

Let me go. I want to be free, but most of all, I want you to be free. She gripped the urn tighter and sucked in a lungful of fresh morning air. The breeze brought all the scents her mother loved: roses blooming in the backyard, lake water, and the faint aroma of cinnamon from the sweet gum tree.

She removed the lid from the urn. "I love you, Mama."

Jamey Johnson began to sing "Lead me Home" behind her as she slowly turned around in a circle and shook the ashes out. The breeze picked up the fine dust and swept it up toward heaven just as the lyrics of the song talked about standing on a mountain and looking over Jordan.

When all the ashes were dumped out, Jenna sat down in the circle floating on the top of the water and filled the urn with lake water. Her tears mingled with the water when she poured out the last remnants of her mother's ashes and watched them sink below the lake's surface. The words to Jamey's song talked about hearing the angels sing. Jenna looked up at the big white fluffy clouds floating above her and imagined her mother's voice joining them.

She stood up, carrying the wet urn close to her body, as she walked out of the water and up to where her friends waited. "Thank you for being here with me."

"How do you feel?" Amber asked.

"Sad and happy at the same time," Jenna answered. "That sounds crazy, but it's true."

Amber draped an arm around Jenna's shoulders. "I understand perfectly. When I went to tell Gloria about Ethan and the kids, I felt the same way. But then a kind of peace settled over me, and it was almost as if I heard my baby giggle. It was kind of like I was finally letting go."

Kelly gave Jenna a quick hug. "I had the same feelings when I accepted the job in Africa."

Jenna sat down in one of the chairs around the firepit, set the ceramic urn on the arm of the chair, and watched the gentle waves on the lake take her mother's ashes and wash them away. "Do you ever hear voices in your head?"

"Of course," Kelly answered. "My grandmother pops in every now and then to give me some advice or just to come off with one of her sayings that makes me smile."

"My granny does the same for me," Amber said.

"Mama whispered to me last night," Jenna told them. "She said that she wanted me to set her free, so I did."

A hard gust of wind blew Jenna's dark hair across her face. The temperature instantly dropped at least ten degrees. She shivered from the chill she got from her wet jeans and started to stand up. The urn wobbled when a blast of wind from the north hit it, and then Jenna's elbow brushed against it. All three of the women saw it about to fall, and they grabbed for it at the same time, but none of them were fast enough. It fell onto the concrete apron around the firepit and shattered into a million tiny pieces.

Now I'm really free. Marsha's voice was so real that Jenna looked out across the lake to see if her mother had risen from the ashes like a phoenix bird.

Kelly and Amber froze, and everything was silent for a few seconds. Then they both began to talk at the same time.

"I'm so sorry," Kelly said.

"I'll pick up all the pieces and glue it back together," Amber whispered.

Jenna slowly shook her head. "She's free now. She just popped into my head and told me. Evidently, she didn't want me to keep that urn. And look"—she held up her hands—"the wind has died down. I'm going to believe that she broke that urn. We'll sweep up the pieces after breakfast."

Amber swiped away a tear. "Stranger things have happened."

Kelly took a deep breath and let it out slowly. "It wouldn't feel right to just throw them in the trash."

"We could bury them under the rosebushes," Amber suggested.

Jenna looked at all the pieces scattered around her feet. "Mama didn't want to be buried in the ground. If there was even the smallest ash left clinging to a piece of that, I wouldn't feel right putting it under dirt. Sounds crazy, doesn't it?"

"No, it does not," Kelly protested.

"I'm going to put them all in a plastic bag, along with the rose I dried from her memorial service, and tape it up good. Then I will walk out to the end of the dock and throw it out into the lake. Mama told me that the water is about thirty feet deep out in the middle, so no one would step on the shards and get hurt."

"That's a good idea," Amber said, and took a couple of steps toward the house. "Let's do it right now, and then go to the café to have crepes for breakfast. That can be like the family dinner following a funeral."

"And we can talk about her," Kelly followed after Amber.

Jenna hung back for just a moment, waiting for her mother's voice. A cardinal flew down from the sweet gum tree and lit on the edge of the firepit. Marsha had told her on numerous occasions that seeing a pretty red cardinal meant she would either have good luck, or maybe get a spiritual lesson. The bird seemed to stare right at her as if trying to tell her something; then it took flight toward the house and landed on one of the red rosebushes.

"I get the message, Mama." Jenna finally smiled. "Loud and clear."

"Who are you talking to?" Amber asked and followed Jenna's eyes back toward the house. "A cardinal means . . ."

"Good luck or something spiritual," Kelly finished the sentence for her.

"It's telling me not to throw the urn pieces in the lake. Mama threw a hissy fit every time a glass bottle washed up," Jenna said. "We'll bury them under the rosebushes, but not in a plastic bag. She's flown away to the clouds. That urn was just the tent that she's lived in for ten years. She doesn't care what we do with it, but she loves her red roses."

"That's beautiful," Amber said, as she swept up every single tiny piece and put them into the bag. "I'll make sure that all the pieces are gathered if you want to go dig a little hole to put them in."

Jenna nodded, and then noticed movement in her peripheral vision. She turned around and saw Carson jogging along the lake shore. She'd gotten the spiritual lesson about the urn. Was Carson bringing her the good luck part of seeing a cardinal?

"Hey," he said, and waved. "What are y'all doing up so early? Did you fall in the lake? Are you alright?"

"We had a little ceremony with my mother's ashes," she said, amazed that there was no hitch in her voice, or tightness in her chest. "I sat down in the water to wash out the urn, and then a wind knocked it off the chair arm, and it broke."

Carson pulled a red bandana from his pocket and wiped sweat from his forehead. "I'm so sorry. Scattering my folks' ashes was very emotional for me."

"I'm so sorry," Jenna said. "I didn't know your folks had passed."

"Three years ago," Carson said. "Uncle Victor and Aunt Dorena are all I have left, but today is not about me. Is there anything I can do to help?"

"I was about to dig a little hole under the rosebushes to put the broken pieces in," Jenna answered. "And then we're going to the café to have crepes."

"Got a shovel or a garden trowel?" he asked.

Jenna nodded.

"I'll be glad to take care of that for you."

"Thank you," Amber said.

"The shovel is in the work shed by the house," Jenna told him. Carson walked along beside her on the way back to the house. Several times, his hand brushed against hers. Finally, she laced her fingers in his. "Thanks for doing this."

"I'll have it dug by the time you get changed, but I would like a bottle of water, if you wouldn't mind. I forgot to bring one with me."

"Come on inside and help yourself to a bottle of water or sweet tea," she said. "They are both in the fridge."

He stopped in the kitchen, but she went straight to her bedroom, with Kelly and Amber right behind her.

She shook her finger at both of them. "Not a word. I'm moving on."

Kelly raised both hands into the air. "Praise the Lord!"

Jenna rolled her eyes toward the ceiling, stripped out of wet clothing, and redressed in dry underwear, jeans, and a plaid shirt, brushed her hair and twisted it up into a messy bun, and even applied just a little lipstick.

She cocked her head to one side, expecting to hear her mother's voice, but there was nothing.

Don't forsake me now, she thought.

Never.

That one word put a smile on her face, and she was humming "Toes" by the Zac Brown Band when she went back outside, again with Amber and Kelly behind her. Her mother had said that the lyrics to the song reminded her of how happy she was in the summer when they could leave the busy life behind and live simply at the lake.

"I recognize that song." Carson pointed to the shallow hole he had already dug under the middle rosebush.

"Mama loved it," Jenna said.

Amber handed her the bag, and she poured the pieces into the dirt and carefully pushed the dirt back over them. When she looked up from the job, she locked eyes with Carson.

"Now what?" she asked.

"Now, we go to the café, have breakfast, and talk about Marsha," Amber answered.

"You want to come with us?" she asked Carson.

"No, Aunt Dorena is making biscuits and gravy." Carson blinked and looked away. "She'll shoot me if I don't show up. Uncle Victor thinks it's a sin to waste good food, so he'll eat it all if I'm not there. She worries about his health. But thanks for the invitation. I've got a junior ranger group coming out from Point Blank for a field trip this morning at nine. Victor is going with me to show me the ropes on an excursion like this. Y'all have a great day. Maybe I'll catch up to y'all later this evening." He waved over his shoulder and jogged toward Victor and Dorena's place.

"We'll be looking for you," Jenna called out.

"What just happened?" Amber whispered.

"I took the first step to truly move on," Jenna answered.

Chapter Seven

Carson glanced down at Bubba, who was sitting on the tiny vanity in the travel trailer watching him shave. "Be glad that you don't have to do this every day," he said.

Bubba cocked his head to one side and meowed.

"I don't understand cat talk, but I'm going to believe that you agree with me. I hope you're in the same frame of mind tomorrow when the movers take Uncle Victor's things out of the house and bring mine in. This is our last night in the travel trailer. We'll be in a bigger place tomorrow evening." He poured shaving lotion in his hand and then slapped it onto his face.

Bubba raised his paw and touched Carson on the arm.

"Are you asking me if I like Jenna? The answer is yes, I like her very much."

But she needs to work through all her issues, Carson thought. *Other than finally scattering her mother's ashes, I'm not sure what else has her spooked, but I can tell she's got other issues from the haunted look in her eyes.*

He picked up the cat, carried him to the living area, and set him on the tiny table. Bubba turned around a few times and curled up in a tight little furball. Carson had just pulled on his boots when Victor knocked on the door and then stuck his head inside.

"Are you ready?" he asked.

"Yes, sir," Carson answered.

"You ain't in the service now, son," Victor said with a chuckle. "I'm your plain old uncle, with an emphasis on old."

Carson took a second to pat Bubba's head before he left the trailer. "How long did it take you to stop saying sir?"

"Longer than two months," Victor admitted.

"Are you and Aunt Dorena ready for tomorrow? Won't it be bittersweet to see that moving van pull away with all your things?" Carson asked.

"Yes, it will," Dorena said as she joined them and looped her arm into Victor's. "This has been our home longer than any place we ever lived, but I'm ready for a change. I want to spend time with our daughter and the next generation of kids. So, I'm going to think about the trip and the fun your uncle and I are going to have on the trip to Virginia, and all the good times we'll have with our family when we get there."

"I'm glad that we'll be busy with the party, and with the movers taking our things out and then bringing yours in," Victor said. "If we didn't have anything to do on our last day, there could be time for sadness."

Carson slowed his stride so that his uncle and aunt wouldn't be winded when they arrived at Jenna's cabin for supper that evening. "I agree, but I'll still be a little sad when I see you pull away in that travel trailer."

"You just be sure Bubba is with you in the house when we leave," Dorena said in a scolding tone. "Our daughter is allergic to cats and dogs both, and this old man right here has such a big heart, he wouldn't let me toss the kitten out at a roadside rest."

"Darlin', do I need to remind you of the frog?" Victor asked.

"No, you do not," she scolded.

"What about the frog?" Carson asked.

"One was on our back porch, and she made me carry it all the way back to the edge of the lake," Victor answered. "My heart is a dried-up raisin compared to hers. She would never throw Bubba out of the trailer. She would probably take him to a shelter when we get to the end of our journey, but until then, she would treat him like a king and cry like a baby when she left him behind."

She nudged him on the shoulder. "You know me too well."

"Yep, I do." He beamed.

Carson wanted what they had—the love, companionship, and friendship, even after years of marriage. He had thought he had found it when he proposed to Jody, but he had been wrong. Folks talked about a woman's biological clock ticking loudly. He didn't believe that men had such a thing, but lately, he had been craving all the things that a permanent commitment would bring into his life. He didn't have a fortune to offer a woman, but he did have a heart that he was more than willing to share with the right one.

Change had never been Jenna's enemy. That probably was a result of moving to the lake every summer, and then back to the family's estate in time for her to go back to school. When Jenna was young, she counted the days until she could get to the cabin for three months. When she was a teenager, she couldn't wait to see her favorite person and take a few more art lessons from Ramona. She seldom even unpacked when they arrived but went straight over to Ramona's cabin to visit and set up a schedule for the next three months. Then everything changed in the course of five minutes. She had a funeral to plan and a divorce to navigate—that was a huge change and a heartbreak all rolled into one.

"Your mind is a million miles away," Amber said, as she set the dining room table for six people.

Kelly tossed grape tomatoes into the salad and added croutons and cheese to the top. "What are you thinking about?"

"Change," Jenna answered.

"What about it?" Amber asked.

Jenna filled six glasses with ice and set them around at each place setting. "There's a lot going on right now. Victor and Dorena are leaving. This is our last week together for what could be the last time."

"We've all made beautiful memories here." Kelly carried the salad to the dining room and set it down on the table. "We've shared so much and gotten through obstacles that life threw at us in these past ten years. We can all lean on those in tough times, but honey, the biggest change is yet to come, because you are going to find happiness right here."

"How can you know that?" Jenna asked.

Before Kelly could answer, someone knocked on the back door. Jenna tossed her apron aside and crossed the room to answer it. "Y'all come on in," she said. "We're putting supper on the table right now."

"I wanted to bring dessert, but Victor said y'all have everything covered," Dorena said.

"This is a little goodbye supper for y'all, so you shouldn't have to cook anything. Besides, I bet you've got all your pots and pans packed by now." Jenna bent to give the short lady a hug.

Dorena had always reminded Jenna of her paternal grandmother Stewart. Gray hair, brown eyes, just a little on the curvy side, and always with a happy smile.

"Yes, she does, but we know where to go buy a cheesecake," Victor said.

"And they are very good, but Amber whipped up a peach crisp that's so good . . ." Kelly started toward the table with a bowl of green beans.

"That it will make you kiss the devil's pitchfork," Victor finished the sentence.

"That's right," Kelly said with a giggle. "Y'all gather on around here and have a seat. We just have to take the pot roast from the oven and bring it to the table."

"This all looks amazing," Dorena said, as she picked up the pitcher of sweet tea and filled all the glasses before she sat down.

Victor claimed the chair right beside her. "And smells even better. I do love a good pot roast, and the potatoes and carrots cooked in all that rich broth."

Jenna brought the final platter of food to the table, set it down, and then realized that Kelly and Amber had chosen to sit at the two ends. Victor and Dorena were side by side, across from Carson. That left only one spot for her—right beside Carson.

Her pulse jacked up a few notches when he stood up and pulled out her chair. Then his shoulder brushed against hers when she sat down, and it spiked up even more. She was determined not to fight the feeling, but to embrace it.

A free heart has room for romance. Her mother was back in her head for the first time since she had scattered the ashes.

Could that mean that by giving her mother's spirit wings to fly, Jenna had also loosened the chains that held her own heart back from having a real relationship? She explored that idea while the conversation around the table centered on Victor and Dorena leaving, and how long they planned the trip to Viriginia would take.

Jenna caught every third or fourth word, just enough to know to nod every now and then so everyone thought she was paying attention.

"You look beautiful this evening. That bright yellow dress makes you glow," Carson whispered.

His warm breath on her neck made her shiver. "Thank you. You look . . ." She felt someone staring and glanced across the table to see Amber wink.

"I look what?" Carson asked. He smiled.

"I remember that you made this same meal the first time you invited us to share supper with you and your friends," Dorena said. "I was hoping you'd serve it again tonight. Pot roast is one of my favorite meals. We'll have party food tomorrow, and then we've decided to get in the RV and leave right after that. No need in sleeping in it here in the park and leaving on Sunday morning when we could easily make a hundred miles before dark."

Victor put a second helping of food on his plate. "I'm glad this is what you cooked up for us, too. It's just about my favorite all-time meal."

"I thought kraut dogs was your favorite," Kelly teased.

"That's his favorite snack, except for chocolate cake, peach cobbler, and ice cream," Dorena tattled.

"It's surreal that you're leaving," Jenna said.

Carson finished off his tea and refilled it. "I'm just now hearing that this will be my last night with y'all. I thought you were staying until Monday."

"Dorena just sprang that idea on me a few minutes

ago," Victor told him. "I agreed with her, mostly because we both hate goodbyes. When we leave here tonight, we'll still see all y'all tomorrow at the party, and then we will get into the RV and be on our way. That way there's less tears."

"I read a quote once that said if nothing ever changed, there would be no butterflies," Dorena told them.

"Mama had that on a plaque in her office," Jenna remembered, "and I brought it to the lake with me. It's hanging in . . ."

"My bedroom," Kelly finished for her. "Every time I see a butterfly, I think of that."

"Amen," Carson said under his breath.

"Well, looks to me like we're all about to see butterflies in our future," Dorena said. "I hope that you young women find what you are looking for in your travels. I hope that Victor and I can make our change without a hitch, and that Carson loves living here at the lake as much as we have."

Jenna thought maybe she had left her out, or clumped her in with Kelly and Amber, until she smiled across the table. "And I really hope that you find happiness now that you are coming out of your cocoon."

"How . . . what . . ." Jenna sputtered.

"I'm old," Dorena said, "but I still see twenty-twenty. I can see that whatever is happening in your life has put a sparkle in your eyes that I haven't seen before now. My prayer is that it's just the beginning of a wonderful future for you."

"Thank you," Jenna whispered. "What you just said is beautiful."

"Yes, it is," Amber and Kelly chimed in together.

"I agree," Carson added.

"We're going to have to talk about something else, or

I'm going to cry," Jenna said. "And none of us are saying goodbye. That's way too final. We're going to just say 'see you.' That means that sometime in the future, we will all be together again around this table."

"Amen!" Victor raised his tea glass. "A toast to what Jenna just said."

"The two of us don't have to say 'see you' to each other," Carson said, for her ears only.

Chapter Eight

"This is a fantastic turnout," Kelly said.

"We should take our cake and punch outside to give them more room," Amber suggested.

"Sounds like a good idea," Carson nodded. "Seems like new folks are arriving by the minute. I didn't realize Uncle Victor had made so many friends here at the lake."

Jenna led the way out to several tables set up at the side of the ranger station. "It's not just friends. He's been here at the lake since I was a teenager, so he's seen dozens of rangers retire, as well as worked with some that were here only for a short while. Plus, all the permanent residents here want to give him a proper send-off."

Carson waited for the three ladies to sit down, and then he put his plate and glass on the table and took a seat beside Jenna. "Well, he's sure going out with a big bang. That adrenaline high should carry him halfway to Virginia."

"Are you all moved in?" Jenna asked.

"My stuff is in the cabin. Bubba has been exploring every nook and cranny, but I can't say that we're actually moved into the place. I slept there last night, but like all new places, it'll take a while to get used to," Carson answered.

"Especially after living in a travel trailer for weeks," Amber said.

"It was right the opposite for me." Jenna finished off her slice of cake and took a drink of her punch. "I went from an estate-sized place to the house I live in now. Even though I had spent every summer here for most of my life, I felt kind of cooped up when I moved back."

Kelly took a deep breath and let it out slowly. "That's because when you came back to the lake permanently, you were all cooped up inside. It wouldn't have mattered if you had decided to stay in that big house that your folks left you. The feelings would have been the same."

"But we are so glad that you have thrown off those chains and began to find some closure," Amber added. "I don't think I could have enjoyed the life I'm about to have with Ethan and the kids if you were still as sad as you were that first year we all were together here for a week."

Carson pushed back his chair and stood up. "Can I get y'all anything else? I'm going inside for a cup of coffee. That was good cake, but now I need something to get all that sweet out of my mouth."

"Yes," Kelly and Amber chimed in together.

"I'll go with you to help carry them all out," Jenna offered.

They had only gone a few feet when Carson asked, "Would it be too imposing of me to ask to take you three to dinner this evening? I know it's the last night before Kelly and Amber leave in the morning, but I thought maybe it might . . ."

"No, it would not be imposing, and yes, we would love to go," Jenna said before he could finish. "And thank you."

Carson opened the door for her and stood to the side. "I

should be the one thanking you, since I really don't want to spend this first evening alone."

"The first day that Kelly and Amber leave seems like it lasts three days past eternity, so we could help each other out," Jenna suggested. "We could drive up to Onalaska for groceries."

"Or since we have the whole day, we could go south to Conroe and make a day of it," Carson replied. "We could do our grocery shopping, have a bite of lunch somewhere, and then catch a movie."

Jenna filled four cups with coffee and capped them off with lids. "I would like that very much."

That sounds like a first date. Her mother's voice in her head sounded happy.

Jenna thought about that as she picked up two cups and headed outside with Carson right behind her. Was she ready to date again? Had she finally gotten past Bryce?

Kelly took one of the cups from Jenna's hand. "Five more minutes, and then the RV is leaving. Has everyone got their little bottle of bubbles ready?"

Jenna remembered that she and Bryce were showered with birdseed as they left the church after their wedding. She was still picking it out of her hair when they boarded the plane the next day for a weeklong honeymoon cruise. She found out later than Bryce had charged the price of the cruise to her credit card that she was still paying off after the divorce. She shook the memory from her mind and vowed to never think of Bryce again. The past had no place in her new life with Carson.

"Whatever are you thinking about?" Kelly asked.

"The past," Jenna admitted.

"Well, get out a virtual shovel and bury all that stuff. Then move ahead and don't ever look back," Kelly told her. "You have taken a few steps, but it's definitely time to really give whatever this is between you and Carson a chance to develop."

Amber pushed back her chair and stood up. "Here they come!"

The door opened, and people poured out, forming two lines for Victor and Dorena to run though. A picture of a gauntlet formed in Jenna's mind, but it disappeared when the couple came out of the building. Victor took Dorena's hand in his, and they made their way slowly down a stream of wall of bubbles to the RV. Dorena went on inside, but when Victor pushed a button to cause the steps to retreat under the trailer, he waved at everyone from the open door.

"Thank you all for a great retirement party," he yelled. "Come see us if you are ever in Virginia and take care of Carson like you have me all these years."

The door closed, and within seconds the engine started, and the RV pulled away out onto the road and disappeared around the first curve.

Carson stood in the middle of the road and waved until they were out of sight. When he came back to where Jenna was standing with her friends, he draped an arm around her shoulders. "That was tougher than I thought it would be."

Jenna reached up and laid her hand on his. "You got that right. I'm glad they're getting to spend time with their family, but I'm going to miss them so much."

"Me, too," he said, "But Jenna has agreed to let me take y'all to dinner tonight to help me get through my first long evening without them. Can I pick you all up in an hour?"

Kelly tossed her coffee cup and dirty dishes into a nearby trash can. "That sounds great, but could I be home by ten? I've got a conference call with my team coming in at that time. Our flight is at ten tomorrow, so I'll need to leave here by six thirty. We're being served breakfast on the first leg of the journey, so I won't even take time to eat in the morning. I'll just grab a cup of coffee to go."

"And I'll leave at the same time," Amber said. "Ethan's folks are planning a little going-away dinner for us tomorrow evening, and I miss the kids so much."

"That will be even harder than today," Jenna said. *Rip the Band-Aid off in one fell swoop,* the voice in her head said loudly. *Then heal up and get on with life.*

The café that Carson chose opened at four o'clock and was on the other side of the lake. Only a couple of vehicles were in the parking lot when he snagged a place not far from the front door, and there was two other couples in the place when they went inside.

Jenna had only eaten at the café a couple of times, and both times the place had been packed. For someone who didn't know how good the food was, they might drive right on past it. That would be a big mistake. Even though the café itself looked like a house with a front porch, it had some of the best ribs and chicken fried steak in the whole lake area.

A waitress led them to a table over near the window overlooking the parking lot, and laid four menus on the table. "What can I get y'all to drink?"

"Sweet tea," Jenna answered.

"Same here," Carson said.

Kelly and Amber both raised a finger and nodded.

"The special tonight is chicken fried steak, mashed potatoes and gravy, biscuit, side salad, and green beans," the waitress told them. "I'll have those drinks out in just a minute."

"We've never been here," Amber said as she studied the menu. "But if the food is as good as all these wonderful smells, I'm glad we came."

Carson studied the menu and then laid it to the side. "I've only been here once with Uncle Victor, but I loved the ribs, so that's what I'm having this evening."

Jenna handed her menu to Carson to stack with his. "Me, too, but a word of warning to all y'all: I'm not graceful, and ribs are messy."

"Then I'm glad I'm not sitting beside you," Kelly said, and put her menu on top of the others. "I'm having the special. I'm already a little nervous about twenty-four hours in a plane, so I'm not testing my jittery stomach with anything spicy."

"Same for me." Amber nodded. "I'll be going to the courthouse on Monday morning to get married, and then flying to Germany that afternoon, so nothing really heavy for me, either."

Jenna would go back to her painting and her routine after they left. Watching the sunset at the end of the day, taking care of business at the art galleries.

And spend time with Carson?

She wondered where that notion came from, and then smiled. Even if they were only friends—that thought flew right out the window when his knee brushed against hers under the table and set off a little wave of heat that told her if she had her way, they would spend lots and lots of time together.

"What are you smiling about?" Kelly asked.

"Just that I'm glad I don't have to fly anywhere this week," Jenna said. "I'm not going to lie, I'm sad that our memory cabin days have come to an end. But I'm glad for every one of the weeks we have spent together, and I wouldn't take a million bucks for the memories we've made."

"Amen!" Amber nodded. "We've helped each other evolve into the women we are today. And now it's time for us to step out of our comfort zones and move on."

"Well said!" Kelly said. "Now let's put all the sadness away and enjoy our last evening together."

"Not our last one forever, though. Just the last one for this year," Jenna told them. "Y'all will come back someday, or else I will come see you, but until then, we'll Zoom every month just like always."

The waitress returned with glasses of sweet tea, took the orders, and then rushed off to take care of several more customers who had filed into the café, and soon the buzz of a dozen conversations filled the place.

"That's life," Jenna muttered.

"What is?" Carson asked.

"Life is like all the things folks are talking about around us. Each table has their own stories to tell," she answered.

"That's beautiful," Kelly said with a sigh. "We get so involved in our own life that we forget that we are just a drop in the bucket in the overall scheme of things."

"Yep, but our drop is important, because it makes us who we are," Amber added.

Carson bumped Jenna with his knee under the table. "Who are you?"

She smiled when she remembered asking him who she was. "I'm working on figuring that out, but I'm not the person I was yesterday, or the person I will be tomorrow. Today, I'm moving forward and not standing still," she answered.

"That's progress, isn't it?" Carson asked.

"I hope so, because it feels right," Jenna replied.

Chapter Nine

Jenna stood at the edge of the front lawn and waved until Kelly and Amber's vehicles were completely out of sight. Somehow it seemed right that they would leave before dawn had fully arrived. The memory cabin visits had ended, and a new day had begun.

"But I don't have to like it," she muttered as she turned and started back toward the house. The dew on the grass was cool on her bare feet, and by the time she got to the porch, the bottom edges of her pajama legs were damp. She went straight to her bedroom and dressed in a pair of jeans, and a dark green T-shirt. She had finished lacing up her athletic shoes when the doorbell rang.

She and Carson hadn't talked about what time he might show up, but she expected to see him on the porch when she opened the door. She was surprised when she found a young girl there with braces, hair in two long, light-brown braids, and big blue eyes.

"I'm Martha Stevens," she said.

Jenna still had Girl Scout cookies in her freezer, but she loved the chocolate mint ones so much that she always ordered a few boxes.

"Did you say Martha or Marsha?" Jenna asked.

"Martha June Stevens is my full name," the teenager answered. "Are you alright? You look like you just saw a ghost."

"I am fine. I was just expecting someone else to be at the door. What are you selling?" She realized that the girl had an artist's portfolio in her hand.

If the girl had another twenty pounds on her, and was a little taller, she would look a lot like the picture of Jenna's mother hanging beside the mirror. Surely she was imagining things because the two names—Martha and Marsha—were so close together. She glanced over her shoulder at the black-and-white photograph and shivered. There was a resemblance there—probably because Martha had braids and good cheekbones.

"My parents have moved here from up in Vega, Texas. That's in the Panhandle, if you don't know where it is. They met you at the ranger station yesterday and someone told them that you are an artist. Do you give lessons? The lady who was talking to my mama said you are very good and that you might be willing to teach me. She said she would ask you, but that she and her husband were leaving the park to move away. The party was for her and her husband," Martha rattled on. "I've dabbled in acrylics, but I want to learn to work in oils."

Jenna thought of her first meeting with Miz Ramona, and how much she had learned from that woman. "Come in, Martha, and let's talk. I've never given lessons before, but I might be interested, if you are serious."

Martha picked up a portfolio and carried it in with her. "I'm very serious. I brought a sampling of my watercolors and acrylics, but . . . oh, my, gosh!" She clamped a hand over her mouth when she saw the painting. "You've got an original JayLee. That artist is my idol. I've studied her art, and my folks have taken me to galleries in Lufkin and in

Houston. I felt like I was in the room with her when I was studying her works."

"That's really flattering," Jenna said. "How do you know that JayLee is a woman?"

"Because I can feel her spirit in her work," Martha said.

A cold chill danced down Jenna's spine. She didn't believe in reincarnation or ghosts, but that moment was the uncanniest one she had ever spent. The week before she died, Jenna's mother had told her that she put her spirit in every painting, and that she should let the world meet her.

She led the way to the back porch, where she could see Martha's paintings in good sunlight. She spread the four pictures out on the picnic table and studied them for a few minutes before she spoke. "What do you like to paint?"

"Landscapes, mostly. I watch the sunset over the water every evening here at the lake. I take hundreds of pictures and study the angles, the clouds, and even the ducks on the water," Martha answered.

"I see a lot of promise here, Martha. I could probably manage a couple of hours once a week. What do you think about us starting on Friday morning at about ten o'clock? You have a talent, but you need to pick a medium and stick with it. Your watercolors are really good. Are you sure you want to do oils?"

"Yes, ma'am." Martha looked beyond Jenna, and her eyes grew bigger and wider. Her finger shot up to point at the painting on the easel. "*You* are JayLee! I'd recognize that style anywhere. I had no idea that . . ." She gasped. "Yes, Friday is good, and . . ." She stared at Jenna and teared up.

Jenna put a finger over her lips. "Shh, please don't tell anyone my identity. That can be our secret."

Martha dried her tears on her shirt sleeve. "Yes, ma'am. I'll be here at ten on Friday. Mama is going to ask me how much you charge, so . . ."

"You keep my secret, and we'll call it even," Jenna said.

"For real? You will teach me for free?" She shook her head. "I want to learn. I really do, but I can't lie to my mama."

"You are right. You should never lie to your mother," Jenna answered. "Feel free to tell your parents who I am, and as payment, you can give me one of your oil paintings at the end of summer. How does that sound?"

Martha gathered up her paintings and put them back in the portfolio. "That sounds wonderful, but I still feel like I'm in a dream."

"Then I'll be looking for you every Friday until school starts."

History repeats itself. Ramona's voice was in her head.

Just paying it forward, Jenna thought.

"I'll be here," Martha promised. "Just meeting you is a dream come true. Having you teach me is something I would have never even let myself think about."

"Are you a freshman this year?" Jenna judged her by her height and the braces on her teeth.

"No, ma'am, I'm a senior, but I'm homeschooled. I'll finish up my high school courses next May, and then I hope to go to a good art school that fall. Fridays won't be a problem for me all year."

"How old *are* you?" Jenna asked. The girl barely came up to Jenna's shoulder, and she was slim built. Maybe it was the braids that made her look so young.

Martha picked up her portfolio. "Fifteen, but I'll be sixteen before I graduate."

"You must be pretty smart."

Martha raised one of her thin shoulders in a shrug. "I've aced all my tests to get into a good college. I just hope I qualify for some financial aid to make it possible. Oh, I forgot to tell you: my daddy is a park ranger, and my mama is a new assistant at the ranger station. They are Joyce and

Paul Stevens. I'm going home and pinch myself to be sure I'm not dreaming. If I am, I hope I don't wake up until after Friday." She started out across the backyard.

"I'll be waiting for you. Hey, what cabin did y'all move into?" Jenna called out.

"The one two doors down from you," Martha turned and said over her shoulder.

"Miz Ramona's old cabin," Jenna muttered, and thought maybe she was dreaming, too. "That is an omen for sure."

"What's an omen?" Carson asked as he rounded the end of the house. "Are you ready to start our day with a trip to IHOP for breakfast?"

"Yes, I am," she said with a smile, "and I'll tell you all about my omen on the way to the café."

Carson took her hand in his and kissed her knuckles. "I love signs from the universe."

"I don't know that I've had many, but there's no mistaking the one that just landed in my world." Her words sounded a little breathy in her ears, but then they had a right to have a quality like that. Her pulse raced like she had just finished a marathon.

"I started to knock on the front door, but then I heard you talking to someone." Carson opened the passenger door of his truck for her. "Was the girl walking across the yard your omen?"

"Kind of," she answered, and then when he was behind the wheel, she went on to tell him about the young lady who showed up within minutes of Kelly and Amber's departure. "My mother was Marsha. The girl who wants to learn to work in oils is Martha, and she even looks a little like pictures of my mama when she was a young girl."

"That's a sign for sure, and think about it," Carson said. "Remember that old saying about how when one door closes, another one opens? Your memory cabin door has closed for a while, and now another one is opening." He cupped her face in his hands.

She barely had time to moisten her lips before his closed over them in a long, lingering, passionate kiss that came close to sending desire to the boiling point.

"I've wanted to do that for days," he said when the kiss ended.

"I'm glad you waited for today," she whispered.

"Why?"

"Because it seems right for this moment." She slipped her hand in his. "I'm ready to go."

"Can we call it a date?"

"I think we just might," she said, and smiled up at him.

"I'm glad," Carson said. "Can it be that we are dating exclusively then?"

"I can't imagine wanting to be with anyone else," Jenna said, and was amazed at how full her heart felt at simply admitting that. The theme song from the childhood movie, *Annie*, played through her mind. She started humming, and Carson chuckled.

"Tomorrow is only a day away," he sing-songed. "But today is right now, and spending the whole day with you is great, but the ending will be the icing on the cake."

"Why's that?"

"Because then I get to kiss you good night," he said with a broad grin.

"Why wait until tonight?" she teased.

He braked, pulled the car over to the side of the road, and opened the door. She slung open her door and met him at the front of the vehicle. He cupped her cheeks in his big hands and slowly lowered his mouth to hers for the second time. Suddenly, they were the only ones in the whole state of Texas. No, that wasn't right—they were in a bubble that shut out the universe.

Right there on the side of the road leaving the park, Jenna got a vision of their future together. Two cars passed and honked, but that didn't even penetrate the bubble. When the string of kisses ended, her knees were weak, and her heart pounded.

"Wow!" she gasped. "I've never felt like this before."

"Good or bad?" Carson asked.

"Oh, honey, *good* doesn't begin to describe the way I feel," she admitted.

"Me, too." He hugged her even tighter. "I could so fall in love with you, Jenna."

I'm already there, she thought, but she just nodded in agreement.

Chapter Ten

One year later

Carson pointed at the poster hanging in the window of Mona Gallery in Houston. "The amazing and talented and famous artist known as JayLee is making her first public appearance in fifteen minutes."

Jenna laced her fingers in his, and together they entered the gallery. "I'm only famous when I'm JayLee, and out at a gallery showing the works of a few new budding artists from Texas—Martha Stevens included. All the other days of the week, I'm Jenna Makay who lives in a cabin at the lake with her new husband, Carson."

"Ladies and gentlemen, if I could have your attention," the CEO of the gallery said when Jenna entered the building, "JayLee has arrived, and I'm going to turn this microphone over to her."

Jenna took the microphone from Audra's hand and smiled at the crowd. "I am JayLee, and I'd like to thank you for all coming to our first-ever showing of young, budding artists from the great state of Texas. If you are interested in buying one of the paintings shown here today, or if you would like to make a donation toward a university scholarship for one of these amazing artists, Audra will take care of that for you. My painting is available in a silent auction beginning right now, and whatever it brings will be divided among the scholarships for the ten artists who are represented. Dig deep into your pockets, and let's help the next generation. Thank you again for attending today."

An older man at the back of the room raised a hand. "I'm Fred Taylor from the *Houston Chronicle*. Is JayLee your real name?"

"It's my professional name. My real one is Jenna Makay, and this is my husband, Carson, standing here beside me," she said.

"Where did you get JayLee?"

"My mother's name was Jenene. My father's middle name was Lee. They supported me when they would have rather I studied business or maybe corporate law. Any more questions?" she asked.

Several flashes from phones and cameras lit up the place. Some of them would be horrible pictures because she was talking, but the ones when she looked up at Carson might be decent. He was her rock and the absolute love of her life. Kelly and Amber had watched the wedding on FaceTime on Christmas Day when she and Carson were married at the edge of the lake. That was six months ago, and she was happier than she had ever been.

"Yes," a tall, lanky boy with glasses near the front asked. "Will you sign my brochure?"

"I would be glad to," Jenna answered.

People began to press her with brochures held out. Audra reached for the microphone and pointed toward a small table set up in the back of the gallery. "JayLee will be sitting right back there and will be happy to sign brochures for anyone who wants them."

Everyone stepped back and made a path for her to get to the table. She took Carson's hand in hers and whispered, "Stay beside me, please."

"Wouldn't want to be anywhere else," he said, grinning. "I'm Mr. JayLee today."

"No, darlin', you are my rock today, and down deep inside, I'm really Mrs. Carson Makay. And I love that title most of all," she said, as they made their way through the crowd together.

"While you are waiting for your JayLee autograph, let me draw your attention to her painting on the wall," Audra said. "The silent auction bidding form is on the table right below it. Remember, all the proceeds are to be divided for scholarships for the students who are here today."

"This is surreal," she said when she sat down.

"I can only imagine, but you are the strongest woman I've ever met, so it will get easier each time," Carson assured her. "And honey, what you've done for Martha can't be put into words."

Martha and her parents, Joyce and Paul, were the last ones to come by to say a few words and get Jenna to sign their brochures. Martha stepped around the end of the table and hugged Jenna tightly. "Thank you for everything, and I'm so excited for Paris."

Jenna hugged her back. "Thank you, Martha. You helped me at a time when I needed it. Keep learning and don't just paint—enjoy the talent you've been given."

"I will," Martha promised.

"We can't thank you enough for everything," Paul said. "I had misgivings about leaving Vega and moving to the lake, but there was a promotion, and they promised Joyce a job. Because of that, we met you, and now we are going on to even better jobs next week. If you ever need anything, we are here for you."

"Thank you, but it's been my pleasure to work with Martha. We have become such good friends, and I will miss her and y'all," Jenna said.

Audra nodded at Jenna from across the room. "The gallery will be closing in fifteen minutes. I'm happy to report that all of the students' paintings have been sold. The buyers can pick them up and pay for them at the table where JayLee has been sitting. I take cash or credit cards and would like to say thank you again for coming out today and supporting our new artists. Also, I would like to remind you that there will be a showing of JayLee's newest work next Saturday. The silent auction will be finished in ten more minutes, and then Martha Stevens will bring me the winner's name. So, if you haven't gotten your bid in, you've still got time. Jenna has a few words to say before she leaves."

"I'd just like to say thank you to everyone again. Have a safe journey home."

The applause that followed her out of the building was deafening.

"I'd say that was a big success. I checked that silent auction bidding form as we were leaving. Each one of those students just got ten thousand dollars added to their scholarship fund," Carson said.

"Who was the highest bidder?" she asked.

Carson got her settled in the passenger seat of his truck and kissed her before he closed the door. He rounded the back of the truck and slid in behind the wheel.

"No name, just the initials C.M. Whoever it is got a beautiful painting. It was my favorite of all the ones that you have done."

"Think about it," Jenna said with a grin.

He whipped around to stare at her. "You didn't?"

"I did," she said. "I would have donated that much money to the artists anyway. What better way to do it than to buy the painting to give to you? Audra will deliver it to us next week on her way to Lufkin for a conference with the CEOs of all my galleries."

He leaned across the seat, tucked his fist under her chin, and kissed her again. "Thank you, my darlin'. Let's hang it in our bedroom, since it's a rendering of the place where we got married."

"Great minds and all that," she agreed. "I was thinking that would be a good place to put it."

He started the engine and drove away from the gallery. "I love you, JayLee, but I love Jenna more."

She reached across the console and laid a hand on his shoulder. "I'm glad, because Jenna is announcing this bit of news, not JayLee. You are going to be a father sometime around Christmas or New Year's."

He whipped into a church parking lot, braked so hard that gravel went flying every which way, and turned off the engine. "Are you serious?"

"Yep, and I hope you are as happy as I am," she answered.

He slung open the door, jumped out of the truck, jogged all the way around to open her door. He scooped her up in his arms and carried her a few feet from the vehicle, then sat her down and hugged her tightly to his chest. "Darlin', I'm so happy right now that I can't breathe."

"So am I," Jenna said. "But you better suck in some air, because parenting is a big job, and it's going to take both of us."

He leaned back and then lowered his lips to hers. When

the kiss ended, he drew her back into another embrace. "We are going to make wonderful parents. We are going to wrap our children up in love."

"Yes, we are," she agreed. "And that's because of the love we have for each other."

Look for these other books from Fern Michaels, Lori Foster, and Carolyn Brown . . .

Don't miss *Smuggler's Cove,* the first book in #1 *New York Times* bestselling author Fern Michaels's brand-new series Twin Lights . . .

In a brand-new series, Fern Michaels introduces siblings Madison and Lincoln Taylor, whose Jersey Shore inheritance plunges them into a world of mystery and mayhem . . .

Growing up, Madison Taylor and her younger brother Lincoln lived privileged lives, but their sheltered existence abruptly ended when their father was arrested for fraud and the family assets were seized. Since then, Madison has carved out a new path, studying fashion and working her way up to editor in chief of *La Femme* magazine, while Lincoln teaches wealth management at a small college outside the city. Both have separated themselves from their family and their past—until an unexpected bequest arrives from their late uncle.

Madison and Lincoln are the new co-owners of a marina at Smuggler's Cove on the Navesink river. Instead of a fabulous, Hamptons-style property, Smuggler's Cove offers little beyond a dilapidated dock, a few gas pumps, and a handful of clam boats. Madison's plan to sell the property goes awry when a dead body is found floating under their dock and transforms their new inheritance into a crime scene.

Suddenly, Madison is swapping her city-girl wardrobe for cargo pants and flannel shirts while she and Lincoln receive a crash course in small-town Jersey Shore life, complete with quirky characters, pirate legends, and a mysterious treasure map. They're discovering more about themselves and each other every day, but with a mystery to solve and big decisions to make, these are lessons they'll need to learn fast . . .

From *New York Times* bestselling author Lori Foster comes *The Guest Cottage,* the uplifting series debut in which forgiveness and unlikely friendship blossom in the haven of a quiet lakeside town when two very different women bond over one man's betrayals.

Marlow Heddings is starting over. She's carried the outrage of her husband Dylan's affair with a younger woman— and the expectations of his family's powerful Chicago holdings company—long enough. Now, after another devastating twist of fate, she's unapologetically moving on.

Arriving in tiny Bramble, Kentucky, Marlow revels in her freedom, swapping her executive suits for sundresses . . . and scouting places to open her dream boutique. Best of all is her new residence, an adorable cottage with gorgeous lake views—and a breathtaking landlord, former Marine Cort Easton. Soon they're sharing dockside morning coffee and nighttime firefly gazing. Marlow's new life feels like a dream.

Then Pixie Nolan arrives on her doorstep. With a shocking secret.

To Marlow's astonishment, Dylan's "other woman" is a desperate girl of nineteen, destitute, exhausted, and disowned by her family. Defying her manipulative in-laws' demands, and surprising even herself, Marlow vows to lay down roots in Bramble and help Pixie get on her feet. Then they'll part ways. But empathy has a way of forging bonds. As Marlow grows close to the hardworking, devoted young woman, she becomes something of a big sister to Pixie.

Now, with each sunrise, Marlow awakens to the life she was truly meant to live, one filled with deepening connections, supportive friendship . . . and even a second chance at love.

Mother's Day Crown—a sexy, witty, fun contemporary romance novella from *USA Today* and *New York Times* bestselling author Carolyn Brown, originally published in the anthology *In Bloom.*

Monica Allen still hasn't forgiven Tyler Magee for breaking her heart when they were teenagers. Ten years on, they're back in Luella, Texas, visiting their respective grandmothers. And there's just a white picket fence and a whole lot of awkwardness between them. Will two weeks be long enough for Monica to learn to stop holding a grudge—and hold on to love?

Look for *Mother's Day Crown*, on sale now!

Visit our website at
KensingtonBooks.com
to sign up for our newsletters, read
more from your favorite authors, see
books by series, view reading group
guides, and more!

Become a Part of Our
Between the Chapters Book Club
Community and Join the Conversation

Betweenthechapters.net

Submit your book review for a chance to win exclusive
Between the Chapters swag you can't get anywhere else!
https://www.kensingtonbooks.com/pages/review/